THE

INLAND

SEA

WILLIAM MORROW

An Imprint of HarperCollinsPublishers

THE

INLAND

SEA

STEVEN VARNI

It is the policy of William Morrow and Company, Inc., and its imprints and affiliates,
recognizing the importance of preserving what has been written, to print the books we
publish on acid-free paper, and we exert our best efforts to that end.

Library of Congress Cataloging-in-Publication Data

Varni, Steven.
The inland sea / Steven Varni.
p.   cm.
ISBN 0-688-16906-6
1. Italian Americans—California—San Joaquin Valley Fiction.
I. Title.
PS3572.A7335I55   2000
813'.54—dc21   99-32243
CIP

Printed in the United States of America

First Edition

1   2   3   4   5   6   7   8   9   10

BOOK DESIGN BY JO ANNE METSCH

www.williammorrow.com

FOR VARLEY O'CONNOR

AND

ANN RENNA VARNI,

AND

IN MEMORY OF

LOUIE VARNI (1921–1989)

ACKNOWLEDGMENTS

MUCH THANKS TO Jeannette Watson and Meaghan Dowling; Mary Evans; Tanya McKinnon; Maeve McQuillan; Peter Mendelsund; the late Professor Joseph Duffy; Brian Wright; Ken Burke; Lou, Frank, and Suzanne Varni; and Marie Frazier.

CONTENTS

PART ONE: INNOCENCE • 1

PROLOGUE • 3

THE BIG PROJECT • 11

HEROES, BRAVERY, GREAT FEATS • 30

GOING UNDER • 60

THE PAINTER • 70

THE REAL THING • 87

PART TWO: EXPERIENCE • 115

CIRCUMSPECTION • 117

SNOW • 146

TORNO BROS. DISTRIBUTING CO. • 164

COUNTERPARTS • 189

SCHMERZHAUSER • 210

THE INLAND SEA • 236

Lately I've come to believe that I can remember a time before I learned to read when the alphabet's string of letters running above the blackboards of my first classroom seemed purely decorative, a kind of meaningless fretwork. When letters were just simple, primitive, two-dimensional images of objects in the world, so that *Io* [I], for example, was no word at all, but just a picture of a column beside a great boulder or sphere. I'm reminded of this now, after rereading these pages I've written, in which all the *Io*'s (even in my tiny script) are as strange and daunting to me as if they themselves were those ancient, massive columns and boulders I once thought they represented—so foreign to me is the solidity, certainty, self-presence suggested by these letters; so little do they have to do with any actual *me*, who writes to you, trying to make myself known. . . .

I could easily substitute *Il* [he] for every *Io* in these pages and be no further from the truth of how my life presents itself to me—and, perhaps, be even nearer.

—*Domenico di Pietri*,
    in a letter to his brother
    (translated from the Italian)

PART ONE

INNOCENCE

Understanding is entanglement.

—*Hermann Broch*

ONE NIGHT WHILE he practices reading with her, Vincent's mother tells him not to be scared when the ambulance comes to their house.

He's in the middle of a slim book about a haunted mansion when she interrupts.

"You read so well!" she says. She's been moving constantly as he reads, the chair beneath her creaking and scraping at the dim edges of the boy's consciousness. Now she taps her fingers on the kitchen table and exclaims, "So very, very well!"

Vincent smiles. He doesn't remind her that together they've read this book before or that he's read it many times by himself. He wonders how she's forgotten this, but he likes her praise. He knows every turn of this story. He's memorized whole pages. Soon the boy and girl will discover the house isn't really haunted, that a poor crippled boy has made all the strange sounds. As he opens his mouth to tell his mother how much he knows, she continues:

"I just can't believe how well you read now! It's really something!"

Her fingers tap a manic irregular beat that makes him uneasy. He tries to ignore it. He has so much to tell her about this book. "Yeah, and when—"

"I'm impressed! This must be your best subject!"

He's sure she already knows this. She's not making sense, but he'll remind her, "In class I'm in the highest—"

"Yes, I know," she interrupts again. "I can tell." She shakes her head. "You're growing up so fast! So fast. You make me practice with you every night, but I don't think you need me anymore. You read better than I do!"

"We're *supposed* to practice every night." He's becoming angry at her interruptions, the way she ignores him even as she praises him. "That's what Sister Lorna says, every night."

"Oh, I know, I'm just teasing. But you *are* growing up," she insists. "You're getting too smart for me." She wears such a big smile he can see all of her large front teeth and how they narrow toward the gum.

He'd felt good; now he feels embarrassed.

He picks up the book. His mother turns toward the den, where his father sits with the loud television. Vincent starts to read again, and she quickly turns back and puts her hand on the page.

"You're getting big enough that I can tell you things now, can't I?" she asks. "You're such a smart boy, I can talk to you, right?"

This praise scares him, but he nods.

"Good. Because you're not a little boy anymore. You should know." She turns in her chair, so her whole body faces him, and leans close. She's hugging herself as if she's cold, and her legs, in navy slacks, are pressed tightly together. "Don't be afraid when the ambulance comes for your father tonight. It will be late, the middle of the night, and it may wake you, but don't be afraid. Things'll be better after this. This is what we have to do, and then things'll be better. Okay?"

"Dad's sick?"

"Yes, he's sick. Not right. He needs to go to the hospital; then things'll be better. I promise."

Vincent's face is hot. He looks to where the television sounds, then to the other end of the house where his sister listens to records and rushes through homework, closed in her room. He thinks of his brother at work.

"Sometimes . . . this is just . . ." His mother, suddenly, is almost crying. "Just what you have to do. When people won't listen. Then we won't fight anymore. . . . About . . . such . . . *stupid* things!"

Vincent tries to remember when his parents last fought. Tonight at dinner his father was silent. When he expected his father to yell— when his mother kept getting up from the table, walking to the sink, coming back empty-handed—he'd said nothing, just followed her with his eyes. Only once, near the end of dinner, when his mother again got up, came back, got up, came back, did he lay his hands upon the table, palms up, and with a low voice ask, "What are you doing, Lucy? *Lucy*, what are you doing?"

His mother grasps his hand and beats it softly upon her knee for emphasis. "I *finally* see that things have to change. *Finally*. I see it all clearly. But this is our secret, okay? Between you and me?"

"Dad's sick," he repeats. Her words reach him across a distance he can't seem to close.

"Yes. But he'll be fine. Believe me." She squeezes his hand. "But! This has to be our secret. You're old enough to keep a secret."

Vincent looks at his lap, at their joined hands. He nods.

"And you won't tell Paul or Mary or Dad? Okay? Don't tell them, because this is what we have to do, to make everything right."

He nods again. He looks at his mother. She lets go of his hand and looks across the table at the bare wall. She says, as if from memory, "Because sometimes things have to get worse before they can get better. You understand?"

"Yes," he lies.

The tapping of her fingers upon the table starts again, then abruptly stops.

Then, in a more familiar voice, she announces, "So. Time for bed. School tomorrow." She closes the book and they both stand. "This is our secret?" she asks.

"Yes," he says.

In bed he lies still, but he doesn't hear a siren. If he falls asleep it will wake him. Dogs will cry at the noise it makes. But he hears only what he hears every night: the distant television, the small cracking sounds of the constantly shifting house, the soft tick-ticking of the heater before it flares to life. He is old enough to keep a secret. Things will be better, he repeats in his mind until he falls asleep.

VINCENT WAKES WHEN his brother comes home from his part-time job. Paul clicks on a dim lamp in the corner of their room and Vincent wakes and, half asleep, listens. He hears the soft *rrip* of a belt pulled through pant loops and the dull jangle of its buckle; the quiet squeak when Paul sits, with a sigh, on the bed; the halting rough sound of corduroys taken off and the light smooth one of pajamas slipping up over his brother's legs. He hears his father's heavy steps in the kitchen, a cabinet open and close, his mother's voice, farther away, rising into a question. The wall near his bed fills with a rushing noise as his sister runs water into the bathroom sink and just as suddenly falls silent again; water splashes as she washes her face. He hears the bed receive his brother's weight as Paul lies back with a heavy sigh, the sound of bare feet sticking to the tile of the bathroom floor, the creak of a towel rack beneath a towel, the hollow sound of the bathroom itself as its door is opened and closed, footsteps on the thick hall carpet, then light taps on their bedroom door. He hears his brother sigh again and climb from bed, his bare feet on the hardwood, the hinges of the door as it swings slightly open, and his sister's whisper, and his brother's, too low to be understood except for the cold harsh sound, repeated again and again, of *she* . . . , *she* . . . , until Paul joins his sister in the hallway and closes the door behind him. He hears their weight shift on the carpet and on the floorboards beneath it, the uneven murmur of their voices, and the television far away. He hears all these sounds of his family's life—hears them now for the first time— as clearly as if they are whispered directly into his ear, and he shivers at the realization that he's always slept through them before.

*   *   *

IN THE MORNING, Paul nudges him awake.

"Where's Mom?" Vincent asks.

"In bed. She doesn't feel good."

He sits up. "Where's Dad?"

"Where do you think? He left for work a half hour ago."

He lies back down. "I don't want to go to school today."

"C'mon. Get up. Mary'll make you breakfast."

"No, Paul, I hate school. I won't go."

"Get up," his brother sighs. He stands with his thin arms folded across his chest and rocks slightly from foot to foot: a high school junior almost resigned to playing at parent.

"No. I *hate* it! I hate my teacher, I hate her. I hate everything about school!"

Paul tugs gently on his wrist. "C'mon, boy, let's go."

He pulls his arm free. "No. No, Paul. I won't go. I won't."

"*Vincent*. We don't need this, we really don't. Get up."

"No!" He pulls the covers over his face, then suddenly throws them back and rolls out of bed. "I'll go see Mom. She won't make me go. I'll tell her I won't go."

"Vincent, leave her alone. C'mon, just get ready."

He brushes past his brother and heads down the hall to his parents' bedroom.

"Vincent!" Paul calls after him in a loud whisper. "Vincent, she's not well! Stay out of there." But he doesn't turn around. Paul starts to walk after him, gives up, leans against a wall. "You wanna catch what Mom has?" he asks sarcastically.

His mother lies on her side, covered with blankets, her back to the door. Vincent sits on the edge of the king-sized bed.

"Mom? Are you awake?"

She doesn't move. "Yes."

"I won't go to school today."

The heap of blankets shifts slowly in his direction. His mother's small hands appear at the top of the covers and, as though with great effort, draw them below her chin. She lies now on her other side, facing him, her hands and one side of her face visible.

"What do you mean, you won't go?" she asks.

"I won't. I just won't."

She sighs. "Vincent, I'm tired."

A pause.

"I didn't sleep well last night."

Vincent stiffens. He doesn't want to hear about last night. He doesn't want to know why the ambulance didn't come.

"I won't go," he repeats. Then with force, "I hate it! I hate my teacher. I hate my class. I hate it all."

His mother raises her gold-brown eyes to his for the first time. "When did this start?"

He doesn't answer. He wants to believe he's always felt this way.

"I thought you liked school," she says slowly. "You know, Vincent, you have to learn. You have to go to school. You used to like school. What happened?"

He says nothing.

"What about reading?" she asks.

"I don't care about it. I know it enough, you said I do. I know it good enough. I don't need any more. I hate school, Mom, I hate it." His eyes fill with tears.

His mother raises her head a moment, clumsily pushes her light brown hair from her face, then drops into the pillow again. "You'll go, Vincent. You don't hate it."

She seems heavy and tired. She moved too much last night, now she hardly moves. He doesn't know why she's changed so much in one night, doesn't want to know. He just wants to sit with her in complete silence. But she continues.

"Vincent, you used to cry because you *wanted* to go to school. Remember? You'd cry when Paul left in the morning. When Mary left. You wanted to go too."

He hears her tongue move inside her mouth. She speaks slowly, but she won't stop.

"It's true. And remember when you cried in the Chinese restaurant? Because you couldn't read?"

He shakes his head.

His mother raises herself onto her elbow. "You did." She lies on her side, her knees drawn up, her head resting against the palm of her hand. "You did. We were in the Golden Dragon. You must have been four years old. All of us were there. Mary and Paul. Dad and me, and you. We sat in a booth, and you sat at the end of the table. In a booster chair. And we had our menus and were trying to figure out what to order. And you started fidgeting in your chair. Started whining a little, and no one was even saying anything. We were just looking at our menus. Then you really started to cry, louder, tears and all. And I looked at you and said what's the matter? And you said you wouldn't get any food. I didn't understand. I told you something like, sure, we'll let you starve—stop it now. But you kept crying. But I can't read, you said. I can't order. Everyone can read, but I can't. I won't get any food. You had big tears rolling down your cheeks. You were really crying. And it was almost funny, but we all felt bad for you and tried to cheer you up. Gave you your own menu. But you kept crying, because you couldn't read it." She almost smiles. "You never wanted to be left out. You always wanted to know as much as we knew. You wanted to be like us. You did. And so you cried and cried that night because you wanted to read too."

She lowers her head onto the pillow again, pulls the covers high around her neck. "I'm tired, Vincent. I didn't sleep last night. Now go to school."

Vincent still sits watching her. Through the open bedroom doorway come faint sounds from the kitchen.

She closes her eyes. "I'll never forget that," she says drowsily. "Poor thing. Crying because you didn't want to be left out. Oh how you cried. Because you didn't know everything we did."

She's silent. She sleeps.

Vincent noiselessly slips off the edge of the mattress, carefully closes and locks the door, and returns to his mother's bed. He lies back on the covers, at the edge of the bed, away from his mother yet close enough that he can stretch out his arm and touch her if he wants or needs to. After a few minutes the whole house seems silent. Maybe Paul and Mary have left, he thinks, maybe they've left me behind.

He doesn't move. He's made up his mind. He'll stay here quietly, while his mother sleeps peacefully, for as long as he can.

ON A PLEASANT April evening in the San Joaquin Valley town of Ralston, with all the house's windows opened to the screens, Paul Torno, Sr., sat watching a special program on the Second World War, in which he'd served, while his wife and the younger of his two sons played pick up sticks on the carpet. When the Pacific theater was mentioned he called their attention to the television, glanced from the screen to be sure they watched. At the commercial break he told his son of places he'd been, Okinawa, Saipan, and though Lucy Torno, with a nearly silent exhalation of impatience or boredom, resumed her turn, the seven-year-old listened intently to his father's voice, which itself sounded strange and foreign. His father rarely spoke directly to him, and almost never like this. His voice contained not a trace of anger, frustration, or criticism, and his father could have been speaking Italian, which the boy didn't understand, and his mere tone would have held his interest. His father told him that he'd been an airplane gunner, a petty officer first class, and his carrier's chief mechanic; had spent four long years far away from home. Sometimes he'd been scared, and sometimes, he admitted, he'd missed his parents and brother (he hadn't met Vincent's mother yet; even when the war ended she was hardly more than a girl). But his voice was not afraid or sad, but almost happy, pleased. Then the show came on again and his father abruptly fell silent.

Vincent wanted to hear more. He asked his father, "Where? Where were those places?"

"All the way on the other side of the world. Watch"—he nodded toward the television—"they'll probably show you." He looked from the screen, repeated, "Watch."

From the corner of his eye Vincent saw his mother raise her head. But the show had returned to Europe. After a minute they slipped back into their game. While his mother tried to remove a stick without disturbing the rest, Vincent tried to imagine those places far away where his father had been happy.

The Tornos lived on Weston Avenue, only one house from Collier Road: a popular alternate link between the extensive old valley-long Highway 99 and the two-lane valley-wide Route 132, which expired at its eastern limits a respectful, awed distance before the stern face of the Sierras and, to the west, led to the grassy surges of the Diablo Range and the Altamont Pass's frenzied winds. With the house windows open, car noises wafted through the screens, barely audible. But diesel trucks, hauling one or even two open-topped trailers heaped with tomatoes or grapes, walnuts, almonds, peaches, or apricots, used Collier too. So that sometimes the grinding roar of a shifting diesel engine filled the living room, as it did suddenly on this evening, blotting out for nearly half a minute all of the Allies' careful preparations for D-Day.

Paul Torno stirred in his chair, as if he would have glared at the offending rig. Then he turned with a frustrated grin to his wife. "It's hard to believe, Lucy, but do you remember when we used to live in the *country?*"

Vincent recognized this tone.

She looked at her husband, dropped her head toward one shoulder, considering, then said, "Barely." She shook her head. "It seems so long ago." She'd been on a roll, picking out one stick after another.

Now she bent to the game again, clutched at one, and jarred the whole pile.

The next afternoon Vincent asked his mother why she'd never taken him to their old house.

She had no idea what he meant. "What old house?" she asked.

All day Vincent had imagined his family packing their belongings into boxes, as he'd once seen some neighbors do. He'd pictured a big moving truck, and the old house itself, one-story, simple, surrounded by a dirt yard and beyond that, orchards or vineyards on every side. Then he'd thought of a long move, and found that it explained a lot of things. His cracked football helmet had once belonged to his older brother—obviously a workman had dropped it on the way to the truck. His favorite painted plastic cowboys and Indians, numbering just five, lacking the horses they fit upon, had belonged to Paul too—he'd find the horses, and other figures besides, scattered about the old yard. In the course of the day he'd convinced himself a great store of treasures remained at the old house.

"The house where we used to live, in the *country*," he said.

His mother looked blankly at him. He explained as well as he could, grew frustrated, but persisted until she understood. But even then her response wasn't what he wanted to hear.

"Oh Vincent, Dad didn't mean *that*. We've never moved. Everything *around us* changed. Collier wasn't here when we were first married. The Nollinses', the Ruggios', the Pruitts', none of those houses were here. That whole neighborhood on Whitmore Avenue . . ." And she told him, not without bitterness, how the land around them had been transformed in the nineteen years since they'd first built the house on a quiet road in the country. She listed all the changes, her mood growing darker, until he nodded that he understood.

She began to make dinner. Vincent went outside, stepped up onto the lower crossbeam of the grapestake fence dividing his yard from the Nollinses', and watched the cars and trucks pass by on Collier Road. He imagined that one day Collier had not been there, then the next day it was. That the Nollinses' house next door had sprouted like a mushroom overnight. That there'd been an orchard where his friend Hammy Oakes now lived, but suddenly the trees had merged into houses, as in a fairy tale. He imagined all around himself a world in unpredictable flux, in which buildings and fences could suddenly push up through the earth like gophers. But no sooner had he thought this than his mind rebelled against it. It could not be true.

His mother spent all of the next day in bed. No one mentioned it. In the morning Vincent heard his father trying to make her get up, but nothing after that. In the late afternoon Vincent saw that she was awake, and dragged from his parents' closet a cardboard box of unsorted photos. His mother paid no attention to him until he had the box at the side of the bed.

"Mom, look—" he began.

She cut him off, saying "Vincent, go away, will you? Put those back and please go away."

As Vincent left the bedroom his father saw him. Winter was over but he was working on the fireplace's damper, his arms and hands sooty. He asked, "Vincent, why don't you help me here?"

It wasn't really a question. Vincent reluctantly knelt and watched. His father seriously explained, as if giving a lesson, what he was doing. It didn't require two people. Vincent thought of asking about the old house, but couldn't bring himself to interrupt his father's work, his intense focus even on this little chore. So he sat bored, compelled to stay by his father's initial show of interest in him. At the end he got to carry a paper bag filled with ashes and a few blackened crispy fragments of metal to the garbage can. Then his father took him outside to help repair the lawn mower, warning him, "You get rummy if you stay inside all day."

Two days later, when she was in a better mood, Vincent again tried his mother. He sorted through the old photographs in the box in his parents' closet, chose a few, and carried them to her as she sat looking over her checkbook in the den.

"What do you have there?" she asked as he approached, then, "God, not those old things!" But she wasn't really mad; she smiled. She took them from him and looked at each. "Oh my!" she said at one, she sighed at another, but her tight-lipped smile stayed frozen on her face.

Vincent took one of them from her hand, held it out to her. "Where's this house?" he asked.

"That house? That's *this* house," she said.

He held a black-and-white photograph of a ranch house on a bare lot. His parents, much younger, stood happily before it, their arms around one another.

"But it has a garage," he said. "This house *doesn't have* a garage."

"It used to. We're sitting in it. This room was the garage. It was changed into a den not long before you were born. You know that, don't you?"

He was doubtful. "How about the carport? And the fences?"

"Those came later. The carport after the den. The fences soon after we moved in. Vincent, the house is brand-new in this photo— just finished," she said, assuming this would explain everything.

He persisted. He showed her Christmas photos, his older sister and brother in pajamas surrounded by presents and wrapping paper. He recognized his football helmet when new, but everything else seemed different. His mother explained how they'd remodeled the room. She showed him a photograph of the whole family taken before he was born, standing in the backyard with the house behind them.

"Look"—she pointed—"you can see where the bedroom was added, can't you?"

He sensed her waning patience and nodded.

She lowered her voice. "You *know* your father would never move," she said, drifting into complaint. "I was ready to move after Collier was put in. I was ready to move when I found out I was pregnant with you—this house was never large enough. But your father always has . . . solutions. He's a very resourceful man, your father," she said sarcastically. While she spoke her hand trembled just slightly above the black-and-white image of the family, distracting Vincent, until she seemed to notice him staring and with a sudden shift of tone steadied it. "So, see?" she asked, straightening her forefinger again, returning both of them to the picture. "See there, where the wall was extended? Look at Paul and Mary. Look how small they are. Look at your father—no gray. And—well, *don't* look at me. That's when I was still slim. But look, all this, all just changed over time. Same house, same people, just changed. Understand?"

He studied the photograph. The four of them dressed for a holiday, smiling, his mother and sister in matching dresses, the house's windows shining behind them.

"See?" she asked with finality, impatience.

He nodded again. "Yeah," he said.

But still he could swear it was no place he'd ever lived.

THE BIG PROJECT was a concession of sorts.

Vincent's parents frequently argued. Even the sweetest days of calm and affection could suddenly be ruptured by argument, as though his parents' usual disagreements about family, money, and housekeeping could never be resolved—only thinly and temporarily covered over. Vincent usually sat out the arguments in Mary's room or the one he shared with Paul. A few times he'd tried, futilely, to stop them.

On this night Vincent and Paul shut themselves in their room. Paul studied. Vincent lay on his back on his twin bed, staring at the frosted glass plate of the overhead light, at the intricate regular curves of its garland design and the animal shapes and twisted faces that appeared there, unintended, among its vines and leaves. Paul told him that his parents would soon stop—why didn't he read or draw or do something?—but they didn't stop. Twice the shouting faded, only to begin again. After the second time Paul slapped his book down onto his lap, said angrily, "Someday he'll just have a heart attack—that'll do it! Or she'll go too far—too far to come back. And that'll be it!" He looked at Vincent. "The end. *Finally*," he said, then sighed, as if anticipating the relief it would bring to himself and Vincent both.

But he only scared Vincent, actually drove him from the room. Vincent wandered into the kitchen, where a minute later the argument came too and wound down before his eyes.

His mother entered first, then, at the sound of his steps behind her, spun quickly on his father. "I'd like to see *you* do a better job!" she shouted. Vincent backed more tightly into the corner made by the dishwasher and a cabinet, but his father didn't flinch. His mother lowered her voice. "Can't you *understand*?" she asked, sounding both sad and mean. "Can't you understand there's nothing I can do?"

For a few moments his father simply stared at her. Then he dropped his head, took a step back, loosely folded his arms. They hadn't noticed Vincent. They both seemed exhausted. It was a long eat-in kitchen with three doors and Vincent hoped this would be a chance to leave, but his father suddenly burst out, "Okay! You can't keep the yard clean, you can't keep the house from looking like a pigsty? I'll *help* you. There's too much stuff, too much *junk*? Okay! Fine. I'll make someplace to put it all. Put *all* of it! How about that?"

She gave no response.

"Look, I'm *trying* to help you," he said sincerely, almost plaintively. But he edged into sarcasm the next moment when still she didn't respond: "So let's make a big project out of it! A great big project! Then there'll be no more excuses."

And two days later he announced at dinner that he'd hired someone to build a storage shed in the backyard.

"I think this'll be a big help," he told his family. "Your mother and I *both* think this'll be a big help."

He glanced at his wife.

She ate silently.

He sighed. "You know, if you kids would help your mother it might not be so hard to find things when you want them. If everyone takes a little extra time, puts things where they belong . . . It's all very simple." He coughed his throat clear, took a drink of wine, looked around the table. "We have a beautiful house here," he said with chagrin. "It's just wrong, *plain wrong*, to act like—" He noticed his wife staring out the window, brought his napkin to his lips then tossed it onto the table. "Ah!" he concluded scornfully.

Now the shed itself became a topic of argument. To build it Vincent's father hired a man who'd once worked for him as a truck driver. The lumber and tin the ex-driver used would come from an old building that had stood, until recently, on one of his father's pieces of property on the fringes of downtown Ralston. To his father it seemed simply good sense to employ a man who was having trouble starting his own carpentry business and to use what he knew to be good material. To Vincent's mother, however, it showed how little her husband was willing to do (or spend) to help her. She called him cheap, and expected a huge rickety eyesore she'd see from the kitchen window every time she stood at the sink. His father promised her it would be out of sight—near the large backyard's side fence—but she remained angry, and still they argued. His father was persistent, he forced every issue; his mother tore each to pieces.

But Vincent was excited by the idea of the new shed. While Paul would smirk at its mention, and Mary would shrug, or at best talk herself into a wavering tone of hope, Vincent thought of it—with none of his father's sarcasm—as The Big Project, something to look forward to. Even when he heard his sandbox would have to be taken away to make room for the shed, he didn't mind. He was too old for the sandbox. On the weekend that the ex-driver and his helper began, Vincent sat outside and happily watched them build the shed's skeleton. And after the concrete was smoothed over the place where his sandbox had been his father wrote his name for him in large letters, right in the doorway:

V I N C E N T

M A Y   7 ,   1 9 7 1

"This way," his father told him, "you'll remember this day, no matter how big you get. Your name will always be here. Forever." His father was very nice to him that morning.

Each school day, as soon as he returned home, Vincent would examine how the building had grown.

In a week the shed was completed. Then for the first time the whole family seemed pleased—even Vincent's mother, though she said nothing. His father guided them through it, asked, *"Why do you act surprised? Didn't I tell you?"* It was as large as Vincent and Paul's bedroom; a wood frame covered completely with corrugated tin, with framed windows on two sides, deep shelves against two walls, and a workbench with a vise opposite the door. His mother couldn't see it from the kitchen. Paul and his friends could use it to work on their new minibike. Mary and Vincent could park their bicycles beneath its overhanging roof, outside, near the door. And most important, there was space for the lawn mower, garden tools, boxes of mason jars, whatever. No reason for clutter, no reason for the mess all around and inside the house, for the lost tools, for all the disorder, for all the arguments and yelling. No reason at all, his father said, and no one disagreed.

Under his father's direction, the family spent the next weekend cleaning the house and yard and arranging everything in the shed. His father screwed in big hooks to hold rakes, shovels, and hoes, and near the workbench mounted a sheet of pegboard covered with the outlines of wrenches, saws, and hammers that Vincent especially liked—though it turned out not to be decorative, like the happy illustrations above the chalkboards at school, but a way of showing where each tool belonged, of keeping them in perfect order. When they finished, his father barbecued hamburgers. It was a hot evening and they ate around a wooden picnic table in the backyard, everyone tired, glad to be done—his father, in particular, almost relaxed, content to sit quietly, straight and tall, and look over the neat yard, his face ruddy-brown and still, like the evening itself. Under the influence of fatigue and the close warmth the whole family lingered around the table until the last traces of red had vanished from the sky and a breeze started up, scattering the paper napkins.

VINCENT BELIEVED HIS parents would never argue again. At the end of May they celebrated their nineteenth wedding anniversary. In early June, school was let out for the summer. When Paul and his friends rode their minibike in the acre of walnut trees behind the backyard, Vincent was allowed to watch. Some nights at dinner his father even talked of having people over for Independence Day, and this rare prospect of company excited Vincent—much more than it did his mother. Over this and other things his parents occasionally bickered. But usually his mother remained stubbornly tight-lipped, and his father, tired from the long hours and six-day work weeks of his wine and beer distributorship's busiest season, let matters drop. So four weeks passed almost peacefully. Four weeks during which Vincent forgot that his family had ever lived together in any other way.

Then, one evening in the middle of June, Paul and his friends pushed their bike to the shed for repairs and found their work space cluttered by three boxes of pots and pans and two boxes of dried flowers. Paul lifted two pans from a box, examined them, sighed, and tossed them back in with the others. Vincent jumped at the clatter. Without a word Paul fit the boxes onto the shelves.

A week later Paul came into the kitchen where Vincent sat drawing at the table and asked his mother, who was loading the dishwasher, about three large boxes in front of the workbench. He spoke quietly so his father in the den wouldn't hear.

"Oh, I've finally gotten started on the closets. Those are just old clothes for the Salvation Army," she said. She didn't pause in her work, didn't look at him. "Just leave them where they are, okay?" she said airily, dismissing him.

"But there's no room to work, with them where they are," Paul told her.

She halted a moment, tried to look imperious, as if she was surprised he was still there. "Well, don't put them on the shelves! Stack them up or something!"

Paul didn't move. "Old clothes," he muttered doubtfully.

"Look yourself if—" She faltered. "The Salvation Army . . ." Then she straightened, suddenly angry. "Listen," she hissed, "you gonna be like your father? Should I okay everything with you first?"

Paul shook his head, walked away. Vincent left the table and followed. As they passed through the den, their father asked Paul, "What's wrong?"

"Nothing," Paul said. "Nothing."

The next night Vincent's father noticed all the new pots his wife was cooking with.

"What was wrong with the old ones?" he demanded, beginning a fight that tore into dinner.

While they shouted, Vincent could hardly eat. He hunched beneath their angry exchanges, looked from Mary, who nearly cried, shifted uneasily in her chair, and picked at her food, to Paul, who sat unmoving, hands in his lap, face fiercely blank—but for slight twitches around the mouth. Neither of them, he saw, could do anything to stop this.

Their father was the one who put an end to it.

"That's it," he said finally. "Enough. You'll do what you want no matter what I say. Fine. I'm tired."

Vincent's mother began to say something, then glanced at her husband and reconsidered.

The rest of the dinner was silent. His mother did not eat. When everyone else was done she rose from the table, said softly, "I have some dessert."

She took from the refrigerator a chilled bowl of watermelon cubes, set it in front of her husband. Brought some small plates. Then sat down and watched. When the others had started eating she said, with peculiar exaggerated precision, "I have no intention of having company on the Fourth of July."

His father sighed. "What?" he asked wearily.

"I can't do it. I've got enough to do. It'd take too much."

His father set down his fork. "Too much *what?* There's no work involved, nothing fancy, just a few people."

She shook her head.

"You wouldn't have to do anything special."

"You have no idea what I'd have to do."

"But I've already mentioned it to—"

"Your friends. To all *your* friends. They're all your friends anyway!"

THE FAMILY SPENT July Fourth alone, at home.

Arguments began again, disrupting what had been the uniform tranquillity of long subdued June evenings. There was never any lack of topics: Mary's summer-school troubles, his father's missing shirts, all the money his mother spent on fireworks. And as the disagreements became more frequent at night, Vincent's mother grew more unpredictable, even while his father was at work. She would suddenly turn demanding and present Vincent with an impossible list of chores. She'd say, "I have a lot I'd like to get done in this house. You going to help me, or you going to be like your father?" Vincent could never answer; her abrupt changes in tone always surprised him. Sometimes he simply refused, then tried for the rest of the day to avoid her and to steel himself against the threat that she might tell his father.

After dinner Vincent took refuge in the shed, where Paul and two friends worked on the minibike they had bought together. Sunset now, in mid-July, quelled only the day's glare and burn; the oven heat remained, constant and dry on the skin like Scotch tape. The shed smelled, exotically, of motor oil, gasoline, sweat. Vincent sat on an upside-down peach bucket near the door, Paul and his friends huddled near the workbench; a thin path, snaking through the boxes their mother had continued to stack in the shed, connected the two small clearings. Only rarely could Vincent actually see their work; a box or a head or someone's back inevitably blocked his view. But he listened to the sober metallic sounds of the tools, to his brother's and his friends' comments, quiet voices diminishing with increased effort. He watched the contortions of their shirtless torsos, the beads of sweat tracing the lines of their shoulder blades and taut necks, where they bent to work beneath a caged droplight. Sometimes they became so intent, so determinedly still, that the heat which brought out the sweat at the edges of Vincent's own scalp seemed to emanate from them, from the intensity of their combined concentration—and it could become almost too much to bear. But then suddenly one of Paul's friends would drop a wrench to the concrete floor and it would clang high and flat like a cracked bell, and he'd throw up his hands—breaking the spell of the work and heat—and say, "Why are we doing this? It'll never run right. We must be crazy," and the others, suddenly animate, would agree and laugh and stretch their arms above their heads or arch their backs and make jokes about how they'd been "taken" when they bought that piece of junk, and Vincent would laugh along with them. All of a sudden everyone would grow boisterous, and from the tin and beams all around them would start up tapping, creaking, scurrying, snapping sounds, as if the shed expanded with their laughter as a balloon expands with air.

After a few minutes Paul and his friends would gradually drop back into their places around the minibike and the noises of the shed would, for the most part—except for some rustling from boxes along the walls, at the backs of shelves—drop to near silence.

About these last sounds, Vincent didn't think twice. If he noticed them while everyone was quiet, or noticed Paul or one of his friends taking note of them, he'd think the shed must "settle" just as his house "settled." But one night after the acre of walnuts behind the backyard had been irrigated and the air that came in through the shed's open windows smelled of mud and earthworms, a great thump sounded upon the roof, and one of Paul's friends nearly shouted, "Look at *that* one!" and with pointed forefinger followed the sound—like a beanbag sliding over tin—down one wall, behind the shelves, to the floor, where Vincent glimpsed its tail and became terrified because, colored like pink chapped skin, it struck him, with all the force of unreasoning instantaneity, as part human. He pushed himself from the peach bucket and scrambled almost on hands and knees out the door, then got his feet beneath him and ran. He heard a stack of boxes fall inside the shed and turned to see Paul hurrying after him. Thirty yards from the shed, on the lawn on the side of the house, Vincent stopped and said, "Paul! There's rats in there!"

"I know," Paul said, almost smiling.

"Huge rats!"

"I know, Vincent, I know."

They stood not far from the door at the side of the house. On the other side of the door, in the den, their father slept in front of the television. Paul placed himself between Vincent and the door.

"You didn't know that before?" Paul asked.

"No."

"You never heard them?"

Vincent shook his head. He lied. Of course he'd heard sounds. He was embarrassed now to admit that he hadn't recognized them.

"Look," Paul said, walking slowly away from the door and with his voice and the position of his body leading Vincent away, "they're more afraid of you than you are of them."

"How come they're in the shed then, when I'm in there? I wouldn't go in there if I knew *they* were there." Vincent stopped walking. "We have to tell Dad."

"No. That's the *last thing* we have to do." With a hand on Vincent's shoulder, Paul coaxed him to walk again, toward the backyard. "Listen. I'll take care of it, okay? I'll take care of it. I'll get poison. Don't bother Dad."

"But shouldn't Dad—?"

"*No.* Absolutely not. God, you're just like Mary." He shook his head. *"Don't—tell—Dad,"* he said slowly. "It'll just make everything worse. Believe me."

Ultimately, Vincent promised Paul that he wouldn't tell his father; promised himself that he'd never enter the shed again.

Just keep quiet, Paul repeated. Just keep quiet.

VINCENT WAS PLAYING in the driveway, heaving a basketball up at the hoop above the carport, sweating, when his father came and said that he had a job for them. For a little over a week Vincent had experienced the unfamiliar pleasure and terror of concealing an ugly secret. For ten days he'd been in league with Paul and Mary: they who knew how, inside, the shed had changed. Outside it looked the same, but *inside . . .* With pride and with shame Vincent kept his mouth shut. For centermost in the secret he carried, physically it seemed, he felt the hollowing enervating dread, still immediate, of the rat's tail, somehow human, though horribly deformed, like a shrunken withered limb, or the scorched, scarred flesh of a man he once saw in Hal's Market, hairless on one side of his head around a melted nub of an ear.

With the ball under one arm he followed his father to the backyard.

"Have you seen the flower bed in the corner there?" his father asked. "It won't take long to make it usable again."

His father walked to the shed, and Vincent automatically lagged. He dropped ten feet behind him, but was still close enough to hear the tumult that arose with the opening of the door, the scattering thuds against every wall, the panicked scratching, scurrying, zigzags of tapping across the tin roof, all the sudden chaotic life that filled the place. Vincent retreated two steps. His father stood astounded within the doorframe, exclaimed after some moments, *"Goddamn!"* For a full minute his father stared, unmoving, futile, thwarted—like the Roman soldier, in Vincent's illustrated Bible, before the empty tomb. Then he strode forward.

"Look at this place!" He shoved the lawn mower out of his way, kicked at some boxes he found at his feet, and staggered through the clutter, turning his head in every direction, almost wildly, his arms raised slightly from his sides, as if all these things, the boxes which overflowed and nearly fell from the shelves, the yard tools and fishing poles tangled together against the wall, bobbed around him like flotsam. Then he paused in the middle of it all, seemed to gather himself—the noise of rats starting to quiet around him— walked over and tore a large box off a shelf, dropped it at his feet.

"Here are my shirts," he said, his voice not loud, but rough with anger. *"Liar."* He lifted a couple of them from the box, let them drop again. "Covered with rat shit. Goddammit." He pulled another box from the shelf. "A whole suit!" he said. "Ruined." He opened other boxes, commented on each, stacked them neatly atop one another, as if taking inventory. He found a bag of potatoes. "No wonder," he said. Then he remembered Vincent. He lifted his head, told him, "Go away. Go play. Go away, Vincent, go on."

Vincent's mother sat in the den watching an old movie with the curtains closed, the wall air conditioner on high, the room cold and damp. She smiled at him when he entered.

"I thought your father had a job for you," she said mockingly.

Vincent stopped and looked at her; miserable, he thought of warning her.

She turned her face toward the television, turned her attention to herself, changing her tone. "Oh, I'm just watching one of those old old movies," she said, as if he'd asked. "When I was young I used to think Ginger Rogers was the most beautiful woman. I look at her now and think, *well . . .* " She shrugged her shoulders. "But those dresses—oh my! They make her look like she's floating. Beautiful." She was playful, girlish. "Now Fred Astaire *never* struck me as good-looking. Too . . . *fey.*" She seemed to be talking to herself, or to an imaginary listener, but not to Vincent. "Of course, they were before my time."

Vincent turned and looked at the television, saw in black and white a man with light hair so plastered to his head that he almost looked bald, dancing before the kind of wide staircase he'd seen only in movies.

The door opened and his father entered, the box of old photographs in his arms. He said bitingly, "You certainly did a good job on the shed, dear."

Vincent quickly left the room. He walked to his bedroom to put away the basketball. Their voices rose behind him.

His father shouted, "You made a goddamn *nest* for the rats! You turned the whole thing into one big rats' nest!"

"Oh no!" his mother objected. "Don't blame me for that shack. You're the one who built it out of rotten tin. You're the one who built that place!" she insisted eagerly—ready for him. "*You're* the one. *You're* the one . . ."

Vincent left the house by a back door.

But there would be no end to this fight.

Until two days later when Vincent awoke one morning to find that his mother was gone.

*   *   *

MARY WORE GARDENING gloves, said, "I hate this! Oh, I hate this!"

Paul, about to lift a box near the workbench, raised his head to her, made a face, said without humor, "So you've told me. About a hundred times."

Vincent peeked in the door, retreated again. He wanted no part of this; he refused to step across his name in the cement. Their mother would be home, maybe, in two days. Maybe three. She'd been gone almost a week. She was sick, Mary had told him that first morning, nothing serious. Really just resting, she said. Resting, Paul agreed. Like a vacation.

Their father was visiting their mother. Before he left, he'd led the three of them to the shed, told them what to do. "Take out any of the clothes that are any good—or haven't been ruined. We can have them cleaned. Make a pile of the garbage—I'll take it away when I get back. And straighten the whole place out. You know, use your common sense," he said. He stood in the middle of the shed, hands on hips, shook his head, almost laughed. "She really did a number on this place." Then he looked at Vincent, who stood outside the door. "And you can help, too," he told him. "You can help—you're not a baby."

Vincent dropped his eyes to his feet.

"Anyway, clean the place up. She'll really appreciate it when she comes home, if it's all clean, everything nice, then she won't have anything to worry about. It'll really help things along if it's clean."

Then his father had left and Vincent had refused to help. He was afraid of the rats, he could still hear them.

Now Mary stepped out of the shed and told him, "If you don't help us, Vincent, how do you ever expect to get rid of the rats? We've got to clean everything up before the poison'll work. Once we clean it up—no more rats. Don't you want to help?"

Vincent shook his head. He knew Mary was afraid of the rats too, but she wouldn't actually say it; she had put on the gloves as soon as she saw the droppings in the first box of clothes Paul carried out. She jumped at every sound, never stopped complaining.

Paul set a box down on the lawn. "Leave him alone," he said, and headed back into the shed.

"Okay," she said to him over one shoulder, then turned back to Vincent. "But when it's all clean again and the rats are gone and you want to—"

"Will you shut up, Mary?" Paul yelled from inside the doorway. "Please? Just work, okay? Just work."

She returned to the shed. Vincent walked to a nearby tree, sat down in its shade. He would have helped, he wasn't a baby, but the rats . . . If they were gone. *When* they were gone . . . when they were gone he wouldn't be afraid of the shed.

Maybe, when his mother came home, they'd be gone. He couldn't wait to see his mother again. Two or three days. She would be rested and happy when she came home and the shed would be all clean, as good as new.

HEROES, BRAVERY, GREAT FEATS

VINCENT TORNO WAS a slight fair-skinned boy with active gray eyes who spent much of his childhood wishing he could have a different father. He was afraid of the one he had, a dark stern hardworking man whose mere presence was enough to transform a room: lamps, wineglasses, vases, all became hazardous, poised to be broken, and open spaces, offering no refuge from his father's gaze, grew harrowing. As he lay in bed at night Vincent would wonder why his older brother, who was patient and kind, couldn't be his father. Why couldn't Father Faolin be his father?

Father Faolin was a very large, barrel-chested priest who visited the Tornos every two months or so. He had a huge head, was slightly jowly even at the age of twenty-eight when the family first met him, had a wide receding hairline, and reminded Vincent of a happy, gentle St. Bernard dog. He played pool with Vincent and his brother—the only weeknights Vincent's father would tolerate the noise—and laughed with and complimented the boy. He also teased and even upbraided Vincent's father in a way no one else dared.

One evening the priest sat on the couch, made Vincent stand before him, his thick hands upon the boy's shoulders, and asked him to say the "Our Father." Vincent stumbled through it, saying "wart" instead of "Who art," "hollow" instead of "hallowed," but Father Faolin smiled encouragement until he finished, then turned to his father:

"Paul, why don't you help the boy with his prayers? This is shameful. He's a smart boy, in the second grade, and yet he doesn't properly know the Lord's Prayer? Shameful."

Vincent's father, seated on the edge of his chair, leaned forward, looked at the carpet a moment, then at the priest with a half-smile, fumbling for words. "Father . . . I . . ." He gave an embarrassed laugh. "I don't know, I don't know the prayers that well myself." Then, after a pause, said resolutely, "I send him to a Catholic school."

"Oh Paul, a boy learns from his father—it's up to the father to pass on his faith. Who do you think will teach him to be a good man, if not you? Dear Miss Petrocelli, with twenty-eight little hooligans scampering about the classroom, hasn't the time to do it for you."

Vincent's father had no response.

Vincent would remember this night for many years; it was the first of the very few times he would ever see his father embarrassed. But if his father was bested momentarily, it was not as if the priest had the final word. His father did not begin to study the prayers with him; when he was not too busy, he was too tired. Nor, ultimately, did he change at all—and perhaps this was his delayed but final response to the priest's criticism. Vincent had anxiously waited to see what would happen, but nothing had changed. And so lying in bed, Vincent, well acquainted with intimidation and fear but not yet bent beneath the idea of fate, stubbornly returned to his wish for a better father and sometimes imagined its miraculous fulfillment.

ONLY DURING THE final weeks of third grade and the first hot days of spring was Vincent invited to spend an afternoon at Hammy Oakes's house. It had been a bad winter. Vincent's mother had fallen ill,

Hammy's father had been injured at work and home on disability, and unusually heavy rains in the San Joaquin Valley had disrupted all normal activities from February through April. So by the time the weather again became predictable, the ground firm and the air dry, and Vincent and Hammy could once more walk together from school as they had for the last three years, they made their way along the familiar route with an almost desperate exuberance, in defiance of all the forces that had recently conspired against their freedom.

They walked slowly along the broad dirt shoulder of Collier Road, past the few straggly low houses fronting it, in their St. Stephen's School uniforms, the tails of their white short-sleeved shirts flapping over brown corduroy pants—Vincent trying to make every big rig driver honk. This was the first thing Hammy had taught him when they began to walk home together. He still smiled when Vincent worked up the courage to do it, and on this day he laughed out loud as Vincent clownishly staggered and doubled into exaggerated coughing after the rigs blew past, trailing dust and grit. When no one with authority was watching, and when he could overcome the thumping heart set off by the thought of almost any public performance, Vincent liked to goof around, and Hammy, who was usually serious, appreciated this. Hammy unbuttoned his shirt to his navel, let the hot breeze blow against his bare chest.

Halfway to Hammy's street, Collier crossed a canal—an intersection of blacktop and water that divided the two friends' known world into quadrants, containing, essentially: their school on the corner of Collier and Route 132, and acres of Gallo vineyards; more Gallo vineyards, more of Route 132, and the houses they'd just passed; the tract neighborhoods in which many of their classmates lived, at the edges of the town's westernmost sprawl; and their own houses (Hammy's in the lone tract—an ugly little polyp of development— west of Collier). The canal, visually unremarkable, was the axis of intensest interest running through this small world, within or along which everything fascinating and dangerous—in fact or legend—was supposed by those younger than fourteen to occur. Vincent and Hammy could not help but pause above it and look westward, toward the bend in the canal beyond which, out of sight, the drug dealers and "burnouts" were supposed to loiter. Behind the two boys, east of Collier, between the school and their classmates' houses, kids would ride bikes in the canal when it was empty in the winter; it had its own dangers and rumors, but it was known territory. West of Collier was different; Hammy always warned Vincent that people got beat up there, stabbed, shot to death. He knew all about that part of the canal's dangers, since only a flimsy redwood plank fence separated it from his own neighborhood.

They squinted against the water's glare for some minutes, but saw and heard no one. Then a diesel approached. Vincent turned to the road, lifted one fist above his head and tugged at the air, got no honk, then got carried away stumbling around in a mock fit of coughing. By the time he paused to see Hammy's reaction, Hammy was kneeling at the corner of the redwood fence, next to a huge squat cactus whose burst of thick green-gray fronds, each edged by a row of large thorns, reminded Vincent of a stegosaurus. Vincent jogged over.

With a pocketknife he always carried, though they were forbidden at school, Hammy cut a long heavy frond from the base of the cactus. Sap oozed from its bottom and from the sides where he cleared a few inches of thorns to make a handle. Then he stood and swung it over his head like a broadsword.

"Cool," Vincent drawled.

Hammy made a few quick swipes through the air, stopped, tested the thorns on his palm.

"I wouldn't like to get hit with this," he said. "Feel those." He held it out to Vincent.

The thorns were like shark's teeth. But the thing as a whole, to

Vincent, seemed a little comical, like a swollen swordfish nose, until Hammy stepped away from him, crouched intently as if he were listening for something, then suddenly turned and slashed fiercely.

Vincent gave him more room.

Hammy crouched again, seemed to listen again, eyes frozen and unseeing, as if he were listening for sounds in complete darkness rather than harsh sunlight—or for imagined or remembered sounds— then turned and slashed again, and again and again, more wildly each time, almost out of control, until he lost his balance and stumbled to a stop.

"Fuck . . ." Hammy sighed, breathing hard. Then he said, "C'mon, let's take the back way home," and started off down the canal bank.

Vincent automatically took a few steps after him, then halted abruptly. "Wait," he said. "What are you doing?"

Hammy turned, smiled. "C'mon, there's no one down here."

Vincent shook his head. "No way."

"We've got this weapon."

Vincent hesitated, refused again.

Hammy looked carefully at him, looked down the canal again, then back at him. "Okay, you're right," he said.

He started toward Vincent. "I was just kidding around. Man, like I've told you before, don't you ever go down there. Though we could've today," he added. "No one was around. Y' know, just to show it *can* be done."

"You're crazy." Vincent smiled.

"No I'm not. I don't believe in doing nothing crazy. But you gotta know what you can get away with. You can't go around scared your whole life." He nodded at the frond: "Though, if there *was* someone down there, I'm not sure this thing would've been much help. But it's pretty cool anyway. Wanta try it?"

"Nope. I don't want that gunk all over me."

"It just gets on your hands."

"No thanks."

"In a few days it'll be dried out. You can try it then." He leaned the weapon against the Collier side of the fence. "We'll leave it here. Who knows? Its thorns are real big—I bet they'd go right through some-one's cheek." He shrugged. "Maybe it'll come in handy sometime." He walked to the canal and squatted to wash his hands.

Vincent followed, looked at the stale brown water, made a face.

Hammy saw him. "What?" he laughed. "It's only muddy. Plain old dirt." He held a cupped hand of it towards Vincent, recited playfully:

> "God made dirt,
> Dirt don't hurt."

AT THE KINDERGARTEN where Vincent first met him, Hammy Oakes had proved himself a hero in both love and war. With all seriousness and with a plastic ring on which he'd spent seven dimes at the bank of gumball machines near the doors of Hal's Market, Hammy pro-posed to Laurie Butterfield, a tall stick of a five-year-old with pale, almost translucent skin. He did so in the morning before school began, oblivious to the agitated crowd of onlookers among whom stood Vincent, awestruck. Not until his own romantic travails in jun-ior high would Vincent appreciate why a boy might behave so se-riously toward a girl, and not until his first year of high school would he witness a similar show of commitment, but even without such experiences and understanding he was struck by the way Hammy stood motionlessly—completely calm and earnest in the swirl of gig-gling kindergartners—and looked unblinkingly with his brown al-most black eyes into the girl's long goofy face. Vincent sensed that here was a boy, husky and strong-looking even then, who had the stillness and steadiness of a man. And when within twenty-four hours everyone else (including the bride-to-be) had forgotten about the betrothal, Vincent alone commiserated with Hammy. For although

Vincent tended to be as excitable and silly as any other five-year-old, he was as hungry for loyalty and its reassuring stability as Hammy himself. They had been fast friends; they became best friends.

Their kindergarten was part of a school which ran to the sixth grade, and each afternoon they rode home on a yellow bus filled with older students—a short raucous trip made unbearable for Vincent by two fourth-graders. Every day these two (one fat, one tall and clumsy) sat behind Vincent and Hammy and taunted them, hovered above them, spitting names. They directed most of their hatred toward Vincent, obviously the weaker of the two; called him "pussy" and "queerbait," which made Vincent think of fishing. He didn't understand most of what he was called. What made him squirm anxiously was their unfounded and disproportionate hostility, the constant, senseless threat of violence—this he recognized, this was unmistakable. He'd sit helplessly and wonder, what did he or Hammy *do* to deserve this? They'd never even spoken to the fourth-graders.

Most of the time Hammy said just ignore them, other times he turned and threatened them, but still the harassment continued. So Vincent sat anxiously before this unending threat until one day for no reason the fat one clubbed him on the head with a book, Vincent, shamefully, began to cry, and Hammy spun around and stood on the bench seat, tugged off his leather belt, folded it in half, and shouted at them, red-faced, "Okay, c'mon! C'mon, fuckers! You asked for it!"

No response came from the fourth-graders, but the usual ambient noise of the bus dropped for a moment, then burst forth more loudly, focused now in one direction. "Fuck 'em up!" someone from the front of the bus yelled, and the bus driver, roused from her usual dreamy state, slammed on the brakes. Vincent was pitched from his corner near the window. Hammy flew into the seatback in front of him, but scrambled back up, angrier, arm cocked, and challenged them again, screaming into their faces, "*C'mon! Dammit! C'mon!*"

The fourth-graders flattened themselves against the back of their bench seat.

The bus driver came down the aisle, yelling, "Hey! Hey you, kid!"

Hammy didn't seem to notice her—"I warned you!" he shouted again—until she moved to seize his shoulders and he whirled suddenly on *her.*

"Don't you touch me! Don't you lay a *finger* on me!"

She retreated three steps. A thrown crumpled paper bounced off her head; the bus was bedlam. Vincent, scared now by Hammy's anger, touched his friend's arm. Hammy jerked his head toward him, glanced back at the fourth-graders, looked again at the bus driver, then lowered his arm and slid down into his seat. He dropped his eyes to his lap, heaved a great breath.

"Calm down now!" the bus driver yelled in every direction, "Calm down! Calm down! *Shut up!*"

When she turned back to Hammy, he just shook his head. "We didn't start it," he said. "Didn't do nothin'. Talk to them," thumbing over his shoulder in the direction of the fourth-graders.

It was a great day. The fourth-graders never bothered them again, and even Vincent's mother was impressed when he told her. After this, she always felt Vincent was safe when he was with Hammy. Hammy, though, never wanted to be reminded of it. He'd say, "Big deal," shrug his shoulders, change the subject, embarrassed.

But it was a big deal to Vincent. He'd marvel at how his friend knew to use a belt like that. Vincent never would have thought of it.

THE RANCH-STYLE HOUSE Hammy lived in was on Whitmore Avenue, the open side of the housing tract bordered on its other three sides by the long redwood plank fence. After he'd unlocked the front door he told Vincent to wait, then disappeared to the right down a dark hallway, calling loudly the names of his two high-school-aged sisters. "Patricia? Lynnette? Anybody here?" The first thing a kid usually showed a friend was his bedroom—his own private space—but Vincent had never seen Hammy's. That whole hallway, and all the rooms it led to, remained a complete mystery. Vincent waited in the entry, a six-by-six square of hardwood nearly filled by a coatstand piled with coats, until Hammy returned, saying, "Cool. They're not here," and led him to the left into the family room, also dark, and turned on the television to Channel Forty, cartoons.

"Hey look, there's Sister Constance!" Vincent pointed to Olive Oyl. "What are you doing on TV, Sister? Where's your little hat?"

Hammy laughed. "You want a Coke?" He walked into the kitchen, and Vincent stood in front of the television and looked around. The drapes were drawn over the one large window at the front of the house and the room was obscured by clutter and darkness. Hammy was the only boy in his class with a mother who worked—at the DMV. Vincent thought she must be smart, because she was serious and plain, with short boyish hair and thick black-framed glasses. Hammy's father he'd seen only briefly, one Saturday when he appeared at the edge of a field to shout Hammy home. He was wiry and wearing old jeans and a denim work shirt, sleeves rolled up above the elbows; his dark hair showed as just an outline around his high round forehead. Though Vincent knew he worked at the milk plant near the railroad tracks, he immediately made Vincent think of a cowboy—his walk made it plain he wore boots—but of the down-on-his-luck ranch-hand type, rather than Vincent's dapper TV cowboy hero, James West of *The Wild Wild West*. Not a trace of either of these two adults seemed to show up in Hammy, whose hair was light brown and whose skin had a year-round golden tint. And this lack of resemblance affirmed Vincent's belief that, in contrast to himself, his best friend was largely immune from any compromising connections to parents—able to take complete care of himself.

Hammy returned and they drank their sodas standing up, flipping

through the magazines on the coffee and end tables: *Field & Stream,*
Time, and *Life,* in sloppy stacks. They looked at the photos of the
war, admired the helicopters, the painted faces of the soldiers and
their camouflage, stared at the dead in the mud, at the bloodsoaked
clothing of the wounded—the dying and dead as foreign to them as
the Vietnamese themselves. They were serious as they looked and
said little, but for them the casualties had little heft. They felt, imagined, instead, the great weight of a machine gun slung over their
shoulders—Hammy said he'd once held one at a gun show—the
sound of the choppers. The way they'd move through the under-
growth and use it for cover.

When Vincent was done with his soda and began squeezing the
can, trying to dent the steel, Hammy said, "Hold on" and headed
toward the dark hallway. He returned with an air rifle. His birthday
present. "Check it out," he said, handing it to Vincent. They went
outside to shoot it.

The backyard looked the same as the last time Vincent had seen
it. Then they were supposedly preparing to landscape. Mrs. Oakes
had brought a neighbor out for a look and, more cheerful than Vincent had ever seen her, pointed out the pond they were going to
make, the walkway that would lead to it, told of the flowers they'd
plant, the color of gravel they'd use, and the way the whole yard
would look kind of Japanese and very peaceful. She'd described the
project in loving detail while Hammy stood behind her and grimly
shook his head. At that time, with a great crater in one corner, with
the lawn torn out and the earth bare and rough, and the fence weath-
ered, it looked to Vincent as if a bomb had exploded there. In the
year since, nothing had changed, except that weeds had grown in
and around the crater. But if it was not the Japanese garden Hammy's
mother had envisioned, it was the perfect place to shoot, and they
spent an hour trying to hit empty cans on the fence, first from a
standing position, then from their knees or bellies over the lip of the
crater, hidden by the weeds.

Hammy was a good shot. He said his father had taught him. Vincent was a poor shot, felt foolish and made jokes about how "crummy" he was, but Hammy tried to help him and was encouraging. Every time Vincent would crack a joke about himself, Hammy would smile but tell him, "That's not true," or "No you're not."

DONE SHOOTING, THEY were pleased to find they still had the house all to themselves. Vincent sat down in a chair in front of the television while Hammy went to put his gun away in his room, but Hammy said to him, "No, come on," and gestured for him to follow.

In the narrow hallway Hammy leaned the air rifle against the outside frame of the first door to the left, then opened the door. Vincent hesitated near the straining coatstand in the house's entry, a few steps away, sure that the long dark hall with its one newly opened door, and all the closed ones, would have remained off-limits as usual if Hammy's sisters or mother had been home. But his friend, standing now half in the room's light and half in the dark hall, wrinkled his brow and gestured again, and Vincent went on, slowly.

At first he noticed only a three-drawer desk opposite the door, covered by two mounds of papers, torn envelopes, a calculator. Then against each of the two walls to the right of the door he saw display cases, glass-topped and inclined slightly. Immediately he thought of the cases in the Ralston Museum, filled with strange, *almost* familiar objects from the daily life of one hundred years ago. "These things suggest what life was really like for them, the first Ralstoners," his teacher had said, and as he looked at the blackened, broken objects he'd tried but failed to imagine cowboys making use of these paltry ugly things. When he took a step toward these display cases, though, he saw patches of color so bright that at first glance they appeared to be butterflies against a rich blue background, and he was immediately attracted. Another moment, another step, and he saw they were not butterflies but medals, maybe a hundred of them, with short broad ribbons of bold hues, in complex patterns with striking contrasts, and as if their designs were asymmetrical, they seemed to throw him off balance—a thrilling feeling.

"Wow," he said and, forgetting himself, peered into a case.

The colors were peculiar, stunning—glowing canary yellows, violent reds, electric lime greens—in stripes and checks which struck him as beautiful, if beauty is felt in the stomach and intestines. And the ribbons narrowed to variously shaped medals: round targets with contrasting concentric circles, centermost a bold "1st"; triangles, also with "1st"; many shaped like pistols, a few like trees. Every one of them exotic, even if on the narrow silver plates at the top of the ribbons were names of places he'd heard all his life:

Stanislaus County Fair 1964
Strickland Gun Club 1959
Oakdale Sportsmen 1967

He'd never before seen, in person, a medal of any kind, and they made him think of heroes and bravery and great feats.

"Wow," he repeated, and looked at Hammy, who wore a slight smile. "Your dad won these?"

"Yeah. Target shooting. Pistols. All over."

"How cool."

"Yeah, I guess. The targets don't move or anything."

"Still . . . Does he ever wear them?"

Hammy laughed. "No. They're not to wear. They're like trophies—for show."

"Not even when he won them?"

Hammy shook his head.

"I'd wear them," Vincent said.

"Yeah, I know you would."

"Like a hero."

"Well, here." And Hammy stepped to the desk, knelt, opened the bottom drawer, took out a wooden box, turned on his knees, and set it on the floor. Inside, attached to a blood-red velvet ground, were two rows of medals.

"More?" Vincent said, kneeling also.

"Oh yeah. Older ones. Ones he didn't like. He gave them to me."

"Really?"

"Yeah. And for your shooting today I think you deserve a couple yourself."

Vincent laughed. But Hammy was serious. He chose two, and when he put them in Vincent's hand the metal was cool and it made Vincent's scalp suddenly tingle, made him remember where he was. He anxiously began to object, asking, "Are you *sure*? Are you *sure*?"— wanting them very much, agitated by how much he wanted them, but agitated as well by other things: Hammy's father; his shouting voice that day he came to get Hammy; his impatient stance, thumbs hooked in his front pockets, weight on one foot, at the edge of the field.

Hammy insisted, "They're mine, aren't they? You're my best friend. What am I gonna do with all these?"

Vincent took them—Hammy had always protected him from trouble, never caused it—and pinned them to his shirt. "Your dad's got a bunch of guns, then? Rifles and stuff?"

"No, not that much. Mostly pistols. That's mainly what he shoots."

Vincent looked around the room, at the closet door, the ironing board leaning against the wall. "Where are they?"

"Not in this room. In my parents'. In a closet. My mom hates them, hates to even see them." Hammy smirked. "Like they're gonna bite her or something. So they're locked up in cases. In the closet."

"You ever shot one?"

"Yeah."

"Really? Was it fun?"

Hammy shrugged. "All right. You don't know how to shoot them—the big ones—they'll break your arm. Really." He stood up to demonstrate. "The kick." He spread his feet slightly wider than his shoulders, stretched his arms before him, making a pistol of his joined hands—forefingers for the barrel, thumbs up for the hammer—and aimed into the hallway. "Like this," he said, suddenly collapsing his elbows and shooting his hands back to his forehead. "See? You can't screw around. They're not toys, like that pump gun."

Vincent stood up, ready to try it himself, then both of them heard the front door.

"Shit," Hammy said, and quickly switched off the overhead light and pushed the door almost closed. "Probably Lynnette," he whispered, slipping out. "Wait here."

Vincent stood in the dark in the center of the small room, bemused, then he heard a man's voice from the entryway. "What're you doing with that gun, Hamlin?"

"Nothing," said a voice Vincent didn't quite recognize at first— Hammy's, higher than usual, tight. "Just gonna clean it."

"Clean it, huh? You sure you weren't gonna shoot it?"

"No. No."

" 'Cause you do—without asking first—it's gone, you hear? I don't want you making trouble with that little pop gun of yours or I'll take it right back. You know that."

"Yes sir, I know."

As the man's voice had come closer, until it was very near the door, Vincent had been taking small slow steps in the dark, trying not to bump into anything, until he was against a wall. Now he felt with just the tips of his fingers—his heart beating hard—for the doorframe, and the hinges, making sure he'd be standing behind it, out of sight, if it was opened. And from this position, back flat against the wall, hardly breathing—well aware of how much his own father hated to get home from work and find some unknown kid hanging around the house—he listened to the whole exchange between Hammy and his father. The father's voice, surly, deep and insistent— *Where the hell's the mail? You got the mail? Go get it. Now. Go on*—and

Hammy's voice, higher and clearer than usual, its rhythm and tone changing in response to the slightest change in his father's. Like boxers, Vincent thought, his friend the smaller and weaker of the two, who could only react, trying to avoid whatever vague but unmistakable danger lay beneath his father's final demands, before he went to take a shower, that Hammy "keep it down," and "don't be messing around." "I'm not in the mood," his father said, on his way to the farthest reaches of the hallway. "I don't want to hear a fuckin' squeak out of you."

A minute later Hammy opened the door and silently waved Vincent out, down the hall and out the front door. In the bright open air, Vincent started to laugh with nervous relief, expecting Hammy to be right behind him, but Hammy hadn't even crossed the threshold; leaning against the inside of the jamb, he nodded once and closed the door. A faded aqua step-side pickup, blocky as the two pairs of concrete lions guarding Ralston's oldest bridge, sat backward in the drive before the garage, its headlight eyes watching the street.

WHEN HE GOT home, Vincent stopped in the kitchen for some water, and his mother, preparing dinner, noticed the medals pulling at the front of his shirt.

"Where'd you get those?" she asked.

"From Hammy. Neat, huh?"

"Where'd he get them?" she asked next.

And then: "Is he supposed to give them away?"

And: "Aren't they too valuable to give away?"

And: "Aren't you just borrowing them?"

And: "Does his mother know he gave them to you?"

A succession of questions inspiring such mounting consternation and anxiety in Vincent—even as he answered with brusque assurances and evasions (as he could risk being brusque and evasive with her)—that by the time she'd concluded with the inevitable "Does his *father* know he gave them to you?" he had vowed to himself that his own father would *never* get a glimpse of these medals. For if they'd moved his mother, who'd been in a good mood lately, to such a thorough interrogation, he realized they'd move his father to much worse—and the incontestable demand that he return them. His father distrusted gifts from outside the family, and distrusted "flashy gifts"—that's probably how his father would view the medals—from anyone.

Shaking his head with chagrin, and leaving his mother shaking hers, Vincent went to his bedroom. There he took from its hiding place in a back corner of his closet, out from beneath various empty boxes and an old pair of pants, a cardboard cigar box he'd gotten from his father. Lined with a piece of pale blue corduroy—chosen from among the other scraps in his mother's sewing cabinet as being particularly regal—this box contained the black-beaded rosary he'd received for his First Holy Communion, a 1915 buffalo nickel, an arrowhead he'd bought at Sutter's Fort (which he persisted in almost-believing authentic, despite its two-dollar price and his half-Yokut friend Darrel Shreef's certainty that it wasn't), and a 1932 quarter. He laid out the medals on the corduroy, admired the way they looked against the pale blue, then took extra care squirreling the box away again—finishing the whole process just in time, as it turned out, since he'd hardly walked out of his bedroom when he saw, through the house's large front window, his father pull into the driveway.

NEITHER VINCENT NOR Hammy ever referred to Hammy's father's surprise appearance that afternoon. Though Vincent knew it was the kind of thing a classmate like Harry Burnet, who lived across Collier and was shameless, would have badgered you about, laughing at your discomfort. Or that dim-witted Mike Wund, from the same neighborhood, would have annoyingly expressed surprise over. With guys like that, Vincent had learned, you walked a fault line, anticipating the next inevitable tremors of stupidity or petty cruelty. But between him and Hammy there had always existed an implicit and unshakable agreement never to remark upon, or even seem to notice, the standard childhood humiliations that befell the other. Besides, there was nothing particularly strange about Will Oakes's behavior—except for some of the cursing. Vincent was always being reprimanded and warned by his father: for picking at his food, or not helping his mother, or watching reruns of "those stupid old shows" (*Leave It to Beaver, Dennis the Menace*), or for generally "getting too big for his britches." He was never spanked—as his older brother and sister had been, ten years before—but his father's look and his voice—like Hammy's father's—were terrifying enough. This was why Vincent, always expecting the worst from him, avoided his own father whenever he could.

For the next few weeks Vincent and Hammy went back to spending all their time together in what they called No Man's Land, midway between Whitmore and Weston Avenues. This was a broad low levee, almost like a little hill, extending the length of the half-mile country block and dividing the Tornos' acre (and those of their neighbors) from the fields along Hammy's street. Dotting this long levee were S-shaped cement irrigation walls, four feet high, each of whose half-circles directed water from the valve within it to the fields on either side. On this levee, between the barbed or electric wire fences, between the horse or cow pastures, the smooth clean dirt of orchards—almonds, walnuts—or the tangle of acres left to grow wild, they'd walk with slingshots (and occasionally Hammy's air rifle), looking for birds, or they'd crouch within the curves of an irrigation wall, peering in opposite directions, and pretend they were sentries. Or they'd play army men, or cowboys, or Indians, and carefully pick their way through the tall weeds as if dangerous enemies hid in the fields to either side. Their raids or reconaissance missions into various properties were sometimes disrupted by angry watchdogs, or the dogs' owners, but they could do whatever they wanted in No Man's Land—out of range of all but the loudest, most determined shouts from their parents that it was time to come home.

Regardless of whatever they played, Vincent created a reason to wear his two medals and always encouraged Hammy to bring one for himself. When Hammy inevitably forgot, Vincent lent him one of his two, and reminded him again to bring one the next time. But Hammy could never seem to remember, and his lapses of memory caused Vincent to become increasingly anxious about the medals. Vincent began to repeatedly ask, "Are you sure—positive—it's okay for me to have these medals? Sure your dad's never going to want them back?" And Hammy would always say, repressing a smirk, "Yes, I'm positive, just like I told you yesterday. Old Will Oakes"—which was how Hammy scornfully referred to his father ever since that unfortunate afternoon—"ain't got no use for them. He gave them to me." And for another day Vincent would try to be reassured—even as his vague abiding sense that he really was not supposed to have the medals made him, at all times, more and more cautious with them. Eventually he never even dared to remove the cigar box from its hiding place when his own father was home.

But his father learned of the medals anyway.

From further back in his childhood than he liked to remember, Vincent had the unfortunate habit of singing to himself while he sat on the toilet at home. He hadn't even been aware he did this, much less how loudly or softly he sang, until the year previous, when his sister, Mary, had teased him as he came out of the bathroom with "Were you giving a concert in there?" Since that day he'd made a point of breaking the habit. Yet sometimes he still caught himself lapsing into it. As on this one particular Saturday near the end of the school year, when he'd come in from his family's field, where he'd been up in a walnut tree—a twice-decorated fighter pilot flying a jet—and was disgusted to realize as he was finishing up in the bathroom that he'd absently been singing "Your Song" by Elton John.

It wasn't that anyone could have heard him—his father was playing golf, his mother was at the market, his brother off at college, and Mary lay futilely trying to get a tan in the backyard—but it was such baby stuff. He washed his hands, becoming more absorbed in self-reproach than he'd been in the song, distractedly wiped them on his pants legs, then opened the door and bumped right into the shock that would, among other things, break him forever of his hated childish bathroom singing.

"Ah! There you are," his father said, before him in the narrow hallway. "Where are the pliers? The ones that are supposed to be in that kitchen drawer?"

Vincent stared at him dumbly a few moments—it was far too early for him to be home from golf—then quickly raised his arm across his chest, across his medals, making as if to rub his shoulder

"What's wrong with your shoulder?" his father immediately asked.

"Oh, nothing," Vincent said, stopping the rubbing but keeping his arm up.

"What're you wearing?"

"Just—nothing."

His father leaned toward him. "Where'd you get those? They're real."

"From Hammy. My friend."

His father moved to lift the medals; Vincent flinched, started to turn away.

"Keep still!" his father said.

Vincent felt his blood in his face.

His father examined them—his hand and black-haired forearm right beneath Vincent's chin. "Your friend won a sharpshooting medal in Merced, in 1963?"

"His dad gave them to him."

"Uh-huh. Well," he said, letting the medals drop against Vincent's bony chest, "unless his dad gave them to you, you better give them back."

Vincent said nothing.

"You hear me? They're his father's, not his. You should never have taken them."

"I didn't *take* them," Vincent weakly objected.

"*You know what I mean.* You shouldn't have *accepted them.* Does your friend live around here?"

"Yes."

"Well, you bring those back now. Don't wait. Take them off, right now."

"But—"

"No! No *buts.* Not today. Go on. And maybe you'll use your head a little next time," he added disdainfully while Vincent unclipped the medals.

Vincent walked as far toward Hammy's house as No Man's Land, then sat down near an irrigation wall, deep in the weeds. He couldn't do what his father had told him even if he'd wanted to. It was the weekend, Will Oakes was home from work, and of course Hammy's house—and often, as today, Hammy himself—was off-limits when Will Oakes was home. He opened his left hand to the sky and draped the two medals across the palm. Then he faintly bounced his hand beneath their surprising weight, enjoying the feel of gravity he got from them. He tilted his hand this way and that to make the afternoon's sunlight play on their narrow silver plates. These two medals were the things he liked best in his life, and he sat in the weeds feeling trapped: neither able to keep them nor, at least on this day, return them as his father had insisted. In fact he realized he had no choice but to lie to his father today—say he returned the medals when he hadn't—and give them to Hammy at school on Monday. He rested one of the medals on his crossed leg and considered the semiflat pistol dangling at the end of the other's blue-and-orange-striped ribbon; felt its textured grip and notched chambers between his thumb and forefinger, then lifted it to his face, where he could feel the little pistol's details even better against the soft skin of his cheek. The medals suggested a whole strange world of strength and independence, which he played at in the fields, and imagining the moment on Monday when he'd have to put them in Hammy's hand and provide some explanation (beginning, of course, with "My Dad told me . . .") he was overcome, in contrast, by a sense of failure and cowardice . . . which, after a few moments, made him decide that he wouldn't return the medals at all. To give them back was too much to ask! Not even his father could make him do it. Especially when his father, and Hammy's, just by being home, had already forced him to come up with an alternative: if he had to lie to his father today anyway, he figured, why not make the most of it?

THE FOLLOWING FRIDAY, at 8:00 A.M., was the last First Friday mass of the school year, and as usual, every St. Stephen's student was expected to attend. Sometimes by Thursday night Vincent knew he wouldn't have a ride to the church, located just across the tracks from downtown Ralston (on the west side—or what in most San Joaquin Valley towns was traditionally the "wrong" side—with its Italians, Mexicans, Okies, and small pocket of blacks), and he would sleep in late the next morning. Usually, though, as happened on this June morning, Vincent and his mother would rush out of the house and into the car, drive the two miles to the church, find no children lingering on its front steps and all of its doors closed, and then, slightly dejected, drive to St. Stephen's School, where Vincent would be left to wait until eight-fifty or so, when everyone began arriving from mass.

On mornings like these, Vincent had strongly conflicted feelings. On the one hand he found it exciting to roam the deserted schoolyard, to hang from the monkey bars in complete quiet, to walk along the rows of windows and leap up for a glimpse above the sill into each empty classroom. He felt a wonderful sense of forbidden freedom, and he thought of his classmates sitting through a boring homily under the watchful eye of their teacher. On the other hand, he liked the smell of candle wax and incense which hung in the church, and the Stations of the Cross tableaux featuring painted Barbie-size figurines, and he hated to be scolded by his teacher for not attending. And, most important, he'd heard the rumor that anyone who attended ten consecutive First Friday masses was *guaranteed* an eternal place in Heaven. So at the start of each school year he would set himself the goal of perfect attendance for ten months—even though by November of each year he would inevitably have faltered. In fact, the only student who missed more First Friday masses than Vincent was Hammy, who missed every one of them. This lessened Vincent's disappointment. For even in the face of a long stint in purgatory (he couldn't believe he'd deserve outright damnation), Vincent was comforted by the thought that sometime after eight-thirty he would see Hammy approaching the school, walking slowly, turning his head to watch every big truck rumble past.

Hammy, always absent from mass, was always scolded by the teacher. Whereas Vincent would blush beneath the assault, his mind racing unsuccessfully to find some excuse, Hammy would listen without expression, respectfully, patiently, to all of Sister Constance's exhortations to carpool to church if his parents couldn't bring him, would nod at all the right times, and when she finished, would finally shrug once as if all this talk failed to acknowledge the simple, regrettable, but absolute impossibility of the matter. When Vincent, foolishly hoping that his absence at church hadn't been noticed, tried to mix in with the crowds of children being dropped off in the school parking lot, Hammy sometimes joined him, loyally bolstering him with his company. But often, as Vincent peered around a corner of the school building, watching for an opportunity, Hammy, with a wave of one hand and a resignation that Vincent, in his stubborn child's optimism, found strange, would ask, "Why fake it? They know I never make mass. I can't change that. But you go ahead. You give it a try—maybe it'll work."

And he responded with a similar fatalism when Vincent suggested they might carpool together to ten straight First Fridays and be eternally saved.

So on this final First Friday of the school year Vincent was surprised when he waited at the edge of the playground near Collier until nine and didn't meet Hammy. He waited so long he arrived late for math; Sister Constance, with particular vehemence, scolded him in front of the class, and he felt his face pulse red.

Surprising, too, was Hammy's absence from school the following Monday. And more surprising yet, his complete absence from the final week of classes, and from the fields and No Man's Land. He seemed simply to have disappeared, and if Sister Constance or anyone else in the school knew his whereabouts, they didn't tell the class.

On the final day of the school year, Vincent even considered knocking on the door of Hammy's house. He devised an unconvincing image of Hammy answering the door in pajamas—foolish, he knew, because he never remembered him being sick. But he held on to this image as he walked down Whitmore Avenue, held on to it until he saw the faded aqua pickup parked backward in the driveway. It was only three-twenty in the afternoon. He didn't dare knock at the door.

But he didn't know what to do. He wandered back toward school along Collier Road. Sometimes kids stayed late on the last day, shooting baskets or playing softball. As he passed the canal he heard, at a distance, voices, laughter. He paused, peered down the canal, but didn't see anyone, heard only violent laughter and a sharp play of voices punctuated by curses, then more laughter, which grew fainter until he heard only the cars and trucks passing on the road. He remembered the weapon Hammy had left at the corner of the plank fence. He listened carefully to make sure the voices were not returning, then walked to the fence, smiling at the thought of himself fending off a couple "druggies" with the frond. Maybe it'll come in handy, Hammy had said—but not for Vincent. Maybe for Hammy, who could defend himself with something like that, with anything, but not Vincent.

It still leaned against the fence. Vincent thought he'd take it home with him, put on his two medals and swing it over his head, slice through the tall weeds with it, be a Civil War hero. He bent to pick it up, then pulled his hand back. Instead of drying into a useful weapon, the frond had turned rancid; its tough green-gray hide had become soft and shriveled, like flesh. Vincent didn't dare touch it, and when he knelt to look more closely the smell drove him back and to his feet again. It was completely useless to him, not even good for make-believe or play—much less protection. He couldn't do a thing with it.

VINCENT WOULD NOT see Hammy again. Though, of course, all through that summer he couldn't know this, and couldn't, or wouldn't, fully conceive of it for many years. On the hottest days of August, Vincent slogged through the submerged irrigated fields (swamps in the games he and Hammy had played) only to find, as always, the Oakeses' house shut up, its windows closed, its curtains drawn, and Will Oakes's faded aqua pickup backward in the driveway. In his loyalty to Hammy, Vincent lived in the continual hope, if not expectation, of that one unusual day when he'd see, in place of the pickup, Hammy's mother's brown Dodge, and the open front door, dark masses of furniture visible through its screen. Or he imagined he'd find Hammy waiting for the morning bell on the first day of school, leaning backward as he often did into the give of the chain-link baseball backstop, knees locked, arms stretched taut over his head, with the first two fingers of each hand hooked into the diamond-patterned wires—partly sitting, partly standing, partly hanging.

Instead, in place of Hammy he found, among his classmates, indifference. No one had seen or heard from Hammy. At the end of the school year, his disappearance had been a surprise. In the fall everyone simply assumed that he'd been transferred to another school. To which school? No one, besides Vincent, really cared. Harry Burnet's father, who worked on the railroad, had gotten one of his legs crushed between the couplings of two boxcars. This was the big story.

Stories about what had happened to Hammy came from other sources that fall. Mrs. Tolan, for one, the school secretary, who lived in an old farmhouse down the street from Hammy, beyond the clutch of the housing tract. Vincent sometimes took rides from her; she'd drop him off on her way home, on the corner of Collier and Whitmore. One afternoon while he waited outside the closed door of her office he heard her, speaking as usual too loudly into the phone, mention Marian Oakes.

"A terrible thing," she said.

Vincent leaned against the frame of her door.

"The poor children," more softly.

"Yes— Well— Not—" She was continually interrupted by her distant and (to Vincent) silent interlocutor.

Finally, she burst out, "He was never a good man! There was always something wrong there," she added, then a buzzer sounded and she had to hang up; the principal, Sister Christine, wanted her.

Bobby Bowen told him more.

"You won't see him again," he said, when Vincent asked him about Hammy. Bobby lived three houses down from the Oakeses, in a house identical to Hammy's in everything but color. He went to a public school. Vincent was startled to find him, crumpled unlit cigarette in his lips, pellet gun in his hands, one Saturday morning in the Tornos' orchard (though Vincent said nothing of the trespass, since he was a little scared of Bobby). Bobby said, "Him and his mom and his sisters—they're long gone. Old big daddy, cowboy, gunslinger, threatened to use them for target practice."

"What do you mean? Why?" Vincent asked.

Bobby removed the cigarette and spat, keeping his eyes on the treetops for birds; repeated *"Why?"* as though it had been asked by some stupid naive girl. "Because he blew a *fuckin' fuse* or something, man, I don't know. He was a bad-ass. One day me and Hammy were gonna take out one of those pistols of his and fire off some rounds in Pruitt's field, but Hammy wussed out. Though I don't totally blame him, 'cause if his dad found out he would've beat the shit— Wait. Shut up." And Vincent watched him creep to a tree, steady his gun against its trunk, and shoot. Two crows cawed angrily and flapped up from the top of a walnut tree—"Shit," Bobby said— then resettled twenty yards away. Bobby pursued and missed and pursued; the crows, arrogant, unfrightened, resettling each time not more than fifty yards off, sometimes even in the same tree, Bobby and his unlit cigarette trailing them (Vincent not daring to laugh), until they led him from Vincent's field into the Nollinses', where Vincent followed, waiting for more information—though Bobby would say nothing else except "He's gone, man, he's gone," and "Shut up. Wait. Shit! Shut up!"

Finally, Vincent asked his mother—it being one of those times when he could risk such questions with her. Sometimes his mother could suddenly turn on him, call him hardheaded or speak to him in a tone of hatred. More often, she was as decorous as the form letters she'd learned to compose in business school (where she'd gone since her parents couldn't afford to send her to college) and tended to avoid inappropriate topics like sex and brutality and death. So when in response to his question about whether she'd heard anything about Hammy or his parents, she shook her head, said, "No. No," looked serious for a moment, then, with a renewed effort at casualness, said, "I haven't heard a word," Vincent felt compelled to imagine the worst.

And, in fact, he didn't have trouble believing Bobby's story. He just couldn't picture it: Will Oakes with one of the pistols, which Vincent had never seen; one of those that Hammy said would break your arm if you didn't know how to shoot it. He couldn't imagine Hammy and his mother and sisters running from the house, his father chasing them, like a cartoon—that was stupid. He couldn't imagine them sneaking away during the middle of the night, stumbling out the front door with suitcases—also stupid. But he could believe that somehow Will Oakes had forced them to leave, that he drove them out, frightened them away, "blew a fuse." He knew this could be true, because he remembered how that whole great spring afternoon of shooting and medals had been shattered when Will Oakes came home; remembered the panic he felt hiding in the dark room and the complete change in Hammy. At the time it had all seemed familiar enough, but after nearly six months of Hammy's absence he now realized how much worse it was than anything he could have imagined. His own father was not nearly as bad as Will Oakes. Nowhere near as bad as that.

The next time Vincent took the medals from the cigar box he discovered he no longer wanted them. With Hammy gone they suddenly became beyond all doubt—and just as his own father had said as soon as he saw them—Will Oakes's property. Vincent didn't want anything of Will Oakes's. And he didn't want anything that now reminded him more of his father catching him with the medals than of Hammy. Besides, maybe the missing medals had been what set Will Oakes off. In this case, Vincent was guilty of something much worse than accepting gifts he shouldn't have or not returning them when he was supposed to; he had betrayed his best friend to Will Oakes's wrath. This was the thought that bothered Vincent the most. If it was true it was the worst thing he had done.

Having decided to return the medals, Vincent brought them to school folded tightly in a brown paper lunch bag, which he kept uncomfortably, penitentially, all day in his front pocket. Then on his way home, planning exactly how he'd walk along the edge of Hammy's street, open the mailbox, and slip the medals in without breaking stride, he stopped above the canal, leaned his arms on the concrete guard wall, and looked in. It had been drained over the weekend, and what was revealed now sickened him even more than it had the first time he'd seen it, in first grade, when some brief reference by Hammy to shells along the bottom of the canal had inspired him to anticipate, excitedly and completely mistakenly, the pale seashells and sand dollars of the Pacific. Below him, huge sludgy heaps of dark shells were banked against both of the canal's sloping concrete sides and spilled across the shallow fetid slough in its middle, where it deepened slightly beneath Collier. Highest up the sides the shallow long shells, some open, some broken, had dried to ugly blue-black and gray, dull and flaky, but lower, down in the green-brown slime, tangled with muck, they still shone black—like fingery coffins—with a filthy dragon-fly iridescence. Farther away down the puddled canal, before it curved out of sight, he saw what appeared to be the slimy frame of a recliner on its side; closer to him, an ironing board, its scissor legs extended into the air, twisted, and shagged with muck.

He'd never before seen the canal so freshly drained, though he'd always wanted to. It was rumored that if you got to the canal soon enough after it was emptied, before other kids or Ralston Irrigation District workers got there, you'd find stolen skateboards and bicycles; maybe even a car, or part of one. But instead he now found only household junk and the shells—clouds of bugs hovering above them—stinking and shining much more than when he'd seen them before; every ugly thing glaring and reeking with hopelessness. He seemed to hear his father say, *If you'd returned the medals when I told you.*

He'd been right, Vincent thought. Maybe. He should have returned them to Hammy as soon as he had the chance.

How could you have taken them in the first place?

Because Hammy gave them to me, Vincent thought—then realized how lame this would have sounded to his father.

According to his father, no one ever got away without punishment for mistakes. Your errors always boomeranged right back at you; you were always found out. At school, teachers sometimes said similar things, but they were talking about God's judgment, and the punishment was in the distant future, and if you confessed before you died you had a chance to get out of it.

His father never gave anyone that much time.

Now he would do exactly as his father had told him months before, though it would change nothing. Hammy would not come back. Though now he would obey his father—too late—and return the medals—too late—to the man who'd chased away his best friend.

He took the medals from his pocket, unwrapped them from the brown bag, then looked at them stretched across the palm of his right hand—dangling pistol at the end of a blue-and-orange ribbon, dangling target at the end of a checked one, colored blue and black like the shells.

What good would it do to return them if he was already found out, already guilty? To do as his father said, like a good obedient boy, though that was not what he was—or at least, he now realized, not what he wanted to be?

Hammy had said, *You can't go around scared your whole life.*

Vincent closed the medals tightly in his hand, and with a short angry overhand motion threw them down into the foul-smelling mess of shells.

DURING THE LONG Christmas break, thick tule fog covered much of the San Joaquin Valley, made each day oppressively short, gray, damp, and made Vincent keenly aware of Hammy's absence. Luckily, the New Year brought Father Faolin to the Tornos' house. He was so tall he had to duck beneath the doorframe, so large that upon his entry the dimensions of the living room seemed to shift, as if every object had been stirred from its usual static place or shaken like mercury in a sealed jar into new sizes and relations. Vincent's father crumpled his newspaper to one side and stood quickly to greet the priest, his older brother and sister came from the far end of the house, his mother from the kitchen. Father Faolin came loaded with new jokes about Irishmen and Italians and golf, with stories of the confusion that bubbled in the rectory during the holidays and one about midnight mass when he glanced at his altar boys in the middle of his homily and found them both asleep, like babes. He said he'd want Vincent for next year's mass; he'd leave the windows wide open in the church and give him a cup of strong coffee—and if that didn't work, a little kick in passing. He played pool with Vincent and his sister and brother (he wanted to play for a dime a game, but Vincent's father wouldn't allow gambling). He even persuaded Vincent's parents to play one game each. Many years later Vincent would think of these evenings—not the tense stressful trips to Disneyland—as the only vacations his family had ever had, the nearest they came to being released from their daily lives, from their constricting senses of fear and duty and guilt, from their cramped close places in the family. But they were short-lived respites. Especially for Vincent, whose father strictly enforced his bedtime.

GOING UNDER

MY MOTHER LAY in a hospital on the opposite edge of town from where we lived. The same place she'd stayed a couple of times before, with vague never-explained ailments, when I'd been too young to visit hospitals. Now I was with my father and he drove on the road that ran alongside the big canal, filled with dirty water and crossed every now and then by concrete footbridges—where the watergates were. It was a brutally hot Sunday in mid-September and there were small clusters of Okies on almost every bridge we passed, wearing ragged cutoffs (and T-shirts, if they were girls), clowning around and jostling for their turns to slide with the rushing water down the gates' short falls. At St. Stephen's School we were lectured on canal safety every spring and fall, and my father always said that swimming in the canals was as filthy as washing your face in a mud puddle, so I knew it was something only Okies did. Kids from public schools and shabby families who weren't taught of the dangers: of the big branches, old rotting shrubs, and discarded ropes that would tangle your feet so you couldn't swim. Kids who were never warned of— or were too stupid to heed—the whirlpools that would swirl around you until you didn't have the strength left to resist them. Watery tornadoes, I'd always imagined, that would catch hold of you and spin you down to the canal's slimy floor.

The kids' faces were disfigured in shouts, but I could hear nothing.
My father had the windows up against the heat. From the air conditioner came streams smelling sickly-metallic and dusty, carrying the
scent of whatever had settled unseen inside the vents and the hoses
that coiled beneath the dashboard. The sun had faded the top of the
gray dashboard to a whitish color, with dirty-looking swipes where
I'd once used a rag soaked with Windex to try to clean the layer of
dust that always coated it. The armrest on the driver's side door was
blackened from my father's forearm. There was a map of Arizona, a
penlight, and a cracked collapsible travel cup in the glove box. A St.
Stephen's Church bulletin, rigid, forgotten, curled beneath the passenger seat. These last things I knew from the few times my father
left his car at home, when I crawled around inside it knowing he
would be gone for the entire afternoon and I'd have time to pretend
the long silver Buick was a submarine, so that anytime I left its con-
fines I had to hold my breath or drown. (The whole Central Valley
had once been a sea, a certain teacher always used to remind us:
"Our crops flourish in its *ancient sedimentary bed.*") But on this afternoon
the Buick seemed more like a submarine than ever before. It was cold
inside the car, beneath a dingy cloudless sky, and the only sound
was the air conditioner, whose air was strangely unnatural enough to
seem necessary, as though it provided the only environment—man-
made—in which I could survive, separate from everything outside,
from the wet Okies whom I couldn't even hear as I sat without a
word and no thought of a word or even a look at my brooding father.

We crossed an overpass spanning the 99 Highway, passed a Kmart
and a Putt-Putt Golf course, then the road and canal were bordered
on either side by tall plank fences and cinder-block walls, above
which I could see the rooflines and chimneys of houses. We passed
the neighborhood, where Richie Smith lived, of skinny short trees
that provided no shade and whose useless presence made the sun
and heat seem all the more intense. One summer I'd gone to Richie's
house for his birthday party. A "Swimming Party," the invitation said.

It was held in the backyard, with traffic sounds rushing over the fence, beside a large mudhole that Richie and his older brother, Rusty, had dug. I'd forgotten my swim trunks, so I sat and watched Richie and Darrel Shreef and Harry Burnet and others splash and slip around, and was watched in turn by Richie's father, who sat in a lawn chair beneath the lone tree, a can of Shasta cola resting between his thighs. I'd rejected a pair of Rusty's shorts—much too big—that he'd offered to let me borrow. So he sat and glared at me. "What's the matter," he'd said finally, after I'd refused for the third time, "pool's not good enough for you? Shorts not good enough for you?" He had the same small nose as Richie and the same accent, the same kind of face that always looked a little bruised, the same crew cut.

I looked nothing like my father. In all the photos I'd ever seen of him his hair was short and grew straight back from the broad almost flat horizon of his hairline. It was black and gray, like the engines of the trucks and forklifts at his warehouse. My hair was reddish-brown and had to be cut often because it grew in erratic curls over the tops of my ears. It had been even curlier when I was a baby, and blond, and my mother had saved clippings from that time, in a blank envelope in the top drawer of her dresser. When my mother left for the hospital with my father it was nighttime and I slept on the couch beneath an afghan, sick with the flu. I woke to my parents' voices, to my mother, carrying a small tan box of an overnight case, and my father waiting at the door, his hand on the knob. Then my mother quickly left the room, walking toward the opposite end of the house, and my father followed. When she entered again I was more awake. She came into the room alone, but I knew my father would follow and I waited for him. She noticed me watching her and from the middle of the room said, "I'm going now. I'm going to the hospital, I won't be long, everything will be fine. Everything will be fine." She looked toward the kitchen door as she said this—not at me—anticipating my father's entrance. She took short, hesitant, nervous steps, forward and back, side to side, moving constantly, but going nowhere. Her eyes darted between the kitchen doorway and her hands, joined together on the handle of the overnight case—both looking for my father and looking to avoid him when he entered, which he soon did. Then he was at the door again, Mary, red-eyed, stood in the doorway to the kitchen, and my mother said, "This is all for the best. Everything will be fine, it's okay, you'll see, things will change and everything will be better and you'll see. Everything will be better, don't worry about me, I'll be home soon, see you soon." And she stepped toward me for just a moment, bent at the waist, still keeping her distance, and gave a quick tug at a curl by my ear. Then both of my parents were gone.

Toward the center of town the rooftops receded from the road and the trees became tall, dark green, dense with leaves. In this neighborhood my mother's mother lived, on a short narrow street shaded by great branches that arched over it from either side and met above its middle to form a cover, like the plaster vault of St. Stephen's Church. It was where I always spent New Year's Eve and my parents' anniversary—nights when my parents stayed out late. But I spent nonholidays there, too. I liked my grandmother's house: small and white, with plain unassuming pillars on its low porch, a trim little unfenced yard in the front, and a rose garden and larger plot of lawn bordered by a tall brick wall and a white garage in the back. One heavy arm of her neighbor's cherry tree stretched over the corner formed by the garage and brick wall, and in the corner opposite, in a niche near the house, stood a tall statue of the Virgin Mary with one bare foot on the throat of a sea serpent, writhing, with fins and long curling tail. This was painted in lifelike colors. Inside the house she had an unused pink ashtray with the words CATALINA ISLAND curving above a picture of a sailboat, and a copper statue of the Empire State Building. A crucifix hung above the door of the bedroom where I slept, and on the wall was an old beige photograph of my dead grandfather in a tie and jacket, with a smooth smiling face. When we walked to the shopping centers strung by their large parking lots along Ralston's main boulevard, MacAffee, she insisted I walk between her and the street, where a gentleman was supposed to walk—"so if someone throws garbage out of a passing car it will soil the man, not the lady." Every time we went shopping she bought me something. Sometimes we took the bus, as if we were in a big city.

But this time my mother went into the hospital I didn't stay at my grandmother's house as I had before. During those times my grandmother had helped me make cards for my mother, letting me use her ancient typewriter, heavy as lead, on which she wrote to her friends and relatives back East and in Italy. When I was still learning to read she used to spell each word for me, patiently letting me hunt among the round keys—so much like a patch of clover—for the right letters. This time my father wanted me with him, and he and Mary and I sat together silently at late dinners, after he got home from work. On nights when he went straight from work to the hospital, Mary and I would eat TV dinners, then she'd talk on the phone (sometimes to Paul, at college) or have her best friend over, and they'd have long pained discussions in the rarely used living room, sitting cross-legged at the feet of furniture which existed, for the most part, only for display, while I watched television in the den. Sometimes Mary would ask about my new teacher, or if there were any new students this year, or any changes at school. Then, inevitably, she'd abruptly say, *This is all for the best. It'll be okay*—and I'd be unable to stand her anymore. I'd wish she'd just leave me alone, go into the kitchen, make a phone call.

At MacAffee Boulevard, beneath which the canal disappeared, my father had to stop for a red light, and I began to think about swimmers who must have tried to swim underwater from one side of the four-lane road to the other. One day at school, Sean Koons had said he'd done it. He always made claims like this and I rarely believed any of them. But there must have been some swimmers who really had done it—or at least tried. Maybe someone on a dare. Or in a game of Truth or Dare, which I hated because its whole point was to frighten and humiliate. Someone could probably do it, even though the water was so dirty that he wouldn't be able to open his eyes and would just have to try to swim, blindly, as straight as possible from the start. Whenever my grandmother and I crossed the canal on our walks down MacAffee, I tried to estimate how long it would take to make this swim. Today, though, as my father's car idled at the intersection, I imagined a swimmer who ran out of air beneath the middle of the road and kicked up toward the water's surface only to find no surface and no air and no light. Someone who came up fast, breathless and scared, and slammed into the bottom of the road, where he'd stay for the rest of time, floating against the concrete that vibrated with the cars passing above. I wondered how many bodies were trapped in this way, and imagined how creepy it would be if someone on a dare got tangled up with these rotting corpses. But possibly there was just a slender layer of air between the bottom of MacAffee and the water's surface, maybe an inch or two, so that a swimmer who ran out of air could, if he rose slowly enough, carefully raise his face close to the road's underside and breathe. And maybe just tread water like that, his head lifted, only his nose and mouth above the surface, and try to remember—in the midst of all those failed and decaying swimmers—the way out.

Across MacAffee the trees of the older neighborhoods remained big and green for a while, then gradually began to thin and shrink, then—just before orchards that stretched out of town—we reached the hospital, four stories high beside the canal. As we drove through the parking lot I saw my mother's three aunts coming out of the hospital doors. My father cursed. My great-aunts all lived in moldy-smelling houses, and held birthday parties for their grandchildren in the center of Almeda Park, at the wooden picnic benches and tables, where everyone could see them carrying on. Their husbands (two were still living) worked for the post office, and were always home from work by four o' clock. These men—both non-Italians—did foolish things and laughed at themselves. The bald, squat one, Fred, spent all his free time playing with his model trains in a room filled with plaster-of-paris mountains and miniature redwoods, tiny towns and scaled-down warehouses and little men. "None of that family works too hard," my father would say to my mother after weddings. And whenever my mother visited them, she'd always embarrass me with how loudly she laughed and talked.

My great-aunts didn't seem to see us, though, and left together in one car. I followed my silent father from the harsh light and heat of the parking lot into the cool hospital, then past the gift shop whose toy-filled windows made me think it might be fun to be sick if people would bring you things. Even though the toys and games in the window looked shoddy, down-sized, I could sense the extra pleasure that would come from a gift-shop toy brought to you in a hospital when you had good reason to stay in bed beneath fresh sheets and watch television, good reason to do nothing at all except receive gifts.

I tried to imagine how my mother would look, lying in bed in a hospital gown with tubes in her arms or maybe her nose, like her father beneath his clear little tent before he died. She didn't look sick before she left, didn't suddenly collapse, soaked with sweat, as he had. I was sicker than she was, in bed with the flu—she was active, busy. On the day before I became sick, she took down from the wall behind my father's recliner all the school and baby and wedding photos, Paul's high school graduation portrait, pulled all the nails out, hammered in new ones, then rehung the photos. The next day while I lay in bed, home from school, I heard her take them all down again, heard the hammering, then saw, later, that she'd altered their placement again. Then, finally, the day before she left she did it all once more: pulled out the nails, hammered in new ones, moved our family photos. I was lying on the couch and she worked without paying any attention to me. By this time, after all the rearranging, it had become a challenge for her to conceal the holes in the plaster. I couldn't help but watch her—it was like she was doing a puzzle.

At the fourth floor the elevator opened to two couches near a large tinted window, two coffee tables covered with magazines, and, to the left, a broad hallway ending abruptly in a wall with a door in its center. The door was closed, and had a small square window, crisscrossed by wire. Cut out of the left side of the hallway, before the door, was a nurses' station.

My father walked with me to a couch, told me to sit down.

"I'll bring your mother out," he said, awkwardly standing over me. He took a step back—a better angle to talk. "She wanted to see you. I'll go get her. Just a minute." He gave a quick half-smile—a grimace, actually—dropped his head, turned, and walked to the nurse behind her counter. They spoke briefly, then he stepped in front of the door, his back to me, his head upright, painfully still, until the nurse, distracted for a few moments by a ringing phone, buzzed the door unlocked and he quickly pulled it open and disappeared behind it.

When I was four years old my mother took me to visit my grandfather in the special care section of a nursing home and I saw a man, tottering down the hall, who wore an oxygen mask over his nose and mouth and cradled a slender scuba-like tank in his arms. I imagined, for a minute, my mother coming out in a mask like that. But I knew it wouldn't happen. I wondered if she had a roommate. If she had a television. Or if she had her own room, like her father, where everything was quiet and there was no TV, where he'd sat almost straight up beneath the clear tent, eyes frozen on nothing. When our St. Stephen's pastor, Father Alvarez, went into the hospital for an operation the whole school said prayers for him each morning before class. Twice in one week we took time out of math to make cards for him. It was almost like a holiday—but serious. I'd written a card for my mother, but realized now that I'd left it at home. No one at school knew my mother was in the hospital.

I turned on the couch, looked out the window at the brimming canal. Two kids on bikes rode along the edge of it. When the canals were empty, in the winter, I'd go with a bunch of other kids to ride our bikes up and down the canal near our school. The trick was to set off from the top at an angle, then slant down one side and up the other. If you went straight down you'd be thrown over your handlebars when your front wheel hit the place where the canal's sloping side met its floor. One day Richie Smith came to school with half of his face bruised and said he "ate it" at the canal. But I never saw anyone actually go over the handlebars. Frankie Banelli, a runty, big-headed asthmatic kid, once had his pedals in the wrong position so that halfway down the side a pedal hit concrete and made his whole bike jump. He didn't come close to falling—still, he never went down the side again. But Sean Koons was the best canal rider. He'd lift his feet from the pedals as he set off, and angle down and up with both of them resting on his handlebars. He'd do it standing: his feet on the bike seat, legs straight, and head and shoulders so far forward (he still had to use his hands to steer) that it looked like the slightest bump would pitch him into the concrete. He was at least a year younger than anyone else at the canal, and he dipped Copenhagen. Before and after school his lower lip bulged with it, revealing some of the soft shiny redness of the inside of his mouth and the black of the finely ground peppery-smelling tobacco. He dipped when he rode. He was fearless.

But, though no one else seemed to remember, Sean Koons had been very different when he first appeared at school, with his mother. On that day he'd been pale and skinny and small, holding on to his mother's hand, timidly. And his mother had worn a muddy-colored coat, all askew, and her short dark hair lay flat against one side of her head, as though she'd just risen from a nap. She was older than any other mother I'd seen at school, confused-looking, and she moved with the hesitancy of a foreigner, slowly approaching the door of the school, risking only a few steps down the hall, before coming outside again, and looking all around for assistance, for signs. I expected her to have an accent. She walked up to a group of us on the edge of the playground, still moving feebly, still pulling Sean along, and asked us where the front office was. And when I heard her voice, unaccented, but sounding as lost and exhausted as she looked, and saw close-up the alien and shabby kind of helplessness in which she was clothed, older as she was and strange, with Sean at the end of her arm, and having to ask a smart-ass like Harry Burnet for directions, my breath was forced from me by a sudden shame, so I could never remember if Harry gave her the right directions or lied to her or anything that he said. I remembered only the laughter and jokes that followed her away.

The waiting room was noiseless, except for the nurse thumbing through papers, or answering the softly ringing phone. I slumped on the couch, stared dumbly at the glossy magazines on the table before me, let the photos on their covers blur into a jumble of formless colors, the words—as though I didn't know how to read—scatter into letters, meaningless shapes.

Perhaps I wouldn't see my mother today after all. I hoped I would not.

But the door near the nurses' station buzzed, then came the noise of someone fumbling with the knob. Through the wires on the window I saw the top of my mother's head, then a glimpse of my father's face and shoulder as he reached around from behind her to help. The door opened and my mother stood still in its frame. She wore her heavy red bathrobe from home, wrapped tightly around her same old off-white nightgown. Her face was very pale, except for deep pink at the edges of her eyelids. My father, from behind, touched the small of her back and she vaguely smiled at me, then started toward me slowly and unsteadily—walking, with great effort, as if she waded to me through water, waist-high.

WHEN I WAS eleven years old my father built a warehouse of gargantuan proportions for his wine and beer distributorship. Large as a football field, with a roof twenty-six feet above its concrete floor, it seemed a space fit for a giant. A comic giant. For when I first saw it, after school let out for the summer, its plasterboard walls—each panel printed irregularly with its manufacturer's name in faint red and blue and marred by various accidental scuffs and stains—suggested a crazy kind of wallpaper. In fact, as the interior neared completion I half expected that one day I'd find a huge armchair in one corner and, off to the side, an elephantine coffee table fronting a massive floral-print sofa, whose every blossom was as big as a car. But instead, the motley walls were hidden beneath flat white paint, and as the painter started on the ceiling, I was put to work in the warehouse's attic.

For reasons never revealed to me (or perhaps for no reason at all), the trapdoor entrance to the attic was located in the very center of the warehouse's ceiling and accessible only with the painter's scaffold. This vehicle consisted merely of four car tires, grayed by age and use, and a towering iron frame supporting long wooden planks at various levels, but it made me think of the rudimentary skeleton of a Trojan horse. On the Monday after lunch that I began working in the attic I found the painter seated in the center of it, halfway up, taking a break, his mask loose around his neck, a plastic one-gallon Coleman cooler beside him.

"Hello! You must be Vincent," he called from his perch, his voice friendly and upbeat, a little like a grammar school teacher. He climbed down carefully, slowly, then shook my hand. "Your father said he'd send you out here today. So you're the one who's going to have to clean up after those electricians, huh? My name's Johnny." He was tall and thin, with longish, loosely curled red-blond hair and a beard, and both his painter's pants and T-shirt were white, except for a faded and cloudy two-colored print upon his back, which I tried unsuccessfully to decipher as I climbed behind him up toward the ceiling.

When we both stood upon the top plank, he stuck his head into the attic, looked around, withdrew it, and turned to me. "Okay." He ticked off upon the tips of his fingers: "You've got some gunnysacks in there, some chicken wire, a pair of wire cutters, a box of horseshoe nails, a hammer, a droplight with a whole bunch of cord, and"—he smiled—"I think a kitchen sink. Everything you'll need."

I wasn't tall enough to climb directly into the attic. I had to grab the frame of the door with my hands, place a foot upon the lower of the two sidebars surrounding the top plank, then pull and frogkick my way through the trapdoor.

"Let me know if you need anything," the painter shouted when he'd returned to the ground. "Ice water, whatever. Just give me a holler." Then he pushed the scaffold to another part of the warehouse, where he'd left off.

The attic's roof was peaked along its length at a height of about ten feet, and the dark triangular space with its long rows of two-by-fours, its slanting roof supports, seemed like a perfectly ordered forest. The only light came from the trapdoor and from long narrow vents spaced along the edges of the building. One of my jobs would be to nail chicken wire over each of these—to keep pigeons and other birds out. But first I had to clean up after the various craftsmen who'd worked in the space before me. I was supposed to pick up the odd pieces of conduit, discarded paper, tangled plastic, the cardboard spools from which electricians had unrolled their wire, Styrofoam coffee cups (some still partly full), and all the other scraps and garbage typically left behind at a work site. Any of the materials that might be of future use I was to save. And as a fringe benefit I could claim all of the clipped lengths of copper wire for myself. Later, I'd realize this was a prospect that had excited me beyond reason. But at first it was as though I'd been given sole title to an area which promised to yield metal much more valuable than mere copper, and I spent too much time in the dark attic stripping insulation from shiny wires ultimately worth only pennies a pound.

THE NEW WAREHOUSE shared a wall with what had already become known as the "old warehouse," but by Tuesday I knew I much preferred my work in the attic to my usual jobs. Typically, once a week every summer since I was eight, I'd swept out the (old) warehouse—a dirty job that took almost an entire morning. Pallets of beer, in bottles and cans, were stacked three or sometimes four high, in long rows, so that to sweep out a newly depleted row was to sweep out a narrow canyon—to either side, immense cliffs of glass or aluminum that I imagined collapsing upon me and my push broom. Rat droppings spotted the bottoms of these pallets and the base of the walls, black widows nested among cartons of wine bottles, and the building was filled with the dusty splintery smell of old pallets and the dry headachy smell of cardboard, and with the forklift's black exhaust. Sometimes my brother, Paul, who spent his college breaks at my father's other warehouse (in Strickland, thirty miles to the north) driving a delivery truck for our uncle, would tell me I had it easy; when he was my age our father made him clean the Strickland warehouse, too, and sometimes even took him along on routes. But I believed I had it bad enough: a few hours of sweeping meant I'd be blowing itchy black mucus—at first more dirt than snot—into a handkerchief until the next morning. And whenever an entire pallet of wine or beer was dropped by a forklift driver and my father lost his temper, I was the one who cleaned up—embarrassed by my father's shouting and by the usually stupid and unnecessary mess of broken glass, sodden cases.

In the attic the timber was new and still smelled more of wood than dust. It was dark, but cool first thing in the morning, and still free of poisonous spiders and rats. Even the debris—except for the coffee cups—was clean: wires newly unrolled and trimmed, recently opened packing materials. And away from the loading and unloading of trucks, of boxcars, whose tracks ran along one side of the warehouses, I felt a certain independence. I was under no one's eyes in the attic, inaccessible without the painter's scaffold. For the first time I was free to work at my own pace, by myself, in a place where no one could watch my progress; away from both my father and from the warehouseman—his great pale gut exposed between his pants and T-shirt like one of a beachball's six segments—who called me "*Eeee-zy*" (short for "Easy Money"). For the first time I enjoyed working at the distributorship, and only when the painter shouted "Lunchtime" from far below did I remember that there was anyone else in the warehouse.

I peered out the trapdoor and found the painter looking up at me, scratching his beard. "You probably want to eat, too," he said, then pushed the scaffold beneath the trapdoor. As I climbed down he took a deep breath, exhaled very slowly. "I don't know about you," he said, "but I'm starving. Very hungry. Glad it's lunchtime."

His cooler sat on the lowest plank. The painter filled a plastic cup, handed it to me. "Here you go."

"Thanks."

"And here." He fished a five-dollar bill from his back pocket. "From your father, for lunch."

"Oh. Thanks."

"Have another." He nodded toward the cooler. "It must be hot up there."

"Getting hot now," I said, between gulps.

When I'd finished my second cup of water he said, "If you want, you can come with me. I'm just gonna pick up something. I haven't noticed many restaurants around here, but there's that drive-through McDonald's off the freeway—so if that's okay with you, you're welcome to come along."

The painter drove a Datsun pickup whose bench seat was cluttered: the *Ralston Bee*'s sports section, a hairbrush clouded with long black strands, a balled-up woman's scarf, a lighter, a tube of lip balm, a pair of Birkenstocks, darkened with the imprints of slender feet. He pulled all these things toward him to make a place for me, apologized for the mess, then, aside from asking for my order, said nothing during the drive along South Ninth Street and Highway 99 to and from McDonald's. Instead of speaking, as we passed the tin-roofed wholesale warehouses, the sleazy motor courts (LOW RATES/WEEKLY), the wrought-iron-reinforced glass front of a Quik Stop, the windowless Load of Bull Bar—all so ramshackle that each summer I was amazed to find every one of them still standing amid South Ninth's treeless pavementscape—the painter worked at rubbing out the stiffness from his arms, shoulders, and neck. He rubbed first one forearm, then the other. He rolled his head, then his shoulders, repeating the motions that sounded in a crack until the crack faded. He opened each hand as widely as he could, stretching the fingers, rotating his wrists, completely ignoring me. But I wasn't offended. Far from it. I had been offended by the theatrical fatigue various other workers had performed for my benefit, each one believing he'd come up with a new way of "conning" the boss's son. They overacted intentionally, I'd come to believe, to measure as quickly as possible just how stupid I was. But the painter's stretching wasn't like that. In his complete self-absorption he paid me the highest compliment: he motivelessly assumed a kind of shared experience—we had both worked hard that morning. He was not putting on a show, or playing a game, but simply stretching the work from his muscles in the presence of a coworker, an equal—whose presence he could therefore ignore. I felt newly mature. I stretched a bit, too, inconspicuously.

When we returned to the warehouse the painter excused himself to go call his wife from one of the office phones. I ate my lunch seated on a plank halfway up the scaffold. Then when he came back, I climbed into the attic to work for another two hours before the tin roof became too hot to bear, and he went back to work too.

ON WEDNESDAY, AT eleven-thirty, the same call of "Lunchtime" came from the painter below.

"I'm heading to McDonald's again," he said, while I drank some water. "If you don't have a lunch, or any plans, you can come along."

In the truck this time, he stretched less and talked more.

"I think your father told me you're eleven. Right?"

"Yeah."

"What's that put you in? Fifth grade? Sixth?"

"Going into sixth."

"Where at?"

"St. Stephen's."

"You like it?"

During the drive he asked the kind of questions the manager of Hal's Market, as he rang up my mother's groceries, asked me; the kind asked by the barber at the Model Barbershop—whom I hated. The painter asked them with actual interest, more sincerity, but with each question the previous day's silent camaraderie withered. They were questions that adults asked of children (I couldn't really ask him how old *he* was). I felt slighted, answered in monosyllables.

But after we'd gotten our food and sat down in the air-conditioned McDonald's, the painter luxuriously stretched his legs to one side of the small table, shook his head, and sighed, almost to himself, "My wife . . ." Then he took a bite of his hamburger, a drink of his iced tea.

I glanced at him to see if he would continue.

He didn't. At least not right away. He leaned back in his chair, rubbed his thumb over a spot of paint on his forefinger. Then he leaned to the table again, picked up his hamburger.

"You ever have trouble getting things done because you're worried about something?" he asked softly, raising his eyes to mine, then dropping them to the hamburger in his hand.

"Yeah, I guess," I said.

"My wife," he began, stalled, took a bite of his hamburger, chewed, started again. "My wife is homesick. Or maybe just depressed. Or a little of both, I think. Probably. Not that I blame her." He sighed. "We like kids," he said simply, "my wife and I. She used to teach, before she started helping with the business. We've tried for seven years to have a kid. With no luck. Or we have luck sometimes, actually—that's really the problem. She gets pregnant—but can't keep it. Can't keep the baby, you know?" he said, looking at me.

I nodded. I was used to the insinuating feigned kindness of some of the beer drivers, of the truck loader—prying into my family's home life, or out of maliciousness or just boredom, trying to manipulate me. I was wary, cautious. I watched the painter closely, listened carefully. He seemed guileless.

"She has miscarriages, loses the child early on. We've been going to doctors, and this time she was pregnant longer than any time before. Like I said, that's the problem. You get your hopes up, and we got our hopes up this time. I guess I get my hopes up pretty easy—and probably always will. I'm not one to doubt all the time. That's not a bad thing, really. Trust, you know?"

"No," I said, "it's not."

"So as many times as this has happened—and we're really pretty lucky, it hasn't happened all that often—I get excited and she gets

excited and I probably get more excited than she does even. And
. . . I don't know. But she really *is* something, my wife. That sounds
corny. But she is. You'd like her. Maybe you'll meet her. She usually
helps me on my jobs, takes care of all the paperwork I've got no
head for. So I can't help but think about her—just like, I guess, I'd
think about a kid all day if we had one. But you get your hopes up
and it happens again and then what? You keep hoping. You can't
control it. I'm boring you. I'm sorry. I'm just rambling on like an
idiot."

"No you're not," I said, then shrugged my shoulders, with no idea
of what else to say; pleased, but also disconcerted, to be the recipient
of such sudden honesty.

"Thanks. You're being kind. But I better eat. I do a bad job for
your dad and waste all day at lunch and he'll kick my butt," he said,
smiling, then quickly added, afraid of offending me: "And he'd be
right to do it!"

When he finished his lunch he asked, "You mind if I make a quick
phone call? We have a little time."

We ended up taking a long lunch, getting back to the warehouse
an hour and fifteen minutes after we'd left. But my father wasn't
around anyway.

WHEN IT BECAME too hot to work up in the attic that day, my father
had me wash a delivery truck. It was so hot—a dry one hundred and
one degrees—I didn't mind the water hissing onto me from the base
of the spray nozzle, but the water that splashed from the bristles of
the scrub brush and ran down its long handle and then down my
arms and armpits and ribs was greasy brown. I had to clamber over
the truck to reach the middle of its windshield and hood, the roof
of its cab and closed bays. When I finished my clothes were filthy
and wet, so I stayed out of the office and wandered around the
warehouses' large Cyclone-fenced yard. I visited the bony Doberman

stray, the watchdog, who refused to leave the shade of his house, then roamed into the new warehouse, where, left over from some unknown phase of its construction, I found curious silver-dollar-sized metal disks that I could throw like miniature Frisbees until my father was done working.

I was still in the warehouse when the painter finished for the day.

"Ah, I thought I heard something," he said, descending the last few rungs of the scaffold's ladder.

I walked over to him, held up my handful of metal disks. "These fly pretty good. You know what they're for?"

He turned off the paint pump. "Let me see." He took one, considered it with mock intensity, rubbing his thumb over the hole in its center. "Well . . . they may be some new kind of tiny scratchproof record—maybe by the Rolling Stones. Or . . . maybe some kind of foreign coin. But let's see. . . ." He threw it with a sidearm motion; it coasted upward, turned slightly, then dove into the concrete floor and bounced to the wall.

"They never fly all the way level," I said. "There's always that turn."

"Yeah, I see that. So what're you going to do with all those?"

I heard the scratch of hard-soled shoes, turned to see my father approaching, put the disks into my back pocket, didn't answer. The painter took less notice, seemed still to wait for a reply.

"Here you are," my father said from a distance. Then when he had reached us, to the painter, "So how much longer will you be?"

"Well. There are a couple of variables," the painter said.

"*Variables*," my father repeated.

I stepped away from them.

"Yeah, uncertainties. The paint pump, first of all. It's old, and it's been acting up this week. If it'll just hold—"

"We have a pump you can use," my father interrupted.

"Airless?" the painter asked.

"Yes. *Airless*."

"Because there's different kinds—"

"I *know* what kind of pump is needed for a job like this. We have it. Believe me."

I drifted farther away. I hated my father for his sarcasm, his imperiousness—for the shame these caused me even when directed at others.

"Okay," the painter said, "but I think mine'll make it."

"Great. If yours'll make it, great. Then we don't have to waste our time talking about it. Now. Everything else okay?"

"Yeah, as far as I can tell."

My father shifted his weight from one foot to the other, cast his eyes down at the concrete with impatience.

The painter spoke to my father in the same casual way he spoke to me—it wouldn't work. It made him an easy target. My own impatience stirred. Just say *yes*, I thought, get it over with.

"You have enough *paint?*" my father asked.

The painter smiled. "Yes, that's not a problem."

"Okay, so you'll be done Friday?"

"I certainly hope so."

As the painter's failure lengthened, my anger at my father expanded to include him. He seemed unembarrassed by my father's attacks. I was embarrassed for him.

"I certainly *hope so* too," my father said.

It was the painter's own fault, he was doing everything wrong. I didn't want to see this: the painter's weakness—his sick wife!—and my father's bullying.

"But *hope's* no good," my father continued. "No. Hope does me no good. I've got boxcars coming on Saturday, I've got wine backed up in the old warehouse. I need to *know*. You understand? You said you'd be done by Friday. You *will* be done, right?"

I turned my back on them, walked toward the far wall, stopped listening. I hated both of them.

A minute later my father called, "Vincent! C'mon, let's go home."

The painter said, "See you tomorrow," as I passed.

"Yeah, see you."

On the way to the car, my father picked up a cardboard flat, dusted it with his hand as we walked. He gave it to me at the passenger door, "Here, put this under you, you're all dirty."

He sat straight up as he drove, or leaned forward impatiently, both forearms pressed against the Buick Electra's gray steering wheel.

"How's that painter work?" he asked.

"Okay."

"Does he work steadily? Does he take a lot of breaks?"

I had no idea. I'd been happy to be working without self-consciousness, without the need to anticipate my father's presence and judgment. I made something up. "This afternoon he worked straight through the time I was there."

He hardly seemed to notice my answer. "That's not that big a job *if* you work. But I don't think he likes to work too much. He's got so many excuses not to—like everybody else. His paint pump, his paint, the weather. Who knows what else? And he's a little . . ."—raising one hand, tilting it from side to side for a few seconds, squinting. "I don't trust him as far as I can throw him. Doesn't work too hard, always has a nice smile, a soft voice. Everything's beautiful. Wonderful. I just want him to finish. I've had enough of him. A little of that guy goes a long way."

He caught his breath quickly, spat out his open window, then lit a cigar.

We passed the milk plant near the railroad tracks; we weren't far from home.

He turned to me. "You almost done up in the attic?"

"Yes."

THURSDAY MORNING, IN the car on the way to the warehouse, my father said, "Will you check if that painter works today? Take a look every now and then, see what he's doing."

I did. I listened futilely for the hiss of the spray gun above—or between—the slow steady *ke-chugg* of the paint pump, periodically hung my head upside down out the trapdoor. Once, I saw the painter hunched on the ground, his long spider fingers crawling slowly among the parts of his dismantled spray gun. I checked on him even though I knew I would never give my father a bad report of him. I did it for myself—just to see if my father was right.

But I couldn't decide.

The painter seemed to be working. But my father had created doubt. And the painter's inability to give (in my father's words) "a straight answer" the day before was almost enough to make me reluctantly adopt my father's opinion of him.

I hammered a piece of chicken wire over a vent. From the din of voices in my mind a certain one with phrasing like Father Ryan's, who taught religion class at St. Stephen's, had recently (though without a definite starting point) begun to stand out. It was deliberate, reasonable, measured—even as I felt myself to be temperamental and impatient and sneaky. As I worked now I imagined tutoring the painter in how to talk to my father—instructing him, over lunch, in the clear calm tone I'd begun to imagine myself using in this new kind of self-aggrandizing fantasy, in which every difficulty and all the pain of indecision shriveled before Reason.

This is what I imagined, in great involved detail, even as I knew I wouldn't say a word of it to the painter.

At lunchtime, after I'd responded to his call and climbed down the scaffold, the painter seemed preoccupied.

"Vincent," he said, "I think I'm going to skip lunch today. I've got to call my wife. She wasn't good this morning."

"Okay," I said.

"Is it?" he asked. "You got lunch, something to eat? If you don't, I'll drive you to that Quik Stop down the road, I think they've got cold sandwiches and stuff."

"No, that's okay."

"Really? I don't want you to go hungry."

"Really. I'll go to the Town and Country. It's okay, really."

The painter walked quickly toward the office.

I looked at the ceiling, decided that he'd be done by the following day, no problem.

The Town and Country Diner, all glass and brown paint with a peaked asymmetrical roof, which in some inexpensive and misbegotten early sixties manner tried—but failed—to be jaunty and optimistic, was frequented by a grim and dusty lunch crowd. I ordered a grilled cheese sandwich to go, then walked the block back to the warehouse. Since the painter was talking on the phone in the truck drivers' room and one of the secretaries worked in the main office, I sat down in a corner chair of my father's empty office, to eat lunch in the air-conditioning.

On the wall above my head, among various sales awards, hung a photograph of my father with his father, who in 1935 had cofounded a one-truck distributorship on the edge of downtown Ralston. Right after the war—I knew the story well—my father bought out my grandfather's partner; then, when my uncle became old enough, my father appointed him manager of a new warehouse in Strickland. Then, in my own lifetime, he'd moved the Ralston business to the south end of town, to a much bigger lot, with easier access to Highway 99 and all of Stanislaus County. But in this photo above my head it was wartime and my father, home on leave in his Navy blues, with an arm slung happily around each of them, stood between his pudgy younger brother and his stern father and, smiling, leaned toward the camera: cocky, self-assured, like some kind of Aeneas beside the creased eaglelike face of his sick father, who would be dead in a few months (twenty years before my birth). I was reminded of something my mother once said: "You might not know it, because of how few pictures there are of him as a young man, but your father never met a camera he didn't like."

On my father's desk stood a formal black-and-white studio portrait of my mother, brother, sister, and me. In it, my mother's light brown hair appeared lacquered into one shell-like curl and her chin was tilted upward, in strained unconvincing haughtiness; my sister wore a dark bob and freckles; my brother was gawky, his smile lopsided and forced; and I, in bow tie and jacket, four years old, pouted and held my hands knotted awkwardly together before my stomach.

I looked from one photograph to the other. As much as I might change from my four-year-old self, I knew I could never be like my father with his father. Never, I had always vowed, would I become a wine and beer distributor. And never, I now thought, would I have his self-confidence—or inspire in him any of the pride his own father felt.

Though why should I want to? I hated my father. I liked the painter better.

This fact should have made it easy for me to know whom to trust.

But it didn't.

When I returned from lunch the painter stood leaning against the scaffold, a cup of water in hand.

I apologized. "Did I keep you from starting?"

"Oh no," he said, "I just got out here myself. You're not late or anything."

I hesitated, then pushed to it by a misguided sense of adult decorum, asked, "Your wife okay?"

He sighed.

I colored.

"Oh, she's a little better, I think. I don't know. It's tough. No, she's not very good."

"Sorry," I said, then hurried up the scaffold.

I FINISHED THAT afternoon. The painter helped me lower everything to the ground. I told him, "I'll throw this away myself. I don't want to keep you from your job."

He agreed. Then said, "Well, I hope I can follow your example and finish this today. There's not much left."

My father was out of the office. I threw the attic's garbage into the large trash bin, put everything away, then, to get out of the heat, sat in the drivers' room and looked without interest at beverage magazines and promotional flyers.

The warehouseman came in to use the rest room, saw me, and sidled up: "Tell me the truth, Eeee-zy, you've been napping up there, haven't you? C'mon. I won't tell the old man. Been snoozin' up there for a week." Then he burst out laughing, quieting only gradually to an exaggerated mulelike nodding of his head, and the repetition as he turned and headed toward the toilet of *"Eeee-zy, good ol' Eeee-zy."* I smiled too, and decided that all he could talk was nonsense, nothing else.

My father returned late to the office, his forehead furrowed and damp with perspiration, but he smiled when he heard I'd completed the job.

"All done, huh? Everything finished?" he asked, making sure, then said, "Good. I don't know who else I could've trusted to do it. Fat Bob would've fallen off the scaffold and killed himself. And that painter . . ." He shook his head. "He would've been up there for three weeks. I would've had to climb up there so often just to check on him—to make sure he was still alive, still moving—it would've been easier to do it myself. So . . . thanks. Good. Let's go home."

The next day he let me sleep late, telling my mother to drop me off at the warehouse sometime before eleven.

WHEN I ARRIVED on Friday I found my father walking a circle in a far corner of the new warehouse with his hands on his hips and his head back, looking at the ceiling. In dark pants and a white shirt, his skin of a reddish-brown tint, he appeared vigorous, dramatic, and small before the tall blank walls. The paint pump was silent, the painter nowhere to be seen. My father didn't seem to hear me approach, so I stopped a few feet away and, following his gaze, turned my eyes upward. There, high above our heads, a patch five yards by five yards was yet unpainted—square as a skylight, it receded, scuffed and cloudy-looking, from the even white all around it.

My father suddenly spoke. "So our friend the painter couldn't finish this yesterday. A big deal. This is ten minute's worth of work. Less! It would take him longer to clean the spray gun! I can't understand it. I just can't understand it."

He stopped pacing, looked incredulously at me. "Then he calls me at ten—I thought he was out here working—to say he can't work today. His wife is sick. His wife is sick! Ten o' clock! Well . . . fine. His wife is sick." He shook his head in disbelief. "Who knows if that's true? But then I come out here and find *this?*" gesturing impatiently with both hands toward the ceiling. "What sense does this make? I've got wine backed up. I told him, *by Friday.* I can't figure this out."

I stared at the ceiling. I could believe the painter's wife was sick, but I wouldn't mention this to my father. In the face of this—this stupidity—it wouldn't matter.

My father said, "He's crazy! He must be nuts. This is nuts."

And I found myself agreeing. He must be. How else to explain this? And how else to explain a man who tells a perfect stranger, a kid, about his wife's problems? To explain a man who'd acted so nice to me? And I'd been taken in. While I stared at the ceiling I shook my head—slowly and incredulously, like my father—at myself. *Sucker.*

My father suddenly clapped his hands once. "Well, *we'll* just have to finish it. I can't wait till tomorrow. We'll be done by lunch. Why don't you pull the scaffold over here, let's get started."

I was used to my father underestimating the time it would take "us"—meaning me—to finish a job.

This was no exception.

It would have been faster for him to do it himself, but he thought there was a lesson here ("Don't put off work till tomorrow—*tomorrow never comes*"), and he impatiently showed me how to apply the paint and clean the gun, then went into the office for a meeting with a winery representative.

I was alone in the new warehouse. The paint pump *ke-chugged* below, steadily, rhythmically, reassuringly. I looked over the warehouse, at how much the painter had finished, and started to imagine scenarios in which this unpainted section made sense. If he had been called away suddenly . . . If the spray gun had broken so late in the day that by the time he fixed it . . .

But the ridiculous sloppy fact of the unpainted plasterboard hovered uncomfortably close above my head, so I lifted the spray gun and, with the long steady sweeping motion my father had taught me, finished covering the ceiling in a flawless white.

THE REAL THING

I

ONE MORNING JUST before he began to sleep in the same room as his brother—and just three months before what was known in places like Berkeley and San Francisco, ninety miles west across the Altamont Pass, as "the Summer of Love"—Vincent awoke in the queen-size bed he shared with his older sister and discovered he could not open his left eye. He lay warm and unfrightened beneath the blankets, Mary beside him in a deep Saturday-morning sleep, and reached up with one hand to find that his eyelid felt like an underinflated balloon, puffy and soft. But his eye didn't hurt, it didn't bother him in the least—except that he couldn't open it—and it felt like nothing at all. It would be for his mother later that morning to speculate on the cause of his shut eye, to look for insect bites and ask him with some urgency if he'd noticed any bugs on his face yesterday (he hadn't), or if he'd been playing in bushes or in the orchard or in the big pile of limbs cut from the walnut trees (he had been, of course, like most other days). At four years of age, though, on a gray morning in a warm bed with his sister, with whom he laughed and talked and some days made late for school with all of his talk and play, one soft closed eye did not alarm him. A little balloon, he thought. And it made little difference in how he felt, in that safe place, on that quiet morning.

The doctor who saw Vincent said it was nothing really, certainly nothing serious. Just a mosquito bite, right on the eyebrow, that she wouldn't have expected to close the eye, especially since another bite on his arm wasn't swollen. Probably just a one-time thing. One of those aberrations that sometimes appear in a healthy child to remind us that kids are more amorphous than adults. Certainly more sensitive. Like the little girl whose torso broke out in a rash as her family prepared to move to a new neighborhood. Out of nowhere, red spots—that disappeared the next day.

His mother said she was so relieved, she'd been afraid his eyesight would be permanently affected. The doctor gave Vincent a shot, then she and his mother talked and talked. His eye began to open even as he sat waiting on the padded examining table, absentmindedly swinging one leg, wondering what Mary was doing at home.

As soon as they pulled into the driveway, Mary came out the front door. She ran to the car, awkwardly, wearing Capri pants in which her legs looked as long and her knees as knobby as a crane's—even though she was not and would never be tall. As soon as Vincent clambered from the car she took his head in her hands, looked at his face.

"Whew! I was afraid I'd have a deformed little brother for the rest of my life!"

Their mother made a face at her.

Vincent shook out of her grasp, laughed, and tried to push her away, but she fussed over him all the way into the house, and teased him. "But he's still kind of funny-looking. Couldn't the doctor do anything about that? In fact, now I'm not so sure he didn't look better before." She tousled his hair, tickled him. Vincent twisted and grimaced under her assault but made no real effort to escape.

After lunch Mary was supposed to help Vincent move his clothes into the big dresser in Paul's room, then clean her own room. She and Vincent began the task with the best intentions. Vincent had carried two tidy stacks of clothes into his brother's room before they opened Mary's closet and became completely distracted. Some of their mother's old clothes hung on one side of Mary's closet: skirts, dresses, blouses, shoes, even two or three hats, all as strange and tempting as the costumes in a theater's wardrobe. They couldn't help themselves. Even though Mary knew better, they fell into their old game of dress-up.

Vincent started it. He loved to make his sister laugh. He pulled off his sneakers, dragged a pair of white block-heeled sandals from the closet, clomped around the hardwood floor to his sister's giggles. He found a swim cap with appliquéd flowers, put it on, and shook his head wildly to make its flimsy rubber petals dance. Mary found a sleeveless floral blouse. It fit Vincent like a muumuu. Then she replaced the swim cap with a floppy terry-cloth hat. Now she was really laughing, and Vincent was too. She added a plastic lei that had hung from her headboard. A pair of sunglasses, huge on Vincent's head. She showed him how to dance the hula, and he exaggerated all the movements, hands and hips completely out of sync. Vincent hammed like mad, and Mary began to laugh so hard tears came from her eyes. She held her stomach, doubled up on the floor, and Vincent, thrilled with the attention, really carried on. Whenever Mary began to get control of herself, Vincent would caper or shimmy, and she'd be overcome once more. Vincent enjoyed it immensely, but Mary, seven years older and more aware of how little boys were supposed to behave, enjoyed it even more.

When their mother walked into the room all she could say was "I should have known better." For from the time Vincent was able to walk and first began to sleep in the same bed as his sister they couldn't be together without breaking into some kind of monkey business. When they were together no chore was ever completed, and all of their mother's attempts to punish one of them with solitude were ruined by the other, sneaking in to make a mockery of confinement.

Vincent's move into Paul's bedroom would help this situation a little: at least Mary was no longer late for school. Paul also played with Vincent, but he had more restraint and self-discipline than his younger sister. Then, six months after the move, in the autumn, the problem disappeared completely when Vincent began kindergarten and Mary became interested in boys.

II

SAM NEWSOM WAS the first boy who visited Mary at home. She was fourteen at the time, Vincent nearly eight. Sam lived a mile away and would stop by on his bicycle after school. He had straight auburn hair brushed forward on either side of his head to approximate sideburns. The first time he showed up at the door, Vincent answered in full James West regalia—hat, holster, boots—but before he had a chance to say a word to the stranger, Mary nudged him to one side. Her face was red. She kept the screen door between herself and Sam, smiled and laughed nervously, tried to shoo Vincent away. He didn't budge. Then their mother, who'd heard the doorbell too, came to see what was going on.

Sam Newsom stayed for nearly two hours that day; all four of them, Sam, Mary, and Vincent and their mother, sat in the den and watched cartoons. A couple of days later he returned again. Then again the next week. After that he visited so regularly after school that Mrs. Torno began to treat him as she'd treat one of Mary's girlfriends. Mary and he would play pool (the only time she ever picked up a cue), tease each other, even throw playful punches at one another. At first they let Vincent play pool with them. Later they ignored him, so he, in response, ignored them.

In any case, Vincent had more interest in his brother, Paul, and Paul's friends. Paul and his friends played basketball in the driveway and baseball in a nearby pasture. Sometimes Vincent was batboy. Paul was always nice to him even though Paul's friends, with the exception of Craig Wilburn, usually acted as if Vincent was hardly large enough to be seen and much too tiny to be spoken to. Craig alone made it a point to talk to Vincent—but always with the same mocking intent: to coerce him into saying "I read *Playgirl*." Without fail, every time Vincent saw him, Craig set about this with a strange eagerness, as though hearing Vincent say these three words would set him laughing for all eternity. But Vincent knew better. Already, the year before, Hammy Oakes had told him about "rubbers"— though their exact function remained perplexing—and even the stupidest boy in the second grade had heard all about *Playboy*.

When Paul and his friends wanted privacy and Vincent was forced from the bedroom that he and his brother shared, Craig's face— smiling sarcastically, smugly—was inevitably the last he'd see before the door closed. Like a taunt, it drove Vincent crazy. In retaliation he'd place his ear against the door. But he never heard anything interesting, just hushed unintelligible voices, sparse laughter. He'd sit outside the door, knowing he was wasting time, but wanting so much to be in that room with them, doing whatever they were doing, that often he couldn't make himself leave. He'd sit in the dim hallway charged with a desire that, beyond his general abiding wish to do and know all his older brother did and knew, had no particular object—angry and impatient with those who kept it, whatever it was, from him.

Vincent discovered his object one rainy day when he was driven by boredom and restlessness to dig through the closet and every dresser drawer in his room in search of something interesting. He found it buried beneath a stack of *Sports Illustrated*s in the bottom drawer of Paul's nightstand. It was thicker than any of the other magazines, and Vincent vaguely suspected what it was even before he drew it out from the pile. Still, the sight of the title made his heart pound. He dropped the magazine back into the drawer, ran lightly to his open bedroom door. He listened to see if anyone was near, then closed it, angry it didn't have a lock, and ran back to the nightstand.

It was wonderful. He didn't rush to the pictorials as an older boy might, or as he himself would later learn to do. He turned through it one page at a time, through all the articles and advertisements. It was breathtaking, just holding this magazine in his hands, having before him what had been kept from him, hidden, and thus loaded with an inordinate value—implicitly promised him like a trust whose deferral only increased its worth. He expected these pages to magically reveal all that had been withheld in the conspicuous lapses of adult conversation, in certain tones of their laughter, in certain inscrutable expressions. He nearly trembled in anticipation and fear, pored over each page. He had begun his third trip through it when he thought he heard footsteps in the hall and fumbled in a panic to put it back into the drawer.

As often as Vincent returned to this magazine, though—and he returned as often as possible—sex itself, the act, remained a fathomless, boundless, unimaginable mystery. What Vincent learned from this *Playboy* (which his friend Hammy, after his lone careful perusal of it, called one of the best issues he'd seen), what he came to appreciate, was more simply the marvelous appeal of a nude woman. These beautiful women were the apotheoses of the crude sketches decorating the boys' bathroom stalls, the incarnations of the grotesquely buxom cartoons he'd seen on cocktail napkins and on blinking signs in a certain part of downtown San Francisco. The visible real fulfillment of all the confused and confusing talk he'd heard and overheard. When he looked at them he felt the first stirrings of that satisfaction and—in spite of his isolation—slightly smug camaraderie that come from being "in the know": as if these photos were the solution to an old riddle, the long-delayed punchline to a joke Vincent had been hearing ever since he began school.

And even long after the first great rush of the magazine's novelty had faded, certain of the photographs' qualities continued to lure Vincent. He found an endless appeal in the photos' wonderful warmth and order: in the glowing flesh, the smooth curves of full breasts, of buttocks and hips, even the few glimpses of pubic hair, which looked soft as lamb's fleece; in the wood-paneled cabin interiors, the plush rugs, furs, the fireplaces, and thick quilts; in the relaxed smiling women, friendly and kind. Everything in the photos suggested comfort and ease and quiet. Relief. Acceptance. He'd hunker in the narrow space between one wall and a twin bed—the bed shielding him from the door—utterly intrigued by these women, so calm and beautiful; by their perfect naturalness, casualness, suggesting the mussed warmth of early morning.

III

EVEN DURING THE eleven months she "went with" Sam Newsom, Mary remained something of a tomboy, preferring plain T-shirts and (unstylish at the time) straight-leg jeans. So when, at sixteen, she met Melvin Orton and suddenly became attentive to her hair and clothing, even Vincent, who had little to do with her by this time, noticed. He began to mock her for all the time she spent brushing her long dark hair and applying makeup. Having overheard her tell a friend that she'd never before felt what she felt about Melvin— "This is the *real* thing," she said—Vincent began to use him as a weapon. When he was very bored he'd pester Mary by repeating in a high screechy voice, "Melvy-boy, my Melvy-baby! Oh Melvin I adore you! Oh Melvy, Melvy-baby!" She hated this—and he loved to see that he could still get some kind of reaction from her. Sometimes, though, she threw some girl's name back at him, teased him about one of her friends' little sisters, and completely ruined his fun.

Melvin was a skinny guy with a huge car who always had basketball or track practice after school. He came over sometimes in the evenings, even though Vincent and Mary's father seemed instantly to hate him and wouldn't yet allow her to actually go out with a boy. Melvin would arrive neatly dressed as though for a date, his face set, determined-looking, as if he expected to be run through a gauntlet, then he and Mary would walk out the front door to the driveway, lean against his car's rear bumper, and talk for hours. This drove Vincent's father crazy. Two or three times a night he'd abruptly rise from his chair and go to the window, mutter, "A couple of idiots. What the hell are they doing out there?" and then sit down again. And each time Vincent would watch his father and silently answer his question, *Nothing*. He'd spied on them one evening, and that's what he discovered: they did nothing. All he'd heard was quiet earnest talk, all he'd seen worth noting was the way they stood, side by side, close enough for their elbows and hipbones to touch—that was it. No giggles, no movement, just low mopey voices, heads down.

In March of that same year, while Vincent was in fourth grade, a 7-Eleven opened on Collier Road. It sat, all orange, green, and white like a soda can or a candy wrapper, at the edge of a bare four-acre lot formerly lined with almond trees; at dusk from his front yard, where he'd once been able to smell the trees' sweet blossoms, Vincent could see the store's glowing sign. During its construction, Vincent had thrilled at the idea of a store so close, imagining all the shelves of toys and sugar that would tempt him. And when it opened, he and two friends who lived nearby visited often, to buy Slurpees and look at magazines. They'd look through all the sports and car magazines on the upper half of the rack, sneak glances at the appealing covers of the ones below. But the first day Harry Burnet went to the store with them, he casually bent down and grabbed a *Playboy*. Vincent couldn't believe it. The rack was only partially hidden by a shelf. He thought he felt the cashier's eyes upon him, and, embarrassed, he set off around the store, wandering the short aisles as if he were looking for something. The cashier smoked his cigarette. Customers, including guys in Ralston Catholic High School letter jackets, entered, paid, left. Vincent circled back to the group still huddled at the rack. Harry pointed at a beautiful blonde stretched across the rumpled covers of a bed. Vincent heard his sly comic tone, laughter, but was too nervous to comprehend what was said. He started around the store again.

As alluring as these magazines were, it took Vincent some time to get used to looking at them in public. He expected the cashier to throw his friends and him out of the store, to notify their parents, to humiliate them. Ralston Catholic High School students so regularly entered the store he was sure that one of his sister's friends would discover him squatting near the rack, or his sister herself, or his cousin Joey, who also went to RC. Once, a couple of guys in RC caps walked past them, laughed, and asked, "You little guys springing some boners over here?" and Vincent avoided the store for the next week. But none of this seemed to bother Harry, or Darrel or Mike. Harry in particular acted as though he had a right to linger all day if he wanted, flipping through *Playboy* and *Oui* (which he said was pronounced "ooo-ee!"). He scorned high schoolers and cashiers alike, considered the phrase "Entertainment for Men" that appeared on every *Playboy* cover a personal invitation. And gradually Harry's defiance had an effect on Vincent. He began to react against his anxiety, recognizing in himself a desire to be as brave and unstifled by conscience as Harry. His afternoons at the 7-Eleven became trials of a sort, tests of his fortitude, and inspired feelings he hadn't known as he looked at his brother's magazine in the privacy of his own room. Slowly he began to feel the thrill, new, dim, yet

uncertain, of entitlement. Yes, he hesitantly told himself, these magazines in this store were here for his entertainment, his pleasure—
he had a right to them.

Then at the end of the school year, when Vincent had become as
comfortable as he ever would at the magazine rack, two events in
quick succession shifted everything again. Mike Wund and his father
built a sturdy, windowless three-room fort on the side of their house,
and Harry found a girlie magazine in a field.

Unlike the fort Darrel Shreef made of the bushes behind his house,
Mike's fort was rainproof and completely enclosed. Its adjoining
rooms were built of plywood, fully carpeted with remnants, and
lighted by small lamps, and its main door could be locked from inside
or out. Inside they could do anything they wanted. The day it was
completed, Darrel brought a battered can of beer he'd kept hidden
in his bushes, intending to finally drink it in the fort's privacy—until
Harry embarrassed him by laughing and taunting him, saying, "You
really think you're gonna get fucked up with one can of spoiled beer?
Fuckin' lightweight!"

They almost fought.

But two days later all was made up when Harry brought into the
fort a battered, coverless magazine. *What great luck!* Vincent, Mike,
and Darrel exclaimed, taking it as some kind of supernatural sign that
their fort was, in fact, the coolest around. But actually it was typical
of Harry. He had freckles, and a cowlick above one temple, like a
boy who might appear in a peanut butter commercial, except that
when he smiled his eyes closed to sliver moons and his mouth looked
cruel. He wandered the overgrown fields surrounding the large housing tract where he and Mike and Darrel lived, roamed the littered
alleys that ran between the houses' rear fences, and dragged out of
the winter-empty canal bike frames coated in muck, wrapped in rotten weeds. He strutted with impunity, fearless, through all the wild
chaotic places, ominous and charged with danger and violence,
where Vincent and Mike and Darrel knew never to trespass alone,

and sorted from all the discarded scraps and rubbish bits and pieces of valuable things. So even as his three friends carried on as if he'd stumbled upon a solid gold brick, Harry, slightly contemptuous, claimed that such magazines regularly turned up in his haunts—a ragged indigenous crop waiting to be harvested.

The magazine itself looked very much like *Playboy*, except it also included a narrative pictorial, complete with period costumes, that fascinated Vincent. It began with a man and a beautiful long-haired woman in a canopied bed in a dark, wood-paneled, lavishly furnished room. The woman's skin glows gold, as if candlelit, her mouth opens in various degrees of ecstasy as the man with wavy brown hair kisses her breasts, lies between her legs—both of them enveloped in the warm soft tones of the room. Suddenly, another man enters, white ruffled cloth at his throat and wrists brilliant in the muted surroundings. Both men look outraged; the woman weeps. In a rich green field, with an audience of three men in old-fashioned top hats and long coats, the rivals meet to duel with pistols, both men in white shirts with billowing sleeves. There is a photo of a deep crimson stain on a white shirt. Then the man who burst in on the orginal couple returns to the woman he has won, strips off her layers of old-fashioned undergarments, and makes love to her in the rich colors of the room, beneath the canopy.

It was the first time Vincent had seen a man and woman together, and in Mike Wund's cocoonlike fort he and his friends scrutinized every curve of smooth unblemished skin. Ultimately, the couple's poses were discreet, uninformative, and Harry joked about the woman's expressions—that she must have been moaning like a cow—and about a shadowy glimpse of a flaccid penis. But Vincent remained rather impressed by the whole thing, struck by its dreamy and heroic qualities. To him sexual intercourse—tactfully concealed like the models' genitalia—was indistinguishable from the overall effects of the pictorial; was wholly composed of the muted warmth of the photos, of the heroic story they told, and the escape they offered from the anxious stupid facts of his everyday life. For Vincent, still ignorant of the mechanics of sex, never having seen them, SEX encompassed all the complex emotions evoked by and associated with such magazines; consisted, really, of his history with these magazines. So he paid little attention to Harry's mocking comments and his favorite question about this particular pictorial, whose heroine, according to the captions, was named Carolina.

"What would you rather have, North Carolina or South Carolina?" he'd ask, laughing. "C'mon, North or South Carolina? I'd take South Carolina myself. Oh yeah, South Carolina, some nice sweet pussy."

This question and almost all Harry said about the pictorial seemed nonsensical to Vincent, incomprehensible, annoying, like the sound of a radio playing incessantly at a great distance.

I V

AT THE BEGINNING of sixth grade, before Coach Mott had gotten to the interesting part of Health class at St. Stephen's, Harry Burnet returned from his first week at Roosevelt School with the news that kids there were already fucking. Vincent, Mike, and Darrel didn't believe him at first; thought he lied to cover up his embarrassment over having to transfer to a public school. But it was true, they heard it from others too. While even the coolest guys at St. Stephen's (a group to which Vincent, having achieved too much in the classroom and not enough on the playing fields, partly belonged) could only guess how long they'd have to "go with" a St. Steve's girl before they could kiss her, the guys at the public schools were getting laid! It was startling!—not even halfway across town, girls their own age were willing to fuck. This revelation stirred up rowdy discussions in Mike Wund's fort and left Vincent feeling slightly disoriented, even dazzled, as though a great floodlight had burst upon a once cozy room, replacing vague shadows and soft edges with stark contrasts, with a disturbing edginess.

Nor was this the only turmoil in Vincent's life, since Mary had jettisoned her plans to go to Ralston Junior College and left to drive cross-country with her boyfriend of two years, Billy Ramsey. She'd just taken off, leaving almost everything she owned and a scrawled note behind her. Nearly all her clothes remained, her great store of makeup sat undiminished on her bureau, but everything was in dis-array—clothing strewn upon the closet floor, drawers jutting open, one small jar of powder shattered on the floor—as if her room, alone of the whole house, had been shaken by a strong earthquake. Or as if she'd been carried off by force after a violent struggle. And Vin-cent's father reacted to the news as if she had been, cursing the "goddamned stupid Okie son of a bitch" Billy Ramsey as if he'd torn her from the house, repeating, "Just the goddamned idea of it . . . Just the nerve of that son of a bitch!"

Vincent had always thought Billy Ramsey looked dangerous, like the guys he'd sometimes seen (from the safe vantage point of his father's passing car) on the run-down southern edge of Ralston, loi-tering outside the Load of Bull Bar, or mixing it up drunkenly at noon near the empty pool of the Palm Motor Court: he was large and rough with thick sandy hair and a big mustache. But in fact he was a butcher in a market in the middle of town, not far from Vin-cent's grandmother's house. Billy would swagger into the Torno house at all times of the day, show Vincent's mother the best way to marinate steak or slice roast beef, vigorously pound for her any meat that required it, and hack up chickens for frying. Right in front of Vincent's father, he'd put his arm around Mary, or clasp her hand, and this always made Vincent, as well as Mary, nervous. As was the case with nearly all of Mary's boyfriends, Vincent's father hated Billy Ramsey—but Vincent did too. He thought Billy was arrogant, and condescending. He was disturbed by his cocky, bowlegged walk; the exaggerated depths of his voice; the thicket of dark upthrusting chest hair on view even above crewneck T-shirts. Had his father limited himself to cursing this brute who'd taken Mary, Vincent for once might have found his tirades strangely tolerable. But his father inevitably moved on to his sister, began to curse her with an unsettling tone of disgust that drove Vincent outdoors into the quiet of the walnut orchard behind their house.

So after nearly a week of such turbulence and of being treated as though he were grounded even though *he* had done nothing wrong, the chance to spend an entire day knocking almonds on the Torno ranch outside of Ralston appeared like a vacation to Vincent. The ranch had been left to Vincent's father and uncle by their father, and someday, Vincent's father said, it would belong, at least partly, to Vincent. He woke early, put on his work clothes (an old pair of jeans, old sneakers), and ate his cereal with a pleasant sense of purpose, even independence. By the time his father sat down at the table with the newspaper, Vincent sat in the living room, watching out the window for his cousin. Joey was late. His father grumbled in the kitchen, asked him, "Wasn't Joey supposed to be here at eight?" Grumbled some more. Vincent read the previous day's sports page. The phone rang in the kitchen. His father said, "I'll get it," noisily pushed his chair from the table, walked to the counter, answered. It was after eight-thirty.

At first his father's curtness seemed to confirm it was Joey. But then his pauses became longer, his sarcasm sharper.

"Oh, wonderful. Is that so?" he spat.

The floor creaked and Vincent knew how his father must be shifting his weight from foot to foot, imagined him glowering in the long silences. "Um-hm," his father mumbled twice. "Yeah." Without seeing his father, Vincent knew how he stood, how he looked, heard in his few words what was building. Then the explosion he knew would come:

"Bullshit! Listen! No, I've heard enough. Shut up! Listen! You want to act like a tramp, you go right ahead, darling."

Joey pulled into the driveway.

"No! You hear me? Don't bother. I'm in no hurry to see your goddamn face. Run around like a slut if you want! Yeah, go ahead, cry—"

Vincent left quickly, heard his father's voice even after he'd closed the door behind him. He jogged to Joey's truck, fumbled with the handle—first the door was locked, then it was surprisingly heavy. His cousin, dimly amused, watched him struggle.

"Boy! You're working hard already and we're not even at the ranch," he said.

"Yeah. Ha."

His cousin turned his almost constant, smug, thin-lipped smile full upon him, but Vincent wasn't bothered by it. For, aside from the smile, Joey's face was round and doughy and impassive, and this morning Vincent welcomed its blandness. They said little to one another on the long drive to the ranch, and Vincent was glad for this too. The sun shone warmly through the windshield. They passed fields of alfalfa, fragrant in the morning, well-tended orchards and vineyards, and in anticipation of work, of what this morning seemed to him the sweet pure sensuality and independence of field work, he forced from his mind the problems at home, and gradually relaxed. Away from his father and his family, he experienced a hope that seemed to begin in his body rather than his mind. He felt himself awaken to the rich promise of the physical—as after the anxiety of Confession, and in spite of his soul's intractable failings (so recently recounted), he would sense in himself and in all around him a buoyant spirituality.

Joey's friends had been waiting almost an hour next to their Camaros and pickups and really "gave it to him" when he finally arrived. There were five of them, all clean-cut, all athletes at Ralston Catholic

High School (Joey was a fullback), and they cursed their friend and laughed. Joey smiled tightly, muttered to each of them in turn, "Fuck you, fuck you, fuck you, fuck you, and fuck you," in an ironic kind of voice. They joked with one another, everyone in a boisterous mood. They stood talking for a few minutes. Then one, with showy impatience, kicked at the dirt, said, "Hey! C'mon! Let's get started! I'm ready to work."

"No shit," another agreed. "I'm sick of standing around."

"Yeah," they all said, "yeah."

Everyone seemed to feel as Vincent did, everyone expansive, happy for the chance to use their bodies. Vincent was happy to be with them, felt older, like a man. They climbed into Joey's pickup for the ride through the fields to where they'd work. Vincent sat in back of the pickup with four of them. They introduced themselves, acted friendly.

The long strip of young almond trees was bordered on one side by a peach orchard, on the other by mature almond trees. The fields were clean of weeds, peaceful in the morning light, with the sounds of birds, the cooing of a dove. In preparation for the harvest the almond orchards had been rolled smooth, the earth between the trees level and flawless. Joey parked near the peaches, took mallets and two long skinny poles out of a rolled-up tarp in the back of his truck. The young trees couldn't yet withstand the mechanical shaker; they had to be knocked by hand. He handed one pole to Vincent, then a big comic argument erupted over who would use the other. They all wanted the heavy rubber-ended mallets. The pole was light, so each pushed it away from himself, tried to force it on another with laughter and insults, the pole itself something of an insult, a sign of weakness. Finally they decided they'd each use the pole, take turns—though this didn't prevent them from snickering at the guy named Marc who started the day with it. Joey and his friends used their mallets on the trees' limbs, and Vincent and, initially, Marc followed with their poles, knocking loose any almonds that still clung, with heads upturned, squinting against the sun and the dust and twigs that fell from the branches onto their faces, into their eyes. Everyone worked eagerly.

"Man, this'll wake you up."

"Yeah, it feels good."

The largest of them worked too eagerly, hacking at the slender trees with a huge uppercut baseball swing—Joey had to tell him to ease up or he'd splinter the limbs. Then Joey opened the doors of his pickup, tuned in an FM station, turned it up loud until it edged into distortion.

Between the music and his work, Vincent didn't even notice a Mexican man who worked his way through the big almond trees on a mechanical shaker until he appeared near the levee separating those trees from the young ones. The day had grown hotter; it must have been ninety degrees, dry and dusty. Joey, like most of his friends, had taken off his shirt; he ran a hand over his forehead, leaned on his mallet with a proprietorial air, as if he owned the whole ranch. Vincent watched his cousin, then remembered suddenly that in fact he, Vincent, would own at least part of this ranch someday, and he turned to look where Joey looked.

The Mexican drove his shaker, its long arm extended and bouncing stiffly before it, up to a tree. Vincent watched as he methodically positioned the padded claw around the tree's trunk, watched the claw close tightly. Then he saw the tree, with a startling abruptness, burst into a violent shudder, a sudden hail of almonds and hulls, leaves, heard the rattle of the machine even above the radio. Not the single jolt he'd expected, but a long furious tremor, the whole tree, limbs, branches, leaves, animate with violence, electric. Chaotic, frightening. Then over. Leaves, twigs, almonds in and out of hulls, lying around the tree like rubbish.

The largest of his cousin's friends, standing not far from Vincent, yelled to Joey, "Hey Joey, I'll save you a lot of money—and gas. I'll just grab those trees 'round the trunk and shake 'em by hand. Do a better job than the machine!"

Joey nodded, wore his usual thin-lipped smile, so Vincent wasn't sure whether his cousin had actually heard.

Another sang, loud and off-key, "*Really love your peaches, wanna shake your tree. Lovey-dovey, lovey-dovey, lovey-dovey, all the time . . .*"

Joey said something Vincent couldn't hear.

"What? What?" the singer yelled, then, "Turn down the fucking radio! You're gonna blow your speakers." He jogged to the truck, turned the stereo low. "Now, what?"

"Why'd you turn it down, dickwad?" Joey asked.

"That's better," another said. "Can't hear yourself think."

"Not much to hear in your case," Joey said.

"Ha ha."

The shaker moved to another tree. Vincent again watched the whole procedure, fascinated.

"Shit! Check that out!" one of them said.

"Man!"

"Hey, I tell ya, I'll do it by hand for a lot less."

"Yeah, in your dreams."

Then the singer again, "*Really love your peaches, wanna shake your fuckin' tree! Lovey-dovey, lovey-dovey, lovey-dovey, all the goddamn ti-ime . . .*"

"Whose peaches you mean there, Carl?"

"Yeah, Carl?"

"Can't mean Trish Olson's," the large one said, "they're nowhere near ripe."

They all laughed, except Carl.

"Fuck you," he said.

"Those your only food, man, you *starve!*"

"Ha ha."

Another, who'd been quiet until then: "Hey Brad, you're starving anyway—when's the last time you got any?"

"Yeah, ripe *or* unripe?" Joey said.

"Don't worry about me . . . I do all right."

"Yeah, with the unripe kind. What? Ten, eleven years old?"

"Yeah, poaching from the grade schools. The kid probably sees you there." He turned toward Vincent. Joey turned toward him too, gave him a look for not working. Vincent started again.

"I do all right," Brad repeated.

Then Carl: "They're tight at that age, right, Brad?"

"Hey! Hey! There's a child present!" Marc warned, half seriously.

"Man, you know who's tight?" another broke in. "Got a nice tight ass? Miss Wallace."

"*The* Lori Wallace?"

"The one and only."

"That's why you sit up front, huh?"

They all stood talking now, their concentration scattered by the shaker. Only Vincent worked.

"Fuck that! Let's get back to peaches."

"Forget Wallace then."

"I'd do her."

"Oh!" in feigned outrage. "She's a professional educator! How dare you say that!"

"Yeah, sure, professional—she's a nice piece of ass, that's what she is."

"No shit. I'd do her," repeated.

"Why not? Bend her over her desk, man, spread those cheeks . . ."

"Doggy-style all the way."

"*Bite that pillow!*" one cried.

Others took it up. "*Bite that pillow!*" they repeated happily.

"Oh yeah."

"No shit."

Then they were all laughing, tossing off comments. Vincent kept working. Eventually Joey and his friends started again too. But they kept up their conversation, veering from one subject to another, usually one girl to another, from insult to insult, inside joke to inside joke, in a way Vincent found hard to follow.

The man moved from tree to tree in the next field, working steadily, quickly. Soon, as far as Vincent could see, the smooth dirt of the field was littered with almonds and leaves, scarred with tire tracks.

JOEY AND TWO of his friends took his truck to Hughson, the nearest town, to get hamburgers for lunch. The guy Carl drove his Camaro into the orchard, took an ice chest from the trunk. By noon it must have been one hundred degrees. Vincent leaned against the gnarled trunk of a peach tree, in the shade with Carl and two others. They talked about football practice, and since they had no soda, gave Vincent an Olympia beer. Its taste reminded him of the smell of wet cardboard.

One guy with an acne-splotched face, whose neck and shoulders were bright red from the sun, turned to Vincent. "You're Paul Torno's brother?"

"Yeah."

"What's he up to?"

Vincent told him where he went to college. All three nodded.

Red Shoulders said, "Paul was varsity baseball when I made JV— *as a freshman*," mock boasting.

"Whoa! Whoa! What a guy!" The other two acted impressed.

"Anyway, I played against him in practice. He's good."

"Shortstop, right?"

"Yeah."

"Yeah, okay, I remember him. He always seemed like a good guy."

"Yeah, he is a good guy," they all agreed, nodding. Drank their beer.

"So then Mary Torno's your sister?" another asked.

Vincent nodded.

He saw the guy Carl raise his eyebrows, murmur, "Mmmm . . ."

The one who'd asked kicked a small clod in Carl's direction. Turned back to Vincent, said, "Oh." Nodded.

Everyone was quiet. They looked around the orchard, stretched, drank their beer.

When Joey's truck appeared on the path between the orchards, a rooster tail of dust behind it, one of his friends seemed to be missing. Joey drove, Brad sat close beside him—Vincent wondered where the other guy had disappeared to. The three around him all started laughing. Then Joey stopped and a third head popped up next to the door, a commotion began, the passenger door opened, and the guy whose head had just appeared tumbled out, laughing, Brad right behind him.

As Joey got out of the pickup, Carl shouted to him, "So you and Brad dating now?"

"Yeah, very funny," Joey said. He carried a large bag of hamburgers.

Brad, carrying a tray of sodas, shook his head as he approached. "Yeah, funny. All through Hughson that bozo thinks it's the height of comedy to duck below the dashboard, make it look like we're a couple of faggots. Hilarious."

The third passenger, Marc, came a roundabout way through the field, still laughing a little. "But you guys make such a cute couple. Bunghole buddies—" He stopped in his tracks. "Hey! Beer! Now you're talking."

"Don't give him any," Joey said.

"Yeah, don't." Brad put down his tray, picked up a clod, threw it at Marc's shoes.

"Fuck you."

"Know who we saw at the burger place?"

A girl. A slut this time. Vincent listened and ate. All of them had something to say, usually at the same time, their voices rising to be heard, mouths full of food. The *snick* of beer tabs.

Snick. Snick.

They drank fast.

Who'd had her? Who hadn't! He had, but *he* hadn't. Oh yes he had! Nothing to brag about, why argue? In low voices: blowjob in the car, that's her specialty—but Vincent heard. On the way to the lake. You too? Oh shit! Oh shit! All over the fucking road, man! Who can drive when . . . ! Shit!

"Remember Marcie? Sophomore year?"

"Oh God, yeah!"

"Oh-oh-ho man!"

A slut too.

"Put out at the drop of a hat."

"Or pants. Ha. Drop of the pants."

"No shit. Used up by the time she was sixteen."

When they'd finished eating, two of them set up empty beer cans, threw dirt clods at them, tried to knock the cans over. Took another cooler of beer from the Camaro. Vincent finished his beer. The inside of his head felt packed with wet cardboard, the smell high inside his nose. He felt like he watched a dream. Like the time Mike Wund knocked him to the ground boxing and kept punching him in the head. When he'd stood up then, everything around him seemed ready to float away, everything light, flimsy, mixed up—that's how things seemed now. Vincent drank some of his Pepsi from the burger place. All six threw clods at empty cans, beers in their hands. One threw and missed the cans: "Fuck!" One threw and hit: "Fuck *yeah!*" Then they threw clods at the one who went to set the cans upright, then at one another. Clods whizzed through the air, exploded against trunks. Vincent hid behind a tree. All of them suddenly scuffling around, ducking behind trees, yelling at one another, cursing and laughing, Vincent crouching, pressing himself against a peach trunk, its rough bark against his cheek. Idiots, he thought. The Pepsi had made him nervous. They were scattered all around him, running, stumbling from tree to tree, clods flying, their laughter on all sides.

"You cunt!" they yelled. "Goddamn! Goddamn! Shit! Goddamn shit!
You prick!" Vincent had to keep shifting around the trunk of the
tree, everything confused. Finally, he jumped away from the tree,
arms up around his head, yelled to his cousin, "I'll . . . be back. Call
me when you're starting again," and ran from the peach orchard. Ran
all the way through the young almond trees and kept running. He
barely felt his legs beneath him. Ran into the field of old almond
trees, his head down, shards of dark shadows and cutting sunlight
mixed, jumbled at his feet like different shades of shattered glass.
And the refuse of almonds, twigs, leaves.

He ran well into the orchard before he stopped. Then he rested
his hands atop his head, staggered in circles while he caught his
breath. He wished his head would clear, felt anxious from the Pepsi's
caffeine, from the dirt clod fight, from the whole morning. He wandered through the rows of knotty trunks, saw no sign of the worker
or his machine. But saw the ragged bark on some of the trunks,
ripped by the violence. Thought the trees drooped in the heat,
drooped after their shaking—battered, used up. He followed one of
the grooves from the shaker's wheels through the trees toward the
edge of the orchard, toward a canal bank. Picked up a couple almonds, cracked their shells between his teeth, ate them. Stooped to
pick up another almond and saw, a couple of rows from him, the
pages of a magazine splayed like a fan. He was almost certain he
knew what kind of magazine it was before he picked it up—what
other kind could it be out here in this hot dusty place? He knelt by
it, looked around him, saw no one, heard in the distance Joey and
his friends, their laughter and curses.

Its pages were dry with dust, slightly stiff, as though it had been
outside for a while. The first photo he saw, full-page, harsh black-
and-white, startled him. *"Jesus Christ,"* he whispered. The woman sat
with her legs spread wide, her hands between her thighs, a thin fold
of skin stretched outward into a long triangle between each thumb
and forefinger. *"Jesus Christ."* She wore a halter top, her face thrust

forward, eyes half closed, showing mostly white. He heard Joey's voice, sarcastic, in the distance, turned the page.

Black-and-white too. Man and a woman, the woman on all fours, the man kneeling behind her, "doggy-style." The man has hold of the woman's hair, tugging her head backward, her mouth partly open, teeth showing. Her back arched, the skin over her ribs creased, in the black-and-white, such high contrast, her side looks sliced up. Another photo, his erect cock in her hands, her face hovering stupidly above it, she lies partly on her side, her body contorted. A strange angle. The photo taken at a strange angle, as though they both might slide off the bed at any moment. More of these two. Her breasts long, stretched. The man's face pockmarked, the scars clear in the harsh black-and-white. Their bodies twisted around one another, or rigidly posed, everything angular, off-balance, sharp bones, rolls of fat.

The whole magazine is black-and-white. No articles, few words of any kind except on the advertisements: movies, dolls, pumps, plastic things, mechanical devices, cartoons, filling the pages, crowded together like a junk heap. The models, too, scattered across the pages like garbage, twisted, bent. Two women together. A woman on all fours between two men, one at her mouth, one at her ass. All three straining and sweating in front of a cheap stage flat—Vincent can see the wall's flimsy edge where the ceiling should begin, but he tells himself, *This is the real thing.* No visible penetration—hair or hands or torsos in the way, the movie ads spotted with black dots—but clearly indicated. The real thing. Cold, harsh. Startling. But what did he expect? This is how things are, he tells himself, thinking of Harry, and feels ashamed of his initial shock, his first flush of embarrassment for himself and for those in the photos, ugly, degraded. What the hell did he expect? He realizes, with some shame, how he has been stirred by these photos, in spite of himself—then feels it in a rush, throughout his body, like a sudden burst of strength. He flips awkwardly through the rigid pages, finds himself moved by the very chaos of the figures before his eyes, in his hands. From the harsh contrasts of the photos, from the flawed, contorted bodies— strangely more immediate in this black-and-white than in the soft color photos he'd seen before—comes a thrill as subtle as the electric taste of a nine-volt battery tested against the tongue, as cool and sharp as the mirthless edge of sarcasm. *Stupid sluts,* he says quietly, trying out how it sounds.

He hears Joey call his name, flinches, drops the magazine, looks nervously around. Then his name again, and he realizes Joey calls to him from a distance. He stands with the magazine, tries to decide what to do. He thinks he should take the magazine—or thinks he *should be* thinking this, that he *should* want to take it. He's straining to think clearly and the effort makes him more confused. But he suddenly doesn't want to take it. Joey might tell his father, might take it from him, they might tease him. He drops it near a tree. He'll tell Mike and Darrel and Harry all about it, he decides, all about it. He imagines their reactions, he grins.

Joey shouts his name, and now is joined by his friends. "Vinnn-cent! Vinnn-cent! Vince! Vin-nie!" they call, their voices tumbling over one another. They're screaming now, laughing, they're drunk.

Vincent begins walking back toward them, thinks maybe his head is clearer, but the caffeine from the Pepsi almost has him shaking. He listens to the shouts—thinks both *what idiots* and *how funny*—then answers them with as strong a voice as he can muster.

"Yeah! I hear you! I'm on my way."

V

VINCENT SLEPT LATE the next morning, until the first ring of the telephone jolted him awake. The morning was cool, he'd slept in shorts under just a sheet, and the phone made him bolt upright and reach for some covers, his eyes still closed. Then he heard his father's voice.

"Hello. Hello. Hello?" A pause. "Hello! Ah shit." The receiver banged down. "That idiot. That's real cute. Lucy, your daughter was calling for you."

"Now you don't know . . ." his mother began, without conviction.

But Vincent knew, they all knew. Where'd she call from? He imagined her at the far end of the country, the opposite side of the world. He couldn't go back to sleep. He began to get out of bed, shivering, to put on some clothes, then he realized his right eye wouldn't open. "Shit." He sat at the edge of the bed, stiff with cold and muscle aches—Joey and his friends had let him use a mallet after lunch, as a brief little joke, but Vincent had kept at it, intent on showing them he could do it. He tried again to open his eye. It wouldn't. He dressed gingerly, but as quickly as he could.

The bathroom linoleum was cold beneath his bare feet. When he leaned over the sink toward the mirror, two steel rods seemed to pierce his sides. The edge of his right eyelid was encrusted with sleep, but not swollen. He washed it, then lifted the lid with one finger, found the white of his eye discolored, filmy. His shoulders ached so much he let his hands drop to his sides. His left eye was unaffected; from it he could see as clearly as he ever had. It felt fine. But his right eye burned and itched even with the eyelid closed. Then he wondered whether he could see from his right eye at all— he hadn't noticed as he looked at it in the mirror with his good eye. He lifted his hand to it again, drew up the lid, closed his left eye.

His right eye stung and watered in the sunlight from the bathroom window, felt like it had been scored with a razor, but through what seemed like scratches on its lens he saw. In the mirror he saw the window, sun blaring through it almost unbearably; saw himself, disheveled from sleep, not clearly but sharply as a blade is sharp—the darkness of his hair, his pale face. He turned and saw, his eye burning, everything in the bathroom, tub, towels, all harsh, edgy in the too-bright light, and the shadows they cast. Saw everything in an ugly glare through the scrapes on his lens, his eye watering and itching until he couldn't stand it anymore, then he sat down weakly on the tub's edge and closed both his eyes.

This is nothing, he told himself, *nothing serious, no big deal*. But suddenly a fear took him: that he'd see this way for the rest of his life.

PART TWO

EXPERIENCE

At that moment it all seemed extraordinary
to me and made me want to flee
from it and yet remain forever.

—*Isaac Babel*

CIRCUMSPECTION

1

MY FATHER WAS like St. Augustine's God: omnipresent in everything I saw and felt—in my very manner of seeing and feeling—and seemingly outside of time; permeating my whole world so thoroughly that for all of my youth any question of when his influence began, how it would change, or when it would end was inconceivable. He was always-already present and so intimidating that only after he died did I even began to suspect that this immanence might contain any comfort. For his very stubbornness, which left so little room for hope, came to seem after his death a kind of constancy and security that I could find nowhere else. In contrast, I had a history with my mother; a changing, ever-uncertain relationship which, if it included much more affection, seemed fated to end in much more despair.

Before I was old enough to know that there were times when something was "wrong" with my mother, the disobedience with which I troubled her—not simply because I was a normally active child but because free of my father I tended to be a stubborn, temperamental, and extraordinarily energetic one—often led us into a certain angry game of chase. When she'd carelessly break into the middle of a war I was conducting with plastic army men, or a Grand

Prix race with small Hot Wheels cars, and tell me to clean my room or clear my toys out from beneath the pool table, I'd listen and obediently nod my head. But as soon as she was gone I'd find that the imaginary context she'd ruptured had become whole again, enveloping me once more, as though she'd never violated it, as though she'd never said a word to me. And I'd continue my game.

Soon she'd return, angry this time: "Didn't I tell you to do something?"

This marked the official start of our fights; the first phase of our chase game. Sometimes out of mere willfulness I'd refuse to do as she said. Other times I'd refuse because she'd been bullying me all day and I'd already done what she was now asking me to do again (for maybe the third time that day)—and because I was too young to interpret what this senseless bullying meant. "Later," I'd say. Or just "No." And this angered her the most, since it was a word I never used with my father.

When my mother complained to my father about how I'd disobeyed her while he was at work, or when he overheard me being "smart-aleck," he'd be furious. He'd yell: "You do what your mother tells you! Who the hell do you think you are?" or "Don't you dare talk to your mother that way!" But then, more calmly, he'd turn to her and say, "It's partly your own fault, Lucy. You're too nice to him. He doesn't listen because you don't have his respect"—never in a nasty tone, but with some exasperation, as though he'd done all *he* could to ensure that his children respected their mother.

So my simple infantile "No" could push my mother as close as she ever came to a rage. "You little mule!" she'd say, threatening me with her open hand, and I'd run for the safety of the pool table (more fearful of the *idea* of her slaps than of the slaps themselves, since they never came) and start both of us on what became our customary circular route.

"You stubborn jackass!" she'd say, chasing me.

Sometimes she'd try to cajole me into stopping: "Now come on,

you're too old for this. It's ridiculous." She'd almost start to laugh. I'd
see her struggle to keep a serious face, so as not to encourage me—
but this struggle was, of course, encouragement enough. I'd keep
leading her around the pool table.

Other times, when the jobs she'd wanted me to do were pointless
or unnecessary, she'd only grow more severe. Nothing I did would
make her laugh then.

"You're as pigheaded as your father!" she'd exclaim. "Stubborn! Bad-
tempered! Just like him!" But even as she insulted him, she'd slip into
some of his rhythms and phrases, trying to assume his authority: "You
stop this right now, you hear? Listen! This is enough! I've had it!"

I wouldn't stop. I'd keep the table safely between us.

"You spoiled brat! This isn't funny! A little of this goes a long
way!"

But I was, as she and Mary agreed even when they weren't mad
at me, as stubborn as my father. So I kept her chasing after me, or
else motionless, glaring across the green felt tabletop, waiting to see
in which direction I'd go. Tirelessly, I'd keep her after me like this,
watching every move I made, for as long as I could.

2

AFTER THREE YEARS during which my mother's hospitalizations became regular, roughly annual occurrences, the envelope I took from
the mailbox one day after school when I was fifteen confirmed my
worst suspicions. It came from a bank, and through its clear plastic
window, to the left of my mother's name and our address, I could
see a clownish cartoon shoe, a thin leg with bent knee, and a slanting
line ending in a black dot. A familiar piece of a puzzle whose meaning, for too long, I hadn't understood—even when I saw the whole
image as my mother read the notice it illustrated. By my sophomore
year in high school, though, I understood it well enough to complete

the figure in my mind and anticipate its consequences. It was a jug-
eared cartoon man, with an expression of comic embarrassment upon
his flat round face, seated upon a three-legged stool. He decorated
every overdrawn statement this particular bank sent out and was in-
tended, I suppose, to lighten the impact of the bad news. But within
our house this little man took on a certain mocking, malevolent as-
pect. For he suggested to me a nearly absolute division between some
normal world in which being overdrawn was simply a slipup, an
oversight easily set right, and the world of my family, in which it
was undeniable and final proof of how wildly irresponsible my
mother had become. Like an oracle seated upon a tripod, this stupid
cartoon foretold the fight that would flare when my father came
home from work, and confirmed—in black and white, so that only
a blind man could miss it—my mother's illness.

And all at once it laid bare and annihilated a slender hope I'd tried
to hide, even from myself, beneath the cover of pessimism.

I briefly considered throwing the letter into the garbage; considered, for a longer time, leaving it in the mailbox until the next day
at least—not to save my mother from the news or from my father's
tirade (I told myself that now there was no saving her), but to save
myself from having to see and hear it. But another part of me wanted
to walk into the house, where she was maniacally busy making
Christmas wreaths for some Catholic Daughters charity sale, and
shove the letter into her face. To say, in this way, without a word:
*I know. I've been right to avoid you, right not to listen to you, right all along.
You can't deny THIS.* It would be sharp and wounding. A wake-up call.

But there was no waking her, I reminded myself. She had pine
cones piled on the pool table, a stack of plywood **O**'s near her feet;
when I entered the house she looked up, wanting to say something
to me, but I avoided her eyes and crossed the den without a pause,
straight into the kitchen, where I placed the stack of mail on the
table, then retreated into my bedroom at the far end of the house.

For a long time I'd been unable to read the signs of my mother's illness. When she was particularly unreasonable or unfair and I became angry and rebellious, my brother, Paul, would try to calm me, saying, "Just do what she says, Vincent, she's not well now," or "Don't pay any attention to her—she doesn't really mean what she's saying." But these vague explanations made no sense to me at seven or eight or nine years of age. A sick person has a fever or stomach cramps, is in bed or in the hospital; and the idea of my mother's words as somehow two-sided, coded, meaning something other than what I understood them to mean, troubled me at least as much as any harsh words she might have said. Besides, at other times I unexpectedly benefited from her "bad spells." She'd take me to buy new brand-name sneakers at Ralston Sporting Goods—notoriously overpriced—instead of the department-store knockoffs I usually wore. She'd buy me an expensive binder for school, saying, "You get what you pay for." The signs, in other words, weren't always bad in themselves. Temporarily, she might become more liberal, seem more confident than usual, or happier.

Before the indoor mall off Highway 99 opened in 1976 and nearly all of Ralston's old downtown businesses vanished, my mother sometimes took me shopping at Greene's for Boys. I remember in particular one long seemingly limitless afternoon spent there trying on all kinds of puffy ski jackets, regardless of price, and lingering in narrow aisles between clothes racks and before a three-way-mirror in which my slight self, made massive by goose down, was multiplied to infinity. I usually hated shopping, but on this day my mother was vibrant and attentive and indulgent, and it's my last and clearest memory of a time before I could perceive any of the signs that later would have—and have since, in recollection—ruined an afternoon like this, making my naiveté an embarrassment, turning every trace of giddiness bitter.

My father often warned my mother, "The bill always comes due, Lucy," and I can't recall whether he usually meant this literally or figuratively (it would have been like him to sententiously figure all of individual responsibility as the neat cause-and-effect exchange of a business transaction). But my mother never seemed to heed either sense, and when the actual bill for that afternoon at Greene's for Boys and for the jacket I proudly wore did come due, she responded recklessly and fatefully with a check drawn upon nonexistent funds. "Fatefully" because, as a consequence, I would finally begin to understand that during her little sprees my mother spent money she didn't have, made promises she couldn't keep, and feigned—or maybe even felt—enthusiasm and affection which in either case she couldn't maintain. Soon, every bounced check she'd spent upon me and each of her hospitalizations became reminders of how selfish and stupid I'd been, blind to every indication of her illness—and made me more determined not to be taken in by her again. I began to examine her actions and words, even intonations, much more carefully. Until at a certain point the whole language relating to her that I, like a foreigner, had struggled so hard to comprehend began with surprising fluency to alter not only my sense of her, but of the world—doubling, complicating, what had been the sole terms in which I'd once known it.

By the time I started high school there were weeks when almost anything could be meaningful; my mother's joy, no less than her anger or depression, could carry a dark significance.

3

THE BANK STATEMENT, as I knew it would, did lead to an argument that night—but my mother surprised me by initiating it. In the past she'd sometimes hidden such notices, denying and delaying the inevitable like a frightened child. This time she brought it out after dinner and dropped it, as if it were a piece of incriminating evidence, in front of my father, onto the table where his plate had been. I'd been hurrying to clear the dishes so I could disappear into my room, but this action of hers pulled me up short. "Look at *this*," she said to him, self-consciously dramatic in both her tone of voice and the gesture she made with one hand. Then she called him "stingy" and "tight-fisted." The dinner had been quiet, but I don't think my father was surprised. He had to have been expecting the worst—as I had tried to—for some time. And after my mother's unusual gambit, he readily followed her into the old fight I'd heard so often.

I loaded the dishes into the washer, tried not to listen.

Once upon a time my mother had been voted the shyest girl of her high school class. In her yearbook, among the photographs accompanying such distinctions as "Most Popular," "Best Smile," and "Most Likely to Succeed," only "Most Shy" was represented by an uninhabited landscape: a bare park bench before a clump of trees, with just "Lucy Gallardo" and "Owen Phelps" printed beneath it. My sister, Mary, always said this was *such* a mean joke. But my mother was glad of it—the empty frame a source of relief rather than insult. She would have been too embarrassed to pose for the photo anyway, she'd always say. At the birthday parties and school awards banquets to which she'd take me (my father never came) she was uncomfortable and awkward. With my classmates' mothers she could manage only a polite distance. She'd never been good at making friends, and besides, she'd naturally adopted the opinions and tastes of the only "crowd" she'd ever belonged to—the one into which my father, twelve years her senior, had drawn her. So in attitude, if not age, she was virtually of a different generation from my classmates' parents—so vast was the gap between those who'd grown up during the Depression and fought in World War II and those who'd come of age in the fifties.

Nevertheless, my mother was no longer as morbidly shy as she'd been in her teens, and for this she gave my father the credit. She'd often say (sometimes with pride in him, sometimes with great self-pity and dejection) that if it hadn't been for him, she didn't know what would have become of her. He was the one who'd encouraged her to stand up for herself, to speak up a little. After they were married he took her along to conventions so she could see distant parts of the United States. On their honeymoon he took her to Mexico—the first time she'd ever been out of the country—and by the end of the trip, in Tijuana, had even persuaded her to haggle a bit (blushingly and unsuccessfully) with the merchants, as shoppers down there were expected to. But in spite of his encouragement and example, he often enough had reason to tell her that she was an "easy mark" after she'd bought, from some door-to-door salesman, brooms purportedly made by the blind ("Was the salesman blind?" he'd ask), or a single-volume *Book of Knowledge* whose proceeds were supposed to benefit the mentally handicapped. In my father's opinion, which she often assumed as her own, she would always remain too soft-hearted—except when she was "on a high," as she was during this late autumn when she was supposed to be making Christmas wreaths, and on this night when she started the after-dinner argument.

At times like this, when everyone in the family agreed that my mother "wasn't herself," I wanted to ask, only half sarcastically, *Who, then, is she?* After I finished with the dishes and stood drying my hands with a cloth, the answer came. She was a parody of my father: critical, indignant, frustrated by what she meant to label his errors with the checking account. "How do you explain this?" she asked, offering a good approximation of his scorn before suddenly losing her nerve. "Can't you keep enough in there so—can't you . . . ? Keep enough money in there?" She couldn't maintain it—his dark stare alone derailed her—but she tried to be as disdainful as he. I don't know if he noticed any of her mimicry, or if her essential faintness of character so distorted even her best imitations that they were unrecognizable to him. But their argument ran in a tight circle: each of them wielding blame, closely after the other, until there was no distinguishing pursuer from pursued.

Luckily, they were interrupted by a phone call from Mary.

"How's Mom?" she asked as soon as I'd said hello.

"Just *great*," I said bitterly.

My parents silently looked at me.

"You want to talk to her?" I asked quickly. "Here, Mom. Mary."

My mother took the phone. My father walked into the den. I went into my bedroom.

For a long time I heard the murmur of one of my mother's monologues through my closed door. I tried to ignore it. I did my homework seated on my bed, my back against the headboard. I hadn't cared much for algebra, or for math in general, but I loved geometry: its intelligible shapes, the revelations of its angles and sides, the preordained logic of it all, the ordered movement through numbered steps to a final conclusion.

Without knocking, my mother opened the door of my room. I glanced up to find her standing silently in the threshold, then looked back to my homework. She said nothing, and when I quickly glanced up again her lips were slightly pursed, as if she were indecisively considering something. Again I immediately went back to work. She was crazy—I wouldn't even acknowledge her. She waited another minute, then said, "I want this room picked up by tomorrow."

I didn't respond.

"You hear me?" she asked.

"Yeah," I said, pretending to be absorbed in my homework.

"I mean it!"

"Yeah."

"This is ridiculous, this room!"

"Hm."

"Ridiculous!" she repeated.

But experience told me what she was trying to do, and I refused to let her pique me. So she turned and left, intentionally leaving my door wide open as a little annoyance, forcing me to get up and close it if I didn't want to hear the new round of bickering she went and started with my father.

4

MY MOTHER WAS born in New York City, but her first language was Italian. When she began grammar school in Santa Rosa, California, it was all she knew how to speak. Her classmates avoided her as if she carried a virus, or lice; sometimes they teased her (exactly as, decades later, a few Mexican children were treated in my own grade school). For a long time her only friends were her cousins, who were younger than she, and her father, a carpenter, who let her help him in his workshop. Her father was the kindest man she ever knew, she'd tell me, her eyes filling with tears. She'd tell me stories like this about herself when she was "down," and I used to listen even if I'd heard them before, because I liked to hear about my grandfather, whom I also remembered with great fondness (and always associated with St. Joseph), even though he'd died when I was only four years old. The funny thing was, she'd say, by the time she was sixteen she'd forgotten Italian—at least how to speak it. Her mother never believed her, but it was true. And at that time her hair was blonder— it darkened after she had children—and her skin and eyes so light that people thought she was Dutch or Swiss. She never corrected them. She was too shy then to correct anyone, she'd say, sadly smiling.

My father told stories about his family at the dinner table. He'd tell us about his father's bar or garbage business, his mother's ravioli factory, or his charming lazy uncle's short-lived and nearly fatal stint as a bootlegger. My mother told hers in private, sitting in the den or living room or wherever she'd been overcome by them, to just Paul or Mary or me. Of the three of us, Mary was the best and most reliable listener. Even though, of her children at least, it was Mary with whom my mother fought most intensely, pouring her own self-hatred upon her daughter in a way she never could upon her sons. Yet fifteen minutes after their bitterest arguments, Mary would still be drawn in by my mother's tears, her exhausted posture, her sad stories. And most of the time, so would Paul, who seemed to resign himself to the task, though something other than resignation must have kept him with her, listening. I was the only one who at a certain point made a conscious decision, and thereafter conscious efforts, not to listen to stories that were only self-justifications, rationalizations, exercises in self-pity, excuses. Not to be sucked into long "heartfelt" discussions with her, which never did—and could never do—any good; which *never* prevented some blowup, some breakdown, some hospitalization, but only made all of these inevitabilities, when they sooner or later came, more crushing.

The day after the bank statement cartoon had warned me of my mother's immediate destiny, I came home from school and found her seated with Mary in the den. My mother was in tears.

"If only your father—" she was saying, in a kind of singsong, when I entered. She stopped, straightened up from the hunched position in which she'd been sitting at the edge of the couch, and looked at me. She could always suddenly stop her tears, and when I was in my teens this led me to believe, conveniently, that everything she did was merely an act. Later it suggested something else to me: a desperate emotional agility. She was too insecure, reactive, dependent, for her emotions to be anything other than provisional.

I said hello, more to Mary than to my mother.

My mother continued to watch me, then turned to Mary. *"We're not getting along now either,"* she said (meaning herself and me) in a voice (now tearless) tinged with a teasing ironical gruffness—by which she meant to suggest that the only obstacle between us was my burgeoning masculine capriciousness. She wanted to make me smile.

I wouldn't. I shrugged and headed toward my room to change.

"I'll help you with the walnuts," Mary called after me.

"Not yet," my mother told her. "Just a few minutes. Wait."

I entered the orchard alone. During those years when Christmas approached and the walnut-picking remained unfinished, my father used to say, "That acre of ground back there is covered with money. That's money out there! Coins scattered on the earth!" But for me the brute fact of the walnuts—some with shriveled black hulls, some with tough fleshlike green ones that stained your hands a bruised yellow-black—resisted all his rhetorical attempts at alchemy. Where my father saw gold, I saw rubbish. I set my portable radio at the base of a tree in the middle of the rectangular field, tuned it to an FM rock station. I wore baseball sleeves beneath a heavy T-shirt. I loved the approach of cold weather, the first scents of wood smoke in the evening air, the slightly acrid, resinous smell of fallen walnut leaves—would have loved it more if each autumn didn't bring with it this job. With a fan-shaped metal rake, its stiff ribbon-wide tines rasping, I raked outward from the trunk until I'd cleared a circle with the tree at its very center. Then I walked to where the tree's outermost branches mixed with those of its neighbors and again started around, this time raking everything toward the trunk until I'd made a heaped halo of walnuts, leaves, twigs, and small clods. Then I knelt on the ground, a peach bucket beside me, and started to pick.

I was hardly conscious of the radio as I worked. At the rear of the field, among trees already picked, burlap sacks bulging with nuts stood like headless and limbless torsos—seeming sentient, even without ears or eyes, like some of Dante's damned. I was reading the *Inferno* for English class, so the trees all around me were suicides, the countless splits and cracks in their pallid bark the only signs of the imprisoned souls straining within. I couldn't decide if the sacks of walnuts were suicides too. I, of course, was only visiting, like Dante—though on second thought I realized I was more like Persephone, since I returned annually. And I was probably part of the lost souls' punishment: their forms of immobile and expressionless embodiment so horrible that they envied even the dull repetitious movements of my walnut-picking.

Mary finally appeared.

"Welcome to the seventh circle of hell," I said.

"I thought I'd never get away from her," she said, not hearing, or maybe just ignoring me. She picked up a bucket, then walked over. "She's so sad. Has Dad been hard on her lately?"

"Yeah," I said sarcastically, "that's the problem."

Her empty peach bucket hung loosely from the fingertips of one dangling arm, and as she spoke she absently, repeatedly, spun the metal bucket in one direction, then back in the other. "He can be difficult," she said defensively.

"No kidding."

"He can."

"*I know.*"

"But she's pretty bad now, isn't she? She's not good at all. That whole Christmas-wreath thing is a big mess, huh? It's already the middle of November—when's the sale?"

"I don't know. I don't care. It could be in August, she'd never finish in time. Just a bunch of crap."

I felt her stare at me. I kept working. She said, "She can't help it— you don't have to be like that. You think she likes it?"

I kept my mouth closed.

"She doesn't like it at all. She's miserable. *So sad.*"

"Stay for dinner. You'll see how sad she is." I rose to empty my full bucket into a gunnysack.

"What's that mean?"

I didn't answer. My mother *wanted* us to talk about her, wanted to be the center of attention. I wouldn't give her the satisfaction. I wouldn't waste my breath.

I returned to my place and sat down. The walnuts clanked, sometimes nearly rang, in the bottom of my empty bucket.

Mary stared across the Nollinses' acre of cow pasture and Collier Road at the bare level earth of what had recently been a walnut orchard, now all ready for paving and for more of the shoddy buildings—looking hardly more substantial than the tumbleweeds that used to blow down the same road—and their ever-changing small retail tenants which already littered a long stretch of Collier on the far side of the 7-Eleven. For a change I would have welcomed her usual complaints about that. But when she sat down, about ten feet from me along the circle of walnuts, her mind was still on my mother. "Oh, she can be a real pain. You should have heard her on the phone last night. I know what she's like. She's . . ." She shook her head. "You know what she's been saying to Paul? She can make you *furious*." A deep sigh. "But she doesn't know what she's saying. She doesn't mean it."

I saw my mother walking toward us through the orchard. "Speak of the devil," I said.

"I haven't been outside all day," my mother said when she was near us. "And besides, you think I'm going to let you two make all the money?"

"Maybe we should all be working on different trees?" I suggested.

"Oh, I won't be out here long," my mother said, then, trying again to be chummy—though with a little edge—"Afraid I'll cut in on your profits?"

She sat down with a theatrical grunt not far from me.

"Mom, that's not going to work," I said, as flatly as possible. "If I go this way I'm following Mary, if I go that way I'm following you—either way, there's nothing to pick."

"Oh. Well. Why don't you move? I just sat down—and I've got creaky old bones."

"I'll go start another tree," I said.

"*No.* Don't run away. Just move over there. This is a big circle."

As I got up to move to the other side of the tree, she said, "And can you turn off that music? God!"

I turned it off.

As soon as I sat down again she started talking. "Those wreaths'll kill me. . . ."

I tried to lose myself in the work. Mary was there, she could listen.

I scrabbled with my hands through the twigs, leaves, and dirt. My mother and Mary and I all worked our way around the same tedious circle. My mother talked without pause; I became hopeless, despairing—decided that if the bare trees all around me were in reality just senseless trees, the sacks of walnuts simply inanimate, then I envied them immensely.

5

MARY, NOT SURPRISINGLY, stayed for dinner. She had only just succeeded in persuading our father to let her move into a small old house near the center of town, with the daughter of one of his friends. But when she was not at her florist job on MacAffee Boulevard, she was almost always at our house, or on the phone to us. In fact, she and our father were closer, in their own strange way, than ever before. His concession allowing her to move out was the final, cementing swipe of the trowel upon the gothic masonry of their rebuilt relationship, whose slow tortuous reconstruction had begun four years earlier, after Mary's return from her cross-country jaunt with Billy Ramsey, not with all the tears, apologies, and pleading of her initial homecoming, but with her vow a few days later, when my father finally deigned to speak to her, never to see that "goddamn Okie" again.

The meal that night didn't go too badly. An outside observer—which was the position I tried to assume—might not have noticed any particular tension. But my mother, in her state, didn't want calm evenings and couldn't stand to be ignored. After dinner she called a fellow Catholic Daughter about the Christmas wreaths, knowing my father hated her to be on the phone at night. But the woman must have been busy, because they didn't talk for long. So then my mother came into the den where we watched television and introduced the idea of having the couch re-covered.

I don't know if my mother's goal was to start an argument (and certain topics were simply the means to this end); if having the couch re-covered really was important to her; or if the challenge of expressing any desire to my father, as fearlessly as possible, was actually the whole point. But my father wouldn't fight with her. When she tried to provoke him, he only became dismayed.

He sounded worn and tired, said, "That's not true, Lucy, you know that's not true. You're not even seeing that couch—you can't right now. Just calm down." But this just made her angrier.

Mary's appeal to her was simpler; at intervals, compulsively, she repeated, *Mom. Mom*—as if this lone syllable might work magic.

"You're not yourself right now, Lucy," my father said, as he'd said in previous years. "You're all off. Listen. You're not well."

But my mother persisted, and my father's patience was easily exhausted.

Finally he stood right up in her face and said, *"Lucy!"*

He would never learn resignation until he was close to death. He could feign it, temporarily, but would soon become more insistent than before, his new vigor and aggression inspired—I realized only years after he'd died—by the fear that certain conditions were truly unalterable. Much of what I knew of as his overwhelming strength came from his inability to bear, passively, what he could never possibly change. But try as he might, he couldn't call my mother out of the whirlwind of her illness.

He was still trying, though, when I left the room, even as my mother had turned her attention to Mary, saying, "And why do you always have to take his side? Why do *you all*—always—gang up on me?"

I closed myself in my room and did my homework.

Half an hour later Mary came to say goodbye. She shook her head silently after she entered, a sign of commiseration I refused to acknowledge. I could have said, "Didn't I tell you?" But I just looked at her blankly, giving her no encouragement. When she spoke, it was about a different topic.

"I'll be here Saturday to help you with the walnuts," she said.

"Okay."

"Paul thinks he can make it, too. He says things in Strickland are coming along."

Paul had replaced our uncle as manager of the troubled Strickland warehouse, where, between fresh outbreaks of chaos, things were perpetually "coming along."

"Fine," I said.

"You having any friends help you?"

"I *really don't think* I want any friends here right now."

"Oh. Yeah. I guess not." She took a step toward the door, hesitated, as though she couldn't leave without saying something about tonight.

"I don't want to talk about it," I said.

"I wasn't going to say anything," she answered, childishly defensive—though she was twenty-two—in a way that guaranteed she was lying.

I was taking a sadistic pleasure in making her uncomfortable.

"See you Saturday," she said in a resolute tone meant to deprive me of just such fun. She left.

An hour later, my mother came into my room and sat down on the edge of the twin bed that had been Paul's when he lived at home.

"What ya doing?" she asked, as if a casual enough tone could erase all of this evening and the whole week before; as if I were still so young that her slightest gesture of affection could transform my mood, draw me to her. She was mistaken. She could evoke neither sympathy nor love from me—though I was mistaken to believe that she'd never evoke either again.

"God! Look at those shoes," she said quickly when she realized I wouldn't answer, pointing to my sneakers on the hardwood floor between the beds. "Don't you think it's time to get some new ones?"

I was sitting with my back against the headboard, legs out; I set my geometry book down on my thighs. "They're comfortable," I said.

She shook her head, smiling broadly, as though to underline the wit of my remark for a television audience. "Comfortable," she repeated. "We can go to Ralston Sporting Goods after school tomorrow."

"No. I'm not going anywhere with you."

Her smile disappeared. "That's nice," she said, introducing an edge into her voice. She shifted forward, put more of her weight on her small feet—tightly together and pointed toward me—so that she was almost more leaning against the bed than sitting. "Maybe I don't really want to go anywhere with *you* either."

I picked up my book again.

"What's the matter with you lately?" she asked.

I almost laughed, but turned a page instead.

"The way you mope around. God! I've never seen such a sad sack. The trials of a teenager!"

"Yeah," I said, against my better judgment.

"Yeah what?"

"You're right on it, Mom. How'd you guess? Donahue do a show on it this week?"

"Well, what is it then?"

I rubbed my forehead with the palm of one hand. She'd do this sometimes, turn everything upside down until she was the reasonable sane one, caring, helpful—with feigned concern in her voice. "Look in the mirror," I said.

"Oh," exhaling a dismissal.

"Look in the mirror," I repeated.

She sighed.

"Look in the mirror," I said once more, determined not to let her twist everything.

"*I'm* not the problem," she said. She shifted again and the bed started to slide from beneath her so she had to jump to her feet to avoid falling. She lost her composure.

"Do you know what your father has been saying in there?" she asked. "Did you hear?"

I was silent.

"There's nothing wrong with me. And he knows it. When I start feeling a little better, when I finally feel some energy . . . I want to get things done around here, what's so wrong with that?"

I wouldn't answer.

"When I was down, he didn't even notice. And *you* didn't even notice. And Paul, and Mary. No one noticed! Or maybe you all liked it because that way I'm so quiet. I'm tired of being quiet. Things aren't right. Your father is stingy and mean. He's never been willing . . ." She sat down on Paul's bed again. "You want to hear a story about your father?"

"No."

"Come on. I won't tell you the really bad stuff."

"No."

"Listen, it's very short. It's just that when we were on our honeymoon, we were in this hotel room that had a double checkers set— you know, a regular checkers board on one side, Chinese checkers on the other, like we have? Well, one night we played checkers and he must have beat me ten times, but we had to keep playing. He was so happy."

I stared at her expressionlessly.

"Wait. Then the next night we played *one game* of Chinese checkers and I beat him, and he wouldn't play anymore! It was checkers or nothing! He *would not* play Chinese checkers again!" She looked at me with wide eyes, as though she'd just exposed my father's entire personality and was waiting for my astonishment.

"I don't care," I said.

"You didn't listen then."

"I—don't—care."

"You didn't listen," she insisted. "You *don't* listen."

"You're right." I said, thinking she might leave. But instead she complained some more, while I sat motionlessly staring at an illustrated explanation of a gnomon.

When she finally realized or admitted to herself that I really wasn't listening, she stood and came close. "How did you become so heartless?" she asked.

Her eyes brimmed, but produced no tears.

I didn't answer.

"You're heartless and cold," she said, as though she couldn't believe it and were inviting me, expecting me, to disagree.

"I am," I agreed.

"Heartless and cold," she repeated. And when this got no response, she added, "And *mean*."

"I am."

She shook her head, and slowly walked away from me.

I didn't speak or move, because I knew that was what she was waiting for.

I wouldn't give in.

At the door, a parting shot, she turned and said, "How did you ever become so cold?"—stupidly thinking she was wounding me, when at that time as I sat immobile, and for a long time afterward, I considered it the highest compliment she could have paid me, and my conscious goal.

WHEN I CAME home from school the next day my mother was standing at the pool table with her Christmas wreaths. She didn't look up when I entered, and I walked through the den without a word, believing I'd been so mean to her the previous night she wouldn't bother me anymore. Her illness would develop as it usually did. (Her *illness*: no one in my family ever used the clinical term, except my mother herself. Sometimes she found quiet solace in it, sometimes accepted it with resignation; other times, intoxicated by some self-help book or television program, or in a "bad phase," she practically flew it as her martial banner, or, weirdly smug, insisted on the two words' power to grant her absolute impunity.) I knew that soon she would have to go into the hospital, to "get her medication straightened out." I was determined to remain safely uninvolved.

My bedroom was dark, its curtains closed, but I noticed something on the wall beside my bed as soon as I entered—a framed picture. I put my backpack on my bed and opened the curtains.

By this time, at fifteen, I would have insisted that the only things that mattered to me (insofar as anything did, since I prided myself on my cynicism and light regard for the world) were my friends at Ralston Catholic High School, my place on the school newspaper, soccer in the winter and baseball in the spring, and my classes—which I would've pretended were easy for me. I would have sworn that my mother's tears had no effect on me and that my fearful obedience to my father was gradually becoming merely superficial—a protective shell, eventually to be thrown off, concealing the hatred and rebellion growing strong within me. I believed I was so familiar with disappointment, its old stories and its old vocabulary, that I couldn't even take it seriously. While Mary earnestly fretted over my mother, I observed her from the great distance that sarcasm creates. When my mother tried to speak to me, I would've sworn I never even heard her.

I wasn't prepared, though, to find a four-color print of a bulldog in a bowler hat on the wall beside my bed.

"What the hell is that?" I asked my mother after I'd hurried into the den, without even the pretense of composure.

She looked up innocently from the Christmas wreath she was working on. "What?" she asked.

"In my room, that picture."

"The print?"

I glared at her.

"That?" she said, as though she didn't notice my anger. "That's a present I bought for you today."

"Why?"

She suddenly held up a wreath, "What do you think of this?" she asked. "Too *busy?*"

"Why'd you buy that print?" I asked.

She put the wreath back on the table and walked to the back door of the den, saying, "Just a minute, I have to get something."

I followed her. In the back patio she picked through a large paper sack of pine cones, considered a few. I watched and waited in the doorway.

"Why'd you buy it for me? It's not my birthday—you do know that, don't you?"

She didn't pay attention to me. She selected a large cone, came back into the house. I followed her back to the pool table. Before I could ask again, she said, "I bought it because it reminded me of you." Then, as though suddenly distracted: "Just a minute, I need something else." And she walked past me into the kitchen. I followed her again. She rummaged in a drawer in the kitchen, ignoring me.

"Mom," I said, to remind her I was waiting.

"Just a minute," she said. "Oh, I know," and she walked to her bedroom. I followed. She opened the top drawer of her large dresser, took out a pair of scissors. Then she turned and went back to the den, as though I wasn't following her and waiting for an answer.

I followed her all the way back to the pool table, where she reached beneath some pine cones and exclaimed, "Ha! Look! They were here the whole time," and held up another pair of scissors.

"So it reminds you of me," I said, "the picture."

"Right. Yes, just like you. Same temperament, same glare. Same personality." She smiled at me as though we were sharing a joke.

"That's funny," I said, without a smile.

"It's just a little present. Don't be so serious." She turned her attention back to the mess on the pool table.

"I'm taking it down," I said.

She was busy now; she didn't answer.

"Stupid, cheap piece of . . ." I muttered.

"Oh it's not cheap," she said, without looking at me. "It's numbered and signed by the artist."

"Great."

A pine cone fell from the table. "Can you get that for me?" she asked.

Automatically I circled around to the opposite side of the table, picked it up, put it on the table. "I'm taking it down," I announced again.

"Do whatever you want." She ignored me.

But I couldn't leave yet. I stood and watched her arrange and rearrange pine cones on a plywood **O**. I was angry and thwarted. Deprived of a furious response from her to my own anger—the response I expected—I could only stand dumbly and watch her small hands, noticing a raw-looking cut just below one of her thumbnails. From the time I was very young my temper had made me rash, made me say things like "Once I'm old enough I'll *never* work at the warehouse," or "I'll *never* talk to so-and-so again." In response my mother would say, "Don't burn your bridges"—not understanding that for me burning was the whole point and that I'd readily exchange any deprivation for a sense of finality. I was waiting for just such a reassuring finality while I stood at the pool table, not suspecting that my mother had been toying with me the whole time, until after a few silent minutes I saw her clumsily but intentionally push a pine cone off the edge of the table, heard her say, "Will you pick that up for me?" and realized, finally and all at once, how she'd had me chasing after her.

"No!" I almost shouted, with renewed but impotent force.

I rushed back to my room to hide the print in my closet, leaving my mother alone at the pool table—and ending the game she'd been playing with me in the same way, years before, she used to end the chase games I'd start with her.

6

SOMETIMES MY MOTHER asked to be checked into the hospital, sometimes my father and Paul and Mary convinced her it was for the best, sometimes she went less willingly. In recollection, all of these variations seem comical to me, giving way to images from television of some poor dazed buffoon sinking into a chair and finally admitting that he or she "needs a rest," or of wiry clean-cut actors in white short-sleeved smocks carrying a straitjacket, an object of fun. Repetition finally reduces everything, even loss, to farce. So the exact manner in which my mother entered the hospital blends with all of the other such instances into irrelevance. She simply left, once more, and for the first few days I remained firmly unsympathetic. I always had an excuse for why I couldn't go along to visit. On Saturday when Paul came straight from the hospital to help Mary and me pick walnuts, I didn't even ask about my mother. Instead we worked, and we discussed whether the 49ers, with yet another new coach, had even the dimmest hopes of ever becoming a good football team, and how the San Francisco Giants' organization, in disarray from top to bottom, was doomed to perpetual failure.

But my father, who often seemed to have faith in no one and nothing but himself—in the efficacy of his ingenuity and the strength of his will—still had, at that time, a belief in certain doctors and in medicine. He had a great faith in practical knowledge, and though he knew he didn't have the training to deal with my mother's illness when it bloomed into its perennial profusion of crises, he believed that her new doctor did. This new doctor, he said, "seemed to be on the ball." About my mother, my father—like all of us—spoke little while she was in the hospital. But when he did, he'd say, "She seemed a lot better today. More like her old self." I couldn't even feign invulnerability to my father; his words inevitably had an influence upon me. And when he eventually told me that I had to go with him to see her, I couldn't refuse.

If I had never been in Memorial Hospital, waiting for my mother amid the cluster of couches and coffee tables opposite the elevators, I might have thought she looked rested and healthy when she came through the door near the nurses' station. Instead, I resisted this first impression and watched her with suspicion. At first she seemed happy to see me. But after she'd sat down with my father on a couch at right angles to mine, her thumbs began fidgeting within the shelter of her joined hands. I took this nervousness, unsuccessfully concealed, as a sign that she was still unwell—without even considering how my suspicions (which I believed were invisible) could be its cause.

My father, in a rare turn, was solicitious. "Doesn't she look good?" he asked me.

"Yeah," I said. "Great. You feeling good, Mom?"

"Much better, thank you," she said, as politely as if I were an acquaintance inquiring about a head cold.

"She can probably come home tomorrow," my father said.

"Great," I repeated.

"I hope so," my mother said—then, loosening a bit, to my father, "I'm tired of this place."

"You'll feel better once you get home," he assured her, placing one hand upon her enmeshed fingers—and her twitching thumbs were stilled by his touch.

He was kind, almost delicate, in all of his responses to her. I began to be ashamed of my own coldheartedness.

Of course, we talked about the weather: the autumn coolness, the shorter days. About walnuts, too—my father told her what a good job I was doing in the field. About the beautiful bouquet Mary had sent her. About how Paul had brought her a box of chocolates the day before, and how ("Don't you dare tell him," she warned with a smile) she'd eaten one in front of him, even though she really had no appetite—a result of the drugs, I suspected; a result of the unappetizing hospital food, my father joked. We kept everything light, my father and I, trying in our own clumsy ways to approach the grace required in a sickroom. My mother seemed to relax. When she mentioned in passing that she hadn't seen a newspaper in days, my father jumped up to go buy her one from the gift shop downstairs.

After he'd left, my mother and I fell silent. For a few minutes we sat in what seemed a wonderful stillness in the middle of that wretched place—perfectly quiet. I stared steadily at the plain white square of linoleum beneath my feet. I heard nothing. My mind was quiet. I was happy enough like that, near her.

"I didn't think I'd see you till I got home," she said.

And everything started again: I fumbled to interpret this sentence, to distinguish between the most attenuated sarcasm and the simplest shy affection, between accusation and an embarrassed admission that she'd missed me. "I've been busy," I said cautiously, waiting to see what she'd say next. But my father's return seized her attention. He smiled as he approached, and as he sat down he tossed—in an uncharacteristic and awkward attempt to seem carefree—the fat Sunday paper onto the coffee table so that its inner sections splayed out sloppily.

"All bad news," he said. "Wait till you're good and rested to look at that."

Then he told us something funny that the cashier had said to him. In the car on the way home he asked, "Doesn't she look good?"

"Yeah," I said.

"Doesn't she seem like her old self?"

"Yeah."

That was the problem.

My mother had told me a couple of years earlier that she had no recollection of what she'd done or said during those times when she was very ill. She offered this as an apology—but by then I'd already begun to doubt everything she told me, and I doubted this too. As I rode in the car, though, I realized that even if this was true it would be no consolation. It might relieve her of her guilt, but it didn't free me from what had become an abiding anticipation and fear of her *next* illness. All along I'd *wanted* her to remember her last illness—had sometimes even tried to remind her—as if the constant memory would help her to avoid the next one. But she must have forgotten it, as my whole family sometimes seemed to have forgotten. So that Mary could respond each time with a misguided sympathy, as though it had never happened before. So that Paul, knowing better, would let his skepticism melt in her presence. So that even my father could summon a buoyancy and optimism, which I rarely saw in him, for this lost cause, for this inevitable failure.

But I would not forget.

I reminded myself that my mother's life, and thus the life of my family, moved in circles: from the first fragile hope of the recovery stage, to optimism, to the numb recklessness of the quotidian, to the first misgivings and anxiety, to distrust, anger, sadness, regret, to a sense of futility—or at best, to futile and meretriciously dogged denial—and then, with an almost comic inevitability, back to the hospital.

All the way home from our visit, any hope that my mother had inspired I tried resolutely to circumscribe within the rigid bounds of these facts.

7

WHEN MY MOTHER returned from the hospital, my family wavered uncomfortably between two contradictory impulses. On the one hand, they wanted to welcome her home, to make her return special enough to seem the beginning of a new era, distinct from what came before; as though my mother—and all of them, really—would be starting from scratch, with a clean slate. On the other hand, too much attention to this new beginning inevitably carried with it unpleasant memories of the collapse that had preceded and necessitated it. So there was a temptation to feign a kind of rote ordinariness, to pretend that the days had unrolled smoothly one after another in a long line of comfortable, familiar banality. In truth, I suppose that they—like proper Catholics on their way to Confession—actually longed for a renewal so complete as to leave them untainted by even the memory of previous sins. But in this instance, unlike Confession, they depended upon each other, not God, for absolution—and it was beyond them. At least it was beyond *me.* I didn't trust my mother enough to forgive her, nor did I trust her enough to believe that she could forgive me.

Virtually all of the affection I'd received as a child from my parents had been provided by my mother; virtually all of the kindness, all of the softness and playfulness. She listened and talked to me as my father never did. She acted as go-between when I was too anxious to make a request of him, she relented from punishment as he never would. All of these things I tried to forget. After she returned from the hospital her kindness could, of course, still inspire pleasure and affection, but I found these feelings intolerable. When I was a child her bursts of irrationality had left me dumbfounded, confused—now it was her sweetness and concern that set me spinning, blurring sympathy and distrust.

By the end of the Christmas holidays my family had quickly worked their way along the old circle of recovery to the outskirts of heedlessness. I lagged, apart, watching them and my mother warily.

One day in the first week of January I came home from school to an empty house. A note on the refrigerator read:

I've gone to Hal's Market and Paradise Drugs.
Be back by 4:00.

Love,

Mom

Nothing unusual in this.

When she was ill she'd disappear and leave no note—or else leave a long crazy note, a strange attempt at explanation that in normal circumstances would have been completely unnecessary. This time she'd simply gone for groceries and to refill her prescriptions. Her new seven-day plastic pillbox sat in a corner of the sink. It was supposed to keep everything tidy, like a first-grader's pencil box.

My bedroom, its curtains open, was filled with cool winter light, and on the wall above my bed—there it was again.

The bulldog print.

I froze at the sight of it, then burst out laughing hard with a mixture of bitterness and relief, like a wanderer who's circled lost for days before stumbling upon a path which seems, without switchbacks or detours, to open out straight and deserted before him.

S N O W

. . . AND BITTER, BLIGHTING COLD.

Ever since he had been admitted by a Catholic university not fifty miles from Lake Michigan, Vincent had heard as much about the brutality of Midwestern winters as he'd heard congratulations. Native Californians spoke of them as fantastic phenomena shown on television or in the paper, or recounted by Midwestern relatives—whom they regarded, with condescension and pity, as if they were peasants subsisting in a benighted Baltic region of werewolves and superstition. Transplanted Midwesterners more simply shook their heads or rolled their eyes, then compulsively related their own experiences of horror, or horrific inconvenience: towering snowdrifts, arctic winds, power outages, frozen windshields. Throughout his last months at Ralston Catholic High School and during the dusty one-hundred-degree days of the San Joaquin Valley summer, Vincent was periodically advised on what to pack, how to dress. He listened readily to it all, because the implicit—and sometimes explicit—theme of his teachers and his friends' parents was always *What a change it will be for you!* A message he never tired of hearing, and one he infinitely preferred to the send-off he got from his favorite teacher, a bleary-eyed underachieving historian, who simply told him: "Californians travel horribly."

The prospect of such cold didn't frighten Vincent; he hoped the reality might, in fact, prove to be *much worse*. For he had grown up in a part of the valley through which even the strongest storms would pass, wild with wind and rain, and leave the sad gray landscape largely unchanged. Where winter traffic deaths, on dark country roads out of sight and hearing, were caused by the tule fog—the dullest, most monotonous of killers—which smothered the valley from December through February. So from the Midwest he wanted the extremest of winters, a climate as unlike Ralston's as possible. *He couldn't wait to leave home.* Upon arrival he hoped to be overwhelmed by the new, the unfamiliar, the unexpected, by every sign that he'd left well behind him the anxiety, pain, embarrassment, and stupidity of his first eighteen years.

His one great fear that summer was that he might die before August 22 (the departure date of his plane ticket); that Fate—which he believed with all the self-pity of adolescence had treated him cruelly enough already—would cut him down as he stood on the very threshold of freedom.

It didn't. Instead he arrived at Oakland Airport with his parents and brother two hours before his flight was to leave. His father always anticipated heavy traffic, crowds, vexing complications, human error—even for red-eye flights—so they had a lot of time to kill. Without Paul along it would have been unbearable, pinned between his brusque father and his mother, to whom he barely spoke as a result of the previous night's fight over the way he packed his suitcase. For two weeks before—and because of—his departure, he and his mother had been gentle with each other, kind; a false peace they couldn't maintain, since none of the old grudges or distrust had vanished. In the airport Paul acted as a diversion, a buffer, talking with his father about business, with his mother about recent renovations in the terminal, new gift shops and restaurants. The four of them wandered through these gift shops. Vincent bought a paperback to read on the plane: *The World According to Garp*. On its cover, above

Robin Williams's beaming upturned face, a blurb promised, *"To be full of Garp is to be full of life!"* Vincent wanted to be full of life. That's what he was waiting for.

Eventually, they went to the gate and sat side by side in molded chairs held solidly in a row by a steel girder. They made quiet small talk, stared out the glass walls at the runway lights, at planes landing and taking off. Vincent sat between his parents, rubbed his thumb over the slick cover of his new book, looked hungrily at those seated nearby, and kept trying to shift the position of his immovable chair.

When it was time to board, Vincent said goodbye to Paul with a handshake, hugged his mother, reflecting her half-smile, and hesitantly, awkwardly, hugged his father after he saw that, surprisingly, his father seemed to want him to. *When was the last time I did this?* flashed in Vincent's mind, then he drew away and saw that his father's eyes were watery, and was shocked and angry—as much as if his father had sprouted wings, ready to follow the plane—then touched. When Vincent turned his back to them his own eyes began to water, and walking alone in the narrow jetway he felt for some moments all the sadness of leaving home. But a turn in the ramp put all this just as suddenly out of mind. He saw the plane's open door, the waiting blond attendant, and found his head filled with all the old stories about freeloving stewardesses and reckless, fleeting affairs.

VINCENT MET LIZ GIVENS, as he met the other women he slept with during his freshman year of college, at a party in a loud, windowless, crowded dormitory basement; that place set aside in every dorm for the drunkenness and clumsy preliminaries of sex against which, aboveground, the university maintained the most rigorous proscriptions. One could be expelled for engaging in premarital sex, and not four weeks into his first semester, Vincent nearly had been, after being caught thoroughly drunk and partially naked with a girl— similarly disposed—on a study lounge's grimy floor. To a degree impossible while still living at home, Vincent had become enthralled by the liberating effects of alcohol, and (as usual) only after he felt himself glow with its beneficent influence could he approach the dark-haired, dark-eyed girl who he finally believed—after an hour of more sober skepticism—had been watching him ever since he arrived at the party.

As he walked toward her, still thinking about altering his course to the bar for another beer, she smiled at him, and mouthed hello before he did. So that effortlessly, without the risk of rejection, he happily found himself launched upon the typical frosh exchange of name, major (they both were Undecided), and school, leaning close to hear and to speak, and enjoying the sudden besieged intimacy necessitated by loud music. She told him she went to the old all-girl Catholic college adjacent to the university. She liked it there so far, the grounds were beautiful and the girls were nice. But she seemed to understand when Vincent said he already kind of hated his school, its single-sex dorms, its conservatism and conformity; a whole campus of former student body presidents, peppy and bright-eyed—the very people he'd avoided in high school. She told him about her hometown in upstate New York, three long hours by car away from New York City. He asked if it snowed a lot there, and she nodded vigorously: "Oh yeah, oh yeah." He told her he was from California and—disregarding a hundred miles and a major mountain range—implied that he lived in close proximity to the Pacific Ocean. She said he *looked* like he was from California, and he almost laughed, since he had dark hair and pale skin. But he kept a straight face and for the rest of the night (and the length of their affair) pretended at every opportunity that if he were home that autumn he'd wake up each morning to bracing sea air—rather than the smell of walnut trees, heavy with dying leaves.

When they seemed to have exhausted their conversational resources she asked if he wanted to dance, but he didn't, he wasn't drunk enough for that, and then she said she didn't really want to either. They went together to get more beer. Then they turned their attention to the people dancing and pointed out the most awkward or ridiculous. Liz's roommate, slightly disheveled, came down to the party from her boyfriend's room upstairs, and Vincent was introduced. Then they were alone together again and stood drinking. Vincent grew bored but he was too unsure of himself to ask her back to his room, until the party started to empty and Liz said she had to leave.

"You want to go to my dorm, see what's going on there? It's nearby," he said.

But she was too tired. Would he walk her to the shuttle?

Before they left, Vincent got a quart of Little Kings Ale from a friend behind the bar. He snuck it out of the party and started taking huge gulps once they were safely outside. He thought he could at least get good and drunk so the night wouldn't be a complete waste. They walked silently across one dark quadrangle and along the edge of another. The bus shelter was large and brightly lit, built in the fifties, and it looked like a Rockwell painting, with clean-cut couples in the nostalgiac plaids and khakis and pale button-down shirts of those first years of Reagan's administration scattered inside and around it. Boys waiting chastely with their sweethearts from the all-girl college, just as they used to before the university went coed.

Vincent said, "Let's stop here," and hung back in the shadows of the Law Building.

He drank.

"Well . . ." Liz began, at a certain point—but had nothing else to say.

They waited.

Gradually Vincent recaptured a very pleasant buzz, which was really the only reason the sight of the shuttle bus's approaching headlights stirred him to action. He abruptly turned and kissed her, and met, at first, with a moment of stiffness, reluctance, which almost made him pull back, embarrassed, but then her mouth suddenly opened, her body relaxed into him—he felt her breasts just beneath his chest, her thighs against his, her arms tightly around him—and he knew he'd call her the next day as soon as he woke and try to see her that very night.

ON HIS FIRST day there the university had seemed to Vincent to be everything he could have hoped for. He arrived during one of the heavy, airless, mosquito-filled days of a Midwestern late August—so different from the dry heat he'd left—and strolled around neat quadrangles of dark green lawn, beneath tall black-limbed trees he'd never seen before. He passed century-old Gothic-style buildings of the palest ocher brick, made of clay dredged from the two lakes on campus, and the turrets, arches, and gargoyles reminded him of the castles he'd always longed to live in as a boy. His own dorm, however, had nothing castlelike about it. An unadorned four-story L-shape built less than thirty years earlier, Vincent had requested it because it was nearly all single-occupancy rooms. He had no wish to bear the constraints of a roommate. So in spite of its blandness he was thrilled with his tiny cinder-block-walled room, overlooking a Dumpster— his childish visions of armored knights having given way as he grew up to other fantasies of self-aggrandizement and conquest.

Vincent couldn't wait to get Liz Givens into his room.

But a week would pass before he'd see her again. He spoke with her on the phone twice; they made a date for the next Friday.

That evening he drank a few beers after an early dinner with friends, then went to meet her at the Engineering Auditorium, which served on weekend nights as the university's theater. She smiled broadly when she saw him waiting beneath a tree for her, but they didn't touch as they greeted each other. The damn shuttle was running behind schedule, she said, still flustered or maybe just nervous— she'd had to wait forever, she'd thought she'd be late. But it was a beautiful night in the middle of October and neither of them seemed in a hurry to go in to the movie. They lingered, and Vincent finished a cigarette and enjoyed the soft Midwestern light that faded behind the new (to him) autumnal reds and oranges of unknown trees.

The movie, a highly acclaimed epic of Gandhi's life, was dull. Liz had to see it for a class. She sat, looking serious, with a small spiral-bound notebook on her lap. Vincent struggled to pay attention in case she wanted to talk about it afterward. He didn't want to seem stupid. But after forty minutes she hadn't even opened the notebook. Vincent nudged her with his elbow and raised his eyebrows; she laughed quietly. She pretended to yawn. He reached to take the notebook from her lap; she made as if to slap his hand away, but let him have it. He wrote in large letters, visible in the bright Indian light reflecting off the movie screen:

I'M DYING OF BOREDOM!

Liz laughed quietly. Then wagged her finger in mock sternness. She took the pad and wrote:

This is a class assignment!

Vincent took it back again. Wrote:

I know that. BUT THE BOREDOM IS KILLING ME!!

Liz made a face at him, shook her head. But a couple of minutes later she took the pad and wrote:

ME TOO!

They both started laughing quietly then, and couldn't seem to stop.

"I'm too young to die!" Vincent whispered.

"Me too!" Liz whispered. "My whole life's ahead of me!"

A girl seated next to Liz looked at them as if they were idiots or children.

"Let's get out of here," Vincent said.

They went to his room.

They exclaimed over how bad the movie was. Then they drank beer and talked in general terms about pop music, listened to tapes. Vincent sat on the lone chair, so Liz sat on the bed. The beer and Liz's presence seemed to warm the whole room for him, the muted light of the old-fashioned metal desk lamp turned against the wall softened everything. They kissed, and Vincent kissed and stroked her with a gentle eagerness and fervent care, moved not by any emotion specific to her—he hardly knew her—but by the thrilling feel and smell of her body, his general reverence for the "female form," and the caution proper toward an object so loaded with meaning. His passion was practiced, almost theatrical: his desire real enough—overwhelming and desperate, actually—but restrained. He struggled with it to hit the right note, maintain the right mood, both for the sake of seduction and to protect the sense he got as he slowly undressed her that he was slipping away from the moorings of the ordinary; afraid that any clumsiness, one wrong move, might jolt her into resistance and himself into the usual, lifelong, embarrassed self-consciousness from which he felt himself escaping.

Twice that night they "made love."

After that they saw each other as often as possible. She'd come to his room, and they'd have sex at least two, sometimes three times a night. As she lay naked on his small bed Vincent would tell her, "You look so beautiful you make my mouth water. I feel like I could *devour* you," and she'd laugh and squirm a little, flattered by his seemingly unbounded desire for her. Vincent wanted to be a great lover and worked hard at pleasing her, counting her orgasms and timing himself. A common joke among his friends was that the urge to ejaculate could be vanquished by imagining old women's varicose veins, but Vincent thought about picking walnuts in Ralston. He'd last through the forty-five-minute side of a cassette, then quietly let himself go (with her, ideally) on the last song.

Once, Liz invited him to her room, and though Vincent liked the idea of being surrounded by a campus full of girls, it was a disaster. Liz's roommate kept coming into the room, so they had no chance for sex. They never met there again.

Otherwise their time spent together was always successful. They fucked until they felt drunk (Vincent was usually a little drunk to begin with), they talked about friends in their respective dorms (they had no mutual friends), about music (of which neither had any real knowledge) and classes, and generally pursued their romance in accordance with songs, movies, and books—always careful to discriminate, it's true, between "mainstream" and "avant-garde" models (Brian Eno's ambient music was a favorite), but never having sex under normal lighting or with just the quotidian sounds of the dorm for accompaniment. In these first weeks together the very strength of their desire seemed to distinguish them from other people. On the lazy walks they took after spending hours in Vincent's room they shared a smug sense of superiority, felt themselves floating above what they once agreed were just a bunch of "throats, preppies, and ROTC burrheads"—feelings no doubt beneficial to their fragile egos.

Except that Vincent was sometimes nagged by a related feeling: of how lucky he was to be at this Midwestern Catholic university, a backdrop so dull and conformist that, in contrast, even his own strained posturing could assume, in the eyes of certain Romantically inclined girls, a tinfoil glimmer of adventure.

OFTEN LIZ WOULD affectionately tease Vincent about being a Californian. One night while they clung to each other, just after her breathing had returned to normal and her heart, which Vincent was secretly monitoring, had slowed to an almost regular rate, she said abruptly, smiling with feigned disbelief, "So you've *never* seen snow?"

"No. Like I've told you before," with mock impatience, "I *have* seen snow. I've even gone skiing. I just haven't lived in it."

"Haven't lived in it," she repeated. "So you probably haven't seen it fall."

"I've seen it fall! In the mountains," and he ducked his head and ran his tongue over her breast in a way that made her kick at the sheets and wriggle beneath him.

"Stop that!" she said. "Well, anyway, you're lucky. It sucks to live in." Then she made him get off her because one of her legs was cramping.

Vincent lay on his back; Liz snuggled against him. He was exhausted and happy from hours of sex and drinking. "The closest thing to snow where I lived," he said, "was almond blossoms. Have you ever seen almond blossoms?"

"No."

"They're pretty cool. In, I think, late February or March, the trees bloom. All their limbs are covered in white—or sometimes pink. But I think only bitter almonds are pink. So, usually, white."

"That must be beautiful."

"It is. They smell really good. Very, very sweet, you know? Like honey or something. Like you."

"Very funny."

"But best of all—at least for me, when I was a kid—is when the blossoms, or petals, fall. Because then you can walk out to the middle of an orchard, and look all around, and kind of squint, and it looks like there's snow everywhere, all over, on the ground. At least for a few acres. I thought that was so great when I was a kid. Like the ground was covered in snow."

"Did it smell, too?"

"I don't know. I guess so. That wasn't really the point. It was just how it looked, so great, so *different*, right in the middle of . . . where I lived. California. Though, of course, it didn't last long. Maybe a couple of days, and then the petals dried up and turned brown, and got blown away, and you just had dirt again."

"Well, my little California boy, you'll see snow here. A *lot of it*," she said.

"I know. It'll be great."

Liz laughed. "Maybe at first. But, then, believe me—it'll suck."

FOR FOUR WEEKS Vincent thought he might be in love.

He had been once before, when he was sixteen. Back then, he'd been thrilled simply as he drove to her house—visible for miles above tomato fields, against the soft curves of buff Diablo hills— thrilled by any scent of her left in his car, by her voice on the phone, her angular scrawl on a scrap of paper, her name. In her actual presence, surfeited with her attention, every disappointment he'd ever had seemed to vanish. But though they were the same age, she was beautiful and womanlike (the sight of her in a swimsuit amazed him) while he was still too much a boy. During the six weeks they dated they never had sex.

His high school sex had been with virtual strangers, at house parties where real desire hardly preceded some opportune moment, some deserted room in which fucking seemed inevitable. His one true love had seemed perfect to him: sexy and smart—too sexy and too smart for him, it turned out. Whereas he realized, as soon as he'd "finished," even as he still embraced them, that these other girls weren't *enough*. He became conscious of their every flaw, and, guiltily, he longed to escape—he had enough flaws of his own.

For four weeks, Liz was enough. She was everything. All the time spent in class, with homework or friends, seemed wasted—nothing more than stretches of near-death. His *life*, in all its youthful expansiveness, was concentrated in his tiny room, in the time spent in bed with Liz. Liz seemed to feel the same way. She told him that whenever they were apart and she heard, through the wall of her dorm room or an open window, the last song from the cassette that often accompanied their sex, she felt a strange, pleasant physical sensation deep inside herself. She said she couldn't believe how *passionate* he was. She didn't hesitate to talk about their sex life, and Vincent loved to hear it, at least at first, since she expressed feelings for him that he'd feared he would never inspire, and an image of him he thought he'd never be able to put over.

But she talked about other things as well, and, in accordance with the perverse law of infatuation which would govern Vincent's affairs for many years, the more she revealed about herself, the less—as they say—he saw in her.

Liz talked about her roommate from Chicago, who was dating three guys at the same time, including the owner of the only vaguely stylish restaurant in the whole dead Rust Belt downtown, which lay three miles south of campus. This girl sometimes provided Liz and Vincent with pot or cocaine, but Vincent wasn't impressed. She was freckle-faced, and her New Wave whore outfits were never entirely free of some Midwestern, Bob Segerish touches; she was hardly worthy of the bloated admiration Liz had for her. More frequently, Liz talked about her younger sister, to whom she spoke on the phone each weekend. In the school photograph Vincent had seen, this sister was an ordinary, gawky fourteen-year-old, though he'd politely agreed when Liz asked, "Isn't she beautiful?" She was just starting high school, which Liz referred to more than once as "that most terrible of times in a girl's life." A statement she always delivered with a smile and a playful melodramatic drawl, but Vincent wasn't fooled. He'd noticed that a lot of girls protected their most earnest opinions with ironic tones, and he sometimes found himself imagining all the typical misfortunes that had probably befallen Liz in high school, and hoping she'd never want to tell him about them.

As long as they were actually fucking, though, he was happy; so they fucked a lot. During the Thanksgiving break they spent an entire day in bed, until both of them were sore. He kept telling her,

"I can't get enough of you"—which was true, but not as flattering as it once would have been. For by late November, Vincent felt disappointed and discontented after sex with Liz. He tried not to think about it; didn't remember that it hadn't always been this way. Instead he explained it to himself with a newly learned quotation from Aristotle—"All animals are sad after intercourse"—and, precociously reaping one of the chief benefits of a spotty college education, sank all the immediate feelings that troubled him as he lay beside her into this fragmentary but authoritative declaration. Until, after a rest, he and Liz were ready to go at it again.

But ultimately, even Aristotle was of little help. All sorts of things about Liz began to bother him: the conservative, preppy clothes she sometimes wore; her pinched nose. Sometimes he was bothered by the four one-night stands she'd mentioned, and worried about the sexual carelessness they suggested. Other times he was bothered by her self-consciousness: the way she seemed ashamed of her breasts (though he truthfully said they were *magnificent*), and how surprised, then almost apologetic she was whenever he went down on her. Sometimes he was afraid that she didn't appreciate him enough. Other times he felt only scorn for her, because she was so impressed by a fraud like him. As seven weeks passed his great monomaniacal desire for her became fractured, its brilliant purity was muddied. Sometimes she'd break parietals and spend the night with him; most of the time he found himself waiting with her at the bus shelter, with all the other stupid couples, for the last shuttle of the night. She'd complain that they never left his room, that they never saw anybody, that he hardly even talked to her. The whole thing became dull.

Vincent began to drink much more before he saw Liz. She'd find him glassy-eyed, paler than usual, and excitable (the first few times he was like this she seemed to take a renewed interest in him). Sometimes Liz drank a lot too.

One night in the first week of December she began to tickle him while they were fucking.

He wriggled, and she exclaimed, "You're *ticklish!*"

"I'm not," he said. "Stop. Stop!" he laughed. He pushed deeply into her, trying to distract her. "C'mon, stop."

She did for a minute while they fucked, then she started again.

"Hey!" he cried.

"You *are* ticklish! Look at that!" she laughed. "Look at you squirm!"

"Stop!" He thrust harder.

She stopped, but only momentarily.

"*Hey!* I'm warning you now," he said.

She giggled and continued.

"You don't stop . . . Hey! Wait! C'mon . . ." He tried to capture her hands. "Stop! I'll tie you up!"

"Oh you will?" she giggled. She was still. "I'd better stop then."

"You'd better," he said.

Her legs were hooked around the back of his calves. They kissed. She started tickling him again. They both started laughing and kept fucking. "I'll do it!" he warned, not thinking about whether he meant it. They were grinding against each other in a way that felt great, slippery with his sweat, and he wasn't thinking about anything. His warnings were automatic. Her fingers ran all over his sides and back, and he squirmed involuntarily, in a wonderful blankness of mind. Then she ran one hand up into his armpit and he really jumped, and the cry that came from his mouth was so unusual that Liz laughed more loudly and Vincent laughed along with her until she mimicked his yelp and her imitation brought him so abruptly back to himself, to self-consciousness, that he felt himself blush in the candlelight. "Stop," he said again, still smiling, but with a new emphasis. He kissed her hard on the lips, stifling her laughter. She stuck her tongue into his mouth, then wrenched her face to one side and, giggling, tickled him some more.

She was playing a game.

"You gonna stop?" he asked.

"No," she giggled.

She was urging him on. She seemed to want a little make-believe danger.

"I'll do it!" he warned. "Stop!"

She didn't.

He reached for his belt on the floor. "Look," he said, bringing it onto the bed. "I'll do it." Making the threat was exciting, but he wouldn't really do it.

She wouldn't stop tickling him. He fucked her hard; she kept tickling him.

"I'll—" he began.

"Go ahead!" she dared him, giggling like a little girl.

She let him take hold of her wrists, let him raise them above her head. He was still inside her and clumsily he wrapped the belt, loosely, around one wrist. They were both laughing. He expected her to stop him, to pull free of him. But she let him wrap the belt around the other wrist, then fasten it to the metal bedframe. She hardly even feigned resistance. She laughed and rolled her head one way, then the other. "Okay?" he asked. "Okay?!" He hugged and fucked her, and she kissed him, keeping her wrists in the belt's loose coils. He ran his tongue over her breasts so that she squirmed and wriggled, but she didn't take her wrists out of the belt. He stuck his tongue into her ear, felt her pelvis push against him, but her arms stayed above her head. He labored over her; he became uncomfortable. She wants to be "ravaged," he realized, she wants to be *overwhelmed*. And at once he knew there was nothing spontaneous or joyful or reckless about what they were doing. It was all faked, like her hands in the ineffectual knots he'd made. All just a stupid cliché. Some idea she'd gotten from a magazine or a movie. She egged him on. As they'd been egging each other on, trying to push one another into being *enough*, after it had become clear that neither of them were. He felt a draft on his back where her arms should have been. He couldn't stand it anymore. He reached up and pulled her hands out of the belt, then undid it and threw it onto the floor.

"What are you doing?" she laughed.

"I love to feel your arms around me," he said, implying out of habit the affection he didn't feel—then added, with real distaste, "Otherwise it's like making love to a stump."

THE NEXT MORNING Vincent lay in bed and watched Liz, who stood in front of the sink and medicine-cabinet mirror near the door of his small room. She was naked except for one of his cropped and sleeveless T-shirts, hardly more than a rag, which she always insisted on sleeping in. He looked her over while she washed her face. She wasn't bashful, except about her breasts. What did she think was wrong with them? he wondered, and the number of melodramatic and silly scenarios that crowded into his mind made him depressed; made him feel that he couldn't stand to be around her for another day.

She patted her face with his towel, then sat on the chair near the bed. "You want to go to that movie tonight?"

"No."

"It's supposed to be great."

"I know. I don't want to go."

She began to dress. "What do you want to do then?"

"Nothing."

"Nothing?" She pulled on her jeans. She'd been trying to be cheerful, but she readily gave it up. "Nothing?" she repeated. "That's what we always do."

"No," Vincent corrected her, wanting to be a little mean, wanting to end it, "usually we *fuck*."

"Yeah, well . . ." Liz murmured.

It wasn't hard to build this into a fight. They ended up, once again, pushing each other along, working each other up, until it seemed for a brief time that something important was happening. They vented all the disappointment they felt in each other. How boring they'd both turned out to be! Vincent purged himself with relish, though he knew she didn't deserve it. He realized even as they argued that he'd never loved her and that, now, he certainly didn't hate her—that, in fact, he had no feeling for her strong enough to justify the cruel things he was saying. It was just that he'd gradually felt himself being drawn into some sad personal history of hers, with its own foolish desires and stupid injuries, and he'd begun to feel embarrassed for them both, and resentful. All the excitement he'd felt with her had evaporated. There was so very little to the both of them. Whatever she could offer him of herself was of no value—just more of the same petty experience and longing that he already had.

In less than fifteen minutes they ran through all their complaints. Then Liz left, quietly closing the door behind her.

A FEW DAYS later, Vincent was walking slowly back to his dormitory after class, smoking a cigarette. The weather had been mild all semester. He wore a ski jacket over an ordinary cotton work shirt; no gloves, no scarf, no hat. In the weak sunlight of late afternoon the buildings and trees were tinged with a soft gold just beginning to fade to gray. He didn't think much about Liz anymore. He was already beginning to anticipate next semester: all the new possibilities. As he walked past the Engineering Building he glimpsed something like a small moth angling slowly across his path. He didn't think anything of it. Then, out of the corner of his eye, he noticed something else, almost floating rather than falling, but turned his head and couldn't find it. He kept walking, took a drag from his cigarette, then there was something a little distance before him—almost immaterial, white—then another at a greater distance. And before he could have named what he thought he was seeing, these sights conjured an amorphous sense of a past time and place dense with boredom, frustration, embarrassment, a keen desire for escape, which in the next moment opened out into recollected sensations—low muddy river; blazing, dusty day; his parents—then finally to his parents' stupid misguided intention: the rare, special day they'd planned to spend with him, *fishing*. The whole thing such a miserable failure he smiled at the memory. That was where he'd seen the trees. On the edges of nowhere, Ralston, on the riverbank. From the trees came the puffs, like breaths, of the finest cotton, which drifted lazily onto the water and vanished, instantaneously, to the faintest dimples amidst the river's glare. Cottonwoods. He stopped and looked up at the trees lining the sidewalk at the edge of the quad, expecting to find them there. But the trees he saw were too tall. He looked down at the lawn for the insubstantial things, tiny ghosts, caught among its blades. They weren't there. A few more fell slowly, widely spaced, around him. He wondered how far they could have been carried on a breeze so light he barely felt it. It didn't make sense. Puzzled, he looked helplessly around him.

Across the quadrangle someone coming out of the bookstore excitedly cried, "Snow!"

TORNO BROS.
DISTRIBUTING CO.

FOR YEARS THE logo of a certain brand of beer struck me as a reproach. At college in the Midwest, graduate school in San Diego, the sight of it on bottles or cans in liquor stores or supermarkets, or glowing neon in the window of a bar, inspired a spasm of guilt and resentment, as might the sudden appearance of a photograph of a close relative long estranged.

It was my father's best-selling brand of beer, the cornerstone of his distributing company, the moneymaker. I'd grown up surrounded by it, and by its various promotional paraphernalia. I used to be the envy of certain classmates because of my pens and pencils, which sported its logo, as well as the T-shirts and the windbreaker which I could never wear to school, not even on "free-dress days," because the Holy Cross sisters in charge were less than thrilled by an ambulatory grammar-school alcohol ad. My father had other brands as well, of course, other beers, various wines, some hard liquor, and an English brand of mixers whose promotional items possessed a certain foreign cachet (including a dimly glowing, brick-wall-backdropped diorama of an early automobile, with turning wheels and weak headlights, rocking and jolting in place above a cobblestone street—all plastic, except for the small motor and drive chain—which always occupied a special place beneath our Christmas tree, where I'd lie and stare at it for an hour at a time, imagining myself elsewhere). But none of these other brands was as intimately connected with our family identity as this particular beer. Seeing this beer's insignia was the equivalent of seeing my family name on a billboard, in a grocery, in a bar, and as long as I can remember, it evoked immediately, without reflection, whatever mixture of feelings my family inspired at any particular moment. In my early twenties my reaction to it had almost entirely to do with my brother, Paul.

We weren't speaking to each other then. Family holidays, when we were forced together, were dulled by our mutual grudges, flashing only rarely with a kind of fool's-gold good fellowship, which was thin and brittle and backed with an elemental disappointment. Even sports talk—our old standby—was beyond us. Paul had come to believe that almost all professional athletes were spoiled, lazy, and disloyal, and I was certain he attributed the same qualities to me. In this, as in all his opinions, I detected a pointed martyr's sense of self-righteousness, and it infuriated me. For I had my own complaints. With an angry incredulity I could hardly believe that Paul—not (as anyone would have expected) my father—had been the chief obstacle between me and what I believed at a certain time to be freedom. That it had turned out to be Paul's face, Paul's actions, which impressed most forcibly the distributorship's claims upon me—conflating fraternal and professional expectations so completely that I couldn't break with the business without breaking with him.

Though, of course, if I now consider the story from something like the beginning it's clear that my father was far from being uninvolved in all this. How could he not have been: that man for whom, until the last few years of his life, the phrase *family business* was a tautology?

TORNO BROS. DISTRIBUTING CO. was the way it appeared on the doors of all the delivery trucks and salesmen's cars; on my father's business card, the office stationery, and the large black-and-white sign attached to the front of the warehouse in Ralston. My father had added the "Bros." to the name of the business he'd inherited from his own father, as soon as his younger brother came out of the Navy in 1948. Added it, I can only assume, out of the greatest optimism and deepest fraternal sentiment—since, by the time I was born, only traces of such motives remained.

The fact is I grew up hardly knowing Uncle Joey, except through the tirades my father directed toward his absent figure on innumerable weekday evenings (and some Saturdays). My cousin Joey I saw just often enough to completely distrust; while my aunt remained simply a sour-faced non-Italian stranger, a holiday giver of unwearably ugly clothes, and my eight girl cousins—all older than I—a mass of femininity whose exact correspondence to a tangle of names, some of which I always forgot, was never clear to me. I rarely saw any of these people, because Uncle Joey was—or had become— simply unbearable to my father. *Is he even trying?* my father would exclaim. *Doesn't he have any sense at all?* Not a single one of our Christmas visits was ever untainted by the problems of business. Yet my father, out of what must have been an increasingly attenuated sense of familial loyalty, tolerated Joey's incompetence through more than a quarter century of unmerited and unappreciated opportunity. Until my brother, Paul, graduated from a small Catholic college in Moraga, California, with a degree in business and was rewarded with a silver wristwatch (*easily exchanged*, I remember my mother saying anxiously before he'd even removed it from the box) and, from my father, the rather more incontrovertible gift of the managerial position in Strickland.

Thus Uncle Joey, released from the thirty-mile drive to Strickland he'd always hated, happily assumed a new position in Ralston— where my father could better keep an eye on him. While Paul found himself in charge of a warehouse which had lost money for fifteen consecutive years, in which salesmen outnumbered deliverymen two to one (the exact inverse of the usual ratio), and where two of the senior salesmen hardly left the office at all, unless they were going to lunch. In the drivers' room, on the metal shelves among price stickers and signs, Paul discovered poker chips and playing cards, and it wasn't unusual for a driver to leave his route unfinished for the day and return early to the office to gamble and drink draft beer. (It was rumored that Uncle Joey sometimes had played too.)

Six weeks after graduation, at my father's orders, Paul was forced to "clean house"—which earned him the enmity of both the dismissed and their friends who'd been spared.

Three months after graduation, Paul caught a summer cold. It never went away. For the next few years it waxed and waned, occasionally thickening into bronchitis. Eventually it was diagnosed as severe allergies, but no treatment ever made him feel any better. He suffered from sinus headaches and blew his nose in all weather. When he came to dinner on Sundays he'd be pale and lethargic, his eyes red, the soft skin beneath them puffy and dark. My mother said the pressures of the job were making him sick. My father didn't disagree, but told her not to worry. "Sure, it's hard for him now," he'd say, "but it'll get better. He's still too nice to those men—he bends over backwards for them. He's soft-hearted. But he'll learn. Strickland'll toughen him up."

Yet when I started working for Paul, the summer after my high school graduation, his five years on the job hadn't seemed to make him much tougher than he'd ever been.

THE DARK QUONSET warehouse was nearly oxygenless on my first morning of work in Strickland, choked with the exhaust of route trucks rumbling two abreast, waiting their turns to pass out the narrow door into the glaring street. I weaved among them, trying not to inhale, but saw no sign of Paul until I reached the rear of the cavernous space. There I discovered a silent truck whose last pull-down door seemed to have trapped a man in its metal jaws: only the lower half of a kneeling body protruded, its torso contorted awkwardly. I knew it was Paul even before I was close enough to make out his small feet, his scuffed black work shoes. Nearby a husky blond driver, his back to the pounding that came from inside the bay, absentmindedly flipped the long narrow pages of his route book. Unseen, I watched him—remembering my father's angry sad words of the night before, *Paul hasn't got one damn soul he can trust up there*—until the pounding stopped and the driver turned, suddenly animate with concern, and my captive brother squirmed free and stood, brushing his short hair off his hot forehead, and greeted me happily.

"Got it?" the driver interrupted, now so concerned that he couldn't acknowledge me.

"I think so," Paul said.

"Here"—the driver bustled to the door—"let's see."

He squatted, pushed, and the door flew up and vanished to a rattling crash, violent enough to almost knock it right back out of its tracks.

"Whoops," he said.

My father would have lost his temper. But Paul simply shook his head, grimly smiling his displeasure, then said, very quietly, "You'd better load that last pallet and get going."

Paul never once raised his voice during the four summers I worked for him. It wasn't his style. He didn't like to emphasize differences in position or authority. Like my father, he wasn't ashamed to do the most menial tasks: he would clean the toilets if he had to, drag dead rats from beneath pallets (though the time I saw Paul do this he was greenish for half an hour afterward). Like my father, too, he worked himself harder than he worked anyone else. But while my father worked like this to demonstrate his absolute superiority—advising me more than once, "You have to know how to do *everything* in business, so no one can ever question what you say"—Paul tried to identify with his employees. In the sales meeting he led two weeks into the summer, he called upon his men's sense of responsibility to each other in the face of almost overwhelming forces. "No one's going to be able to check up on everything you do," he said in a soft intense voice. "No one's going to know if you're not rotating the stock in every store, if you're not getting the P.O.P. onto all the shelves—at least not for a while. But that kind of sloppiness hurts us all. We can't compete with Gallo, with Bud, if we do that. Those big guys'll crush us. We don't have a chance."

He was as earnest as a high school history teacher, and though the combination of shyness and allergies made his breathing difficult during sales meetings—stifled gasps swelling and sometimes breaking through his low-voiced exhortations—he tried to be encouraging. Like a man cornered by a fear-sensing beast, his optimism was of a desperate nature—but compelling. At least to me. Standing in an office with an immense fireproof wall safe and a security system, the razor-wire crown of the yard's high fence gleaming through one small dirty window; in the center of a wholesale zone of blank unidentifiable buildings (anxiously concealing their inventory from the purportedly thieving residents of the run-down barrio nearby), where—but for short periods when delivery trucks left or returned, or when the spluttering of an ill-tuned forklift escaped from a briefly gaping warehouse door—the stark hot gridded streets betrayed no hint of life; standing in the middle of all this, when Paul appealed to his employees' sense of honor, I found myself filled with pity and love.

That summer I really tried to help. Strickland, sprawling beneath the elevated I-5 Freeway on its western flank and across the sunken old 99 Highway to the east, was a grimy sun-faded city of billboards, light industry, bars, and liquor stores, with twice the population of Ralston's ninety-five thousand. From its gloriously corrupt heyday at the periphery of the Gold Rush, home port to the San Joaquin Delta's steamboats, only the corruption, now uninspired and brutal, remained. I learned my way around this place in the course of doing routes no one else wanted. One took me the length of "Skid Row" (near the warehouse), to dive bars and to dark little dumps whose entire stock consisted of cigarettes, porno magazines, Lotto tickets, and booze; then to a market on the banks of the 99, where my arrival almost always coincided with a tallow works driver who hauled from the butcher shop reeking garbage barrels of viscous, veiny, flyblown fat. I delivered to Chinatown, in the abandoned downtown, not far from the old port; to Little Vietnam's two strip malls in the shadow of the I-5; to the dusty ramshackle white neighborhoods, descended from Hoovervilles, east of the 99; and to the black neighborhoods of south Strickland, segregated almost South Africa–like from the rest of the city. In the poorest, most crime-ridden areas I had to collect cash payment for every delivery. By the middle of the day my pants pockets bulged with twenty-dollar bills. Yet while my predecessor on these routes had lost his job because he insisted on carrying a handgun for protection, I never felt myself in danger.

Occasionally I went out with Paul, helping deliver large three-door Visicoolers to major accounts, or setting up bar guns and kegs for various festivals and fairs all around San Joaquin County. These were my favorite days. I hadn't spent so much time with him since before he'd left for college. Usually we passed the time by talking about sports; once or twice, briefly, I wandered—unaccompanied—onto the subject of some novel. For a time, when he was in college and I was just discovering the old paperbacks he'd left in our bedroom, he always used to ask what I was reading. He'd ask me questions about the characters, and recommend other books by Steinbeck or Hemingway or Fitzgerald. But after college, as Strickland more and more consumed him, he took to assuming a sudden obvious indifference at the mention of a novel, becoming—if I persisted—quietly, uncomfortably, impatient. So we stuck almost exclusively to sports, resuming an old long-developing conversation—impersonal yet sentimental—in which affection assured complete outspoken agreement on such matters as the designated hitter and the Giants' farm system. The subject of business rarely came up at all. I had no interest in it, and Paul only spoke of his problems (with a driver or a certain account) in short purging outbursts, during which his whole tortured manner revealed how hard and long he'd tried to contain his complaints, and how little he wanted to burden me with them. I'd be quietly sympathetic, not wanting to embarrass him, until, after a hopeless sigh, he'd change the subject back to sports.

Otherwise Paul loaded all his frustrations into the name *Strickland*, which he never mentioned without adding, epithetlike, "home of the nation's highest per-capita murder rate"—his voice pushed into its higher registers by an almost gagging repugnance.

In the evenings, at dinner, my father grilled me about work. He'd ask how many cases went out on the trucks. I'd hazard two or three estimates until one seemed to satisfy him, then repeat that number with something like certainty. If I was too worn out from work to answer with what he believed were appropriate levels of vigor and interest he'd become angry, ask me, "Aren't you helping your brother up there?" If, on the other hand, I responded satisfactorily, he'd flatter me by laying out his plans for my future. "The business could sure use a good tax attorney," he'd say. "You've got the grades for it."

"I don't like math," I'd invariably answer.

"You don't have to like math! It's got nothing to do with math. You'd know all the laws and *oversee* the guys who do the math."

I'd shake my head. "Those attorneys have got it made," he'd insist. He took pride in my grades, and this was the only way he knew to express it. He valued the *practical*—i.e., moneymaking—application of intelligence; nothing else made sense to him. On more than one Sunday evening he turned to Paul, slumped pale and tired in his chair, for corroboration, asking, "Tax attorney, right? Isn't that the thing for a kid with his grades?" And each time he inspired the same discomfort in Paul, who'd glance from him to me, then down; murmuring, after some moments, "Sure. Sure," while staring glassy-eyed and haunted-looking at his plate.

But I paid them little attention. Everything that summer paled almost to invisibility before the dazzling vista of college and its infinite possibilities. Ultimately, my father's plans, my brother's unhappiness, worried me no more than those poor neighborhoods I worked in with pockets full of cash, since I was at that age when even the most insecure and neurotic of us believe in our own uniqueness—if only that we are uniquely unhappy or dissatisfied—and thus that we are blessedly exempt from all circumstances affecting others.

AFTER ONE DISAPPOINTING year of college I returned to California a determined underachiever, resolutely Undeclared, almost looking forward to a summer of mindless physical labor. ("Mindless" and "meaningless" being important and interchangeable words that freshman year to the dull group I hung around with: *mindless* exams, *meaningless* papers, *mindless* sex . . .) But Paul had other plans for me.

It was my first week back and we were repairing a breach someone had cut into the chain-link fence of the warehouse's small yard. We struggled to stretch the fence like a piece of fabric, then stitch the two sides together with wire. "Damn neighborhood kids," Paul muttered while we tugged at the stiff links. Then, with unconvincing casualness, not looking at me, he said, "It would be great if you could train new drivers this summer. A huge help to me. I had Rick doing it"—the husky blond I'd seen daydreaming while Paul pounded inside the truck bay on my first morning of work—"but now he says he won't anymore. He doesn't want the *responsibility*," he sneered, momentarily sounding like my father before shifting into his own beleaguered astonishment: "He was making good money! But he doesn't want it. He says he'd rather have less money and less responsibility. Right now I've got him doing Skid Row and he's happy as can be."

So I trained drivers, and soon discovered that I didn't want the responsibility either. At the end of the workday I now faced two rounds of interrogation: the usual one administered at home by my father, and, before that, the gentle but no less insistent questions put to me by Paul. "How is he?" Paul would ask, diffidently hopeful, leading me to a corner of the warehouse or yard out of earshot of the men counting in trucks. "Can he do the work? Does he hustle? How's he with people? Do you think he'll work out?" We talked about little else that summer. Paul spent nearly all of his limited time off with Kris Andersen, whom he'd met when she temped in the office. While at work, all through our unsuccessful attempts to fill two driver positions during the busiest season of the year, every conversation between Paul and me began with: *How is he?*

All of the trainees were capable in some ways. All needed the job—two or three desperately. Like the man in his mid-forties, hair perfectly molded and teeth perfectly white, who spent the time between stops telling me about the tire business he co-owned and his '57 T-Bird and his ex-model wife, as if he expected me to believe this delivery job was just a hobby. But I knew, as did every driver, that no one much over the age of thirty "humped cases" except as a last resort. And knowing this, though it seemed he always left the heaviest hand-truck loads to me—cases of wine, beer kegs—while he opted for stacks of aluminum cans; though he seemed to cut corners, rotating stock only as long as I watched, stopping for a cigarette or a chat whenever he thought I'd be too occupied to catch him, I had little faith in my judgment. I couldn't quite believe that a man old enough to be my father would actually behave like a teenager on a summer job, while I, a teenager, should have to behave like my father and judge him.

I told Paul he was fine.

He was given his own route. He was fired after three weeks.

Or Les—"Saint Lester," he was called by the salesmen—a young, thickly muscled black man, effusive about his newly found Pentecostal faith. Initially likable, he wore upon everyone, as new converts self-consciously overflowing with God's Word are prone to do. On his right arm, from forearm to quadriceps, was a long pale crescent scar—like the baked gash atop a loaf of French bread—from those benighted days before he was saved, when he'd tried drunkenly to run through a sliding glass door.

"I've had some bad times, but God's guiding me now," Les would tell me; He had guided him to this job.

Who was I to interfere with His will?

Saint Lester lasted less than forty days working amid the wastes of south Strickland before God guided him elsewhere.

Because I looked nothing like Paul, I usually had one or two days with a new driver before he found out my relation to authority. During these brief spans, when I was neither a Torno nor a college boy, new drivers spoke to me as they did to everyone else (except Paul, of course). Usually the topics were the same: wives, ex-wives and girlfriends, in-laws, cars, drinking and drugs. But the talk was easy and comfortable, inclusive—until they discovered who I was. It wasn't that I expected to become close friends with any of them. My age alone would've set me apart, as a certain walrus-mustached trainee, nearly thirty, reminded me at the end of his first day, smiling and shaking his head enviously and saying, "Man, I wish I was like you: young, dumb, and full of cum!" Nor did it bother me that I was never invited to those breathless cold box convocations—the great perk of all drivers, salesmen, and supermarket managers—of men peering between cartons of milk and whipping cream, or bottles of beer, at unsuspecting women shoppers bent over in shorts or tank tops. But I spent most of that second summer feeling as singled out, as indelibly marked, as Cain; trainees often told all the managers and drivers in a store who I was. *The boss's brother!* And thus I was stuck and labeled once and for all; sentenced before I'd offered any evidence of myself, and exiled, not simply from them, but from the anonymity I would have preferred.

Sometimes, wondering what I'd have to do to slip out from this unwanted place, I used to imagine letting trainees do as they pleased, goof off, waste time. But I knew even this wouldn't do it. I'd simply call more attention to myself for being the boss's brother who didn't give a damn: a fool, a fuckup.

Something like Uncle Joey.

Even when Uncle Joey seemed to try, he could do nothing right. In the middle of the summer, perhaps growing bored with his limited responsibilities, or trying to prove something, he arranged a huge beer sale with a major chain of supermarkets and stirred up the kind of evening-long storm from my father that I hadn't seen since before Joey was moved to Ralston (when I used to see them almost every week). I came home from work one night and found my father pacing the kitchen, drink in hand, raging, while my mother made dinner.

"He claims the *volume's* going to make up for it," my father said as she sliced zucchini. "The sheer volume of sales! *But not when you're losing money on every case,* I told him." He paused to drink, then, "Volume! I didn't even think he knew that word. I wish he didn't. But how hard is it to grasp? How many times do I have to tell him we *can't* go as low as Budweiser? How stupid can he be?"

My mother said nothing, and when he noticed me and turned I betrayed no reaction at all. You weren't supposed to when my father was carrying on like this about his brother. You showed every sign of listening intently, but nothing else. A smile could get you into real trouble, and if you should actually *agree* . . . ! I'd learned this years before, the hard way, as they say, one night at dinner when my father had been complaining about Joey's imbecility for a long time and I was so young (maybe six years old) as to let my desire for approval make me incautious. My father seemed so dismayed, and Joey seemed such a problem, that I offered a simple and reasonable suggestion, truly praiseworthy I thought, in its incisiveness: "Why don't you fire him?"

I have never forgotten his reaction: the deep blood-red bloom of his face before he could manage speech—embarrassment? I wondered at first, amazed, until it became an unmistakable look of disdain and repugnance, even horror, as if I'd suggested, "Why don't you kill him?"

"I'd never do that to my brother," he said slowly, engraving the words upon my hard stupidity. "Do you hear me? *Never.*"

He could complain about his brother for as long as his frustration level demanded, but always with the underlying—and, I think now, guilty—insistence that his words really meant absolutely nothing. They escaped from him like steam, heated but insubstantial, leaving no residue. A matter of water not blood. Whereas *work*—as I'd believed for many years by that summer when I was nineteen—was love. Work was all-expressive.

IN AUGUST, TWO weeks before I was to return to college, the huge safe in the Strickland office was torn out of the wall during the night. Even before I saw the gaping hole I knew something was wrong; the morning routine was disrupted. Drivers and salesmen stood around the warehouse in clumps, talking and laughing quietly, with a strange subdued frivolity, like children suddenly freed from their classrooms by some small threat—like the minor cafeteria fire that once, when I was in third grade, released all of St. Stephen's School into the beautiful sunlight of a spring day, where we milled about giddily, safe and unconcerned.

In the office a salesman and secretary stood examining the hole, which opened out into the warehouse.

The secretary said to me, "Look at this! Can you believe this?" She was outraged, but even more she was excited, her eyes wide. When I was silent, she tried to sober a bit. She raised one arm stiffly, pointed to the closed door of my brother's office, said, "Paul's talking to the police now"—more quietly, but unable to suppress the thrill in her voice.

"Put the forks of that lift right through the wall," the salesman said, oblivious with admiration, "and pulled that baby out. Jesus Christ! That's some job!"

Paul, needless to say, derived much less pleasure from this feat. I waited in his office until he got off the phone. He placed the receiver in its cradle with an exaggerated gentleness, then dropped his face into his hands, both elbows resting on the desk, and rubbed hard at his eyes, so that when he looked at me his cheeks and brow were red and the front of his hair was mussed.

"They found it," he said softly. "On the other side of the 99, on a dirt road in some orchard. They used the forklift to load the safe onto the stake truck, drove out of the warehouse, closed the door after themselves, and made it out to the orchards before the truck tipped onto its side and dumped the safe."

"Did they catch anyone?" I asked.

"No," Paul said, hopelessly and dismissively. "They're long gone."

"Why didn't the alarm . . . ?"

Paul shrugged his shoulders, shook his head. "I don't know. The whole thing's so unbelievable . . . so stupid. . . ." He dropped his head back into his hands and did not move for some time. I stared at the top of his head, noticing the gray in his hair. No patches of it, just individual threads, but they were everywhere, evenly distributed among the dark brown. I thought, he's not even thirty yet, he's too young for those. I tried futilely to think of something to say to him. From the other side of the door came three gleeful voices.

As soon as we walked out of his office, though, everyone Paul and I encountered became suddenly serious and concerned—and this was the worst part of the whole incident. Conversations stopped at the sight of us, smiles vanished, as if we were two lepers crashing a cocktail party. They were all so obvious about it it was almost funny. Except it made me realize how alone Paul actually was, how alone he'd always been, from the very start, in Strickland. In a minor way that summer I'd experienced myself the seemingly unbridgeable gulf that responsibility—and the Torno name—created between those who bore it and those who didn't. As Paul walked quickly about, rousing the men on their way in a voice of strained enthusiasm so unnatural to him that it sounded almost ironic—his work voice—I thought of how much help I could be to him, how much comfort. It seemed that the very situation, if not Paul himself, appealed to me for some word, some dramatic gesture, some promise.

As the warehouse was emptying, Paul walked me to my own route truck.

I climbed into the cab without looking at him and headed out.

ONE AFTERNOON DURING the first summer I worked in Strickland, I had to drive an old open-bay truck overloaded with wine to the warehouse in Ralston. Increasing poverty and crime had rendered the truck useless for routes—its exposed contents were tempting, easy targets on the street—and nostalgia alone explained why it had not been sold or simply junked. It had been the company's first full-size delivery truck.

"Just take it slow," Paul said reassuringly, patting the driver's door above the faded and chipped block letters reading TORNO BROS. DISTRIBUTING CO.

I nodded, pulled the truck out of the warehouse, and found myself almost immediately at sea. During the short trip to the freeway I strained to comprehend the truck's dimensions. How far back was the rear bumper? How far to the right or left did it extend? The large mirrors on either door didn't help. I made incredible attempts at projecting my mind to the truck's farthest reaches, trying to fill the machine with my consciousness, so that even a stray plastic wrapper blown into one of the rear bays at a stoplight wouldn't go unnoticed. My ribs were itchy and tickly with trickles of sweat. Driving through a narrow concrete underpass summoned from me the purest leap of faith I had ever made. Under the wine's weight the truck rode low. On turns it rolled sickeningly, as if the real danger wasn't tipping over but being swamped. On inclines I had to stand on the accelerator, my leg straight, and urge the truck forward by bouncing on its screechy bench seat. Then, finally, I was on Highway 99, piloting I don't know how many tons of wine with a steering wheel with ten inches of play in it. If you picture the steering wheel as a clock, from the ten of the truck's huge wheel to the two was like a free fall, without a whisper of resistance. For a few miles I sawed the wheel—with its wine-cask-hoop circumference—back and forth across this abyss, bumping against one extreme, then the other, the truck veering a little left, a little right, a little left, a little right, within the slow lane's white lines. Until gradually, hopelessly, I gave myself over to this lack of control. I stopped cursing the old heap and fatalistically barreled ahead, discovering a certain perverse pleasure in the realization that if the truck left the road, rolled into the ditch between the highway and dusty fields, and killed me—blood mixing with wine from all those shattered vessels—it would be the fault of my brother, and ultimately my father, who forced me into this work. All responsibility for my confused, unfulfilled life shifted pleasantly from me to them; my death became almost preordained, inevitable, a happy martyrdom.

This trip figured in my dreams more than a few times during my first two years of college. I used to think about it a lot; it seemed to perfectly embody the forces I felt at my back, and the peculiarly Catholic temptation—and consolation—of self-sacrifice. I had no desire to go into the business, and yet . . . But it also reminded me that the act of giving myself over to the business never struck me as anything other than a complete disaster, in which any pretense of virtue was demolished by an inescapable sense of far less admirable motives. Loyalty, in this case, was always inseparable from cowardice about my future. Responsibility showed itself to be a reckless fatalism; familial love a kind of self-loathing. And Catholic self-sacrifice would arm me, I knew, with a victim's arsenal of blame.

Rationalizations, I still imagine Paul saying. I sometimes say it myself.

And that may be true. But it's a matter of self-preservation: they're the kind of rationalizations we live by.

THREE DAYS INTO the new year, a few days before I was to return to school for the second semester of my sophomore year, my father woke before dawn with chest pains. My mother woke me after she'd called the ambulance, then sent me into the kitchen to call Paul and Mary while she stayed with him, flat on his back, one arm extended, half crucified in bed. I didn't bother to turn on the kitchen lights, but punched angrily at the phone's lighted keypad and angrily woke them and told them, becoming even angrier, senselessly, at their panicked half-asleep attempts at comprehension while I leaned hard on my elbows on the tiled kitchen counter, listening for the ambulance's siren. Which came at first (after I'd rushed Mary off the phone) so faintly, in such dark isolation, I thought I imagined it, sounding across more than a decade as I'd expected to hear it one night in bed, as a boy. A dozen years earlier my mother had crazily warned me that an ambulance would come one night and everything would change. As it turned out—though her timing was way off— she was right. My father would survive this attack, but with a severely damaged heart and degenerating health. At home things would get better, at work things would get worse, more chaotic; everything changing in ways once unimaginable, as my father, over the next three years, was forced by illness to loosen his grip on life.

After the end of my sophomore year I returned to California to find new rumors about the land around our house and a new equilibrium within it. In the former case, the same developer who in recent years had despoiled much of the eastern side of Collier Road with low-rent commercial buildings was now supposedly looking to do something grander on the other side: two big shopping centers on the western corners of Collier and Weston. My mother could hardly contain her excitement—she rightly considered such development the only chance she'd ever have to get my father to move—while Mary, though she was newly wed and not living at home, bewailed these rumors almost obsessively. The mere mention of such possible developments irritated my father, and (reassuring Mary; dashing my mother's hopes) he'd impatiently end every discussion of them with the same response: "It'll never happen. It's completely irrational. You don't build shopping centers on prime agricultural land! Besides, the Pruitts aren't going to sell after all these years. And neither am I. I'm not going anywhere."

Otherwise, my parents were getting along better than usual. My father seemed more patient with my mother, while my mother—as though my father's health problems and all the doctor's appointments and medications and dietary changes had given her a focus—seemed less scattered, less anxiously and defensively nettlesome. And my own situation had changed as well.

Two weeks earlier I'd officially put an end to my father's fond hopes that I might become a tax attorney, or at least pursue some other business-related career, by declaring myself an English major. A decision that caused him no small amount of discomfort, since the rather vague ends to which an English major might lead (even the structured world of academia as I tried to explain the little I knew of it) were completely foreign to him. His very notion of ethics—to say nothing of existence—was inseparable from the kind of laborious business life he himself had always led, and he was suspicious of the indulgences and lazy habits that other "softer" careers might promote. If to these deep distrusts you add the fact that Uncle Joey had taken my father's declining health as his cue, after decades of only sporadic and superficial interest, to suddenly try on the mantle of absolute authority—issuing all sorts of nonsensical directives that made a mess of the Ralston warehouse's operations—it comes as no surprise that my father chose the very summer I declared my break from the family business to pursue his usual nightly investigations into Strickland's sales with a new intensity, bristling at the least semblance of sloth in me and pouncing upon me at the hint of *attitude.* "Your uncle's done nothing for years," he warned me one night, sounding exhausted and sad, "and look what he's become."

Another night when I was a little slouchy and curt from fatigue his irritation burst forth in: "And what the hell are you doing all night, every night, in your room? Why can't you sit in the living room with us?"

"I'm reading," I said.

"Can't you read with us?"

"No. Not with the TV on."

"*Oh* . . ." he sighed skeptically.

"I can't. Really. Not the books I'm reading."

"What are you reading?" still a little dubiously.

"Louis Ferdinand Céline."

"Who?"

"A French writer, named Céline. Louis Ferdinand Céline. I should know him for school. I should've read him already," I said ingenuously.

"Oh"—actually a little abashed—"I've never heard of him. I didn't know that. You should have told me," he said, reasonably enough.

Though, lest I give the wrong impression, I should note that the very next night he simply demanded I sit in the living room with him and my mother and watch sitcoms.

When my report card arrived in June, with my best grades since high school, I felt a little vindicated. It was proof of hard work, and at dinner that night I got carried away and referred to other proof, too: the laudatory comments adorning some essays I'd brought home. My father, surprised that I hadn't shown him these, asked to see them—and thus my small triumph came to its embarassing end. I couldn't bear to stay in the same room while he read the essay I brought him after dinner; I left him sitting in his chair in the den and spied on him through the kitchen doorway. First he read the professor's final comments. Then he spent a few minutes on the first of the stapled pages. But he'd hardly turned to the second before, with a shake of his head, he gave up, letting the first page fall back into its place, and setting the whole thing, an essay on *Dombey and Son*, on the small table beside his chair.

My distance from him—the degree to which he simply couldn't make me out—never gave me as much pleasure as I usually told myself it should.

I often used to feel him staring at me during dinner that summer and I'd have to exert a lot of effort to continue eating in something like a natural manner. One night he broke a long silence at the table with a little chagrined laugh, said, "If I'd had your grades . . ."

IN STRICKLAND WITH Paul, the subject of my grades, major, or career never came up at all—directly. Whereas it seemed only right that I should try to impress my father, as soon as I saw Paul's unhappy face at work I knew that any mention of such things would only strike him as gloating. Which isn't to say that these things and, more simply, my certain escape from the business weren't almost always on my mind. But the thought that they might cause my brother pain— since he could expect no long-term help from me—made me feel guilty and humble, and, only gradually and rather faintly, resentful . . . while any suspicion that he begrudged me the path I'd chosen inspired an immediate resentment, a lot less guilt, and a certain defensive arrogance.

Most of that summer in Strickland I was arrogant.

For, from my first day there, I would have sworn that in the clear language of work Paul was conveying his displeasure with me. With the same kind soft voice he always used, he sent me to Skid Row, and then, on subsequent days, to all the other routes, familiar from my first summer, that no one else wanted. Once again there were the dead vermin among the back-room cases—though these could also be found in the better parts of town—and store owners who actually lived in their windowless back rooms, and one, with his family, in a tin storage shed in a corner of a parking lot. But I was almost less appalled by these facts than by the fact that I was seeing them at all. The responsibility I'd unwillingly shouldered the previous summer now became a matter of pride: I'd progressed beyond these basic routes, and though I reminded myself that since there wasn't a chance in hell I'd go into the business, *any* route, *any* job, now amounted to an equal waste of my time, I still felt slighted.

I felt this even more keenly a couple of weeks later when Paul hired a new driver and assigned *Rick* to train him.

Outside of the warehouse, Paul and I rarely saw each other at all; he and Kris were preparing for their autumn wedding, and I was occupied with a reading list I'd made for myself. At the warehouse our rare attempts at conversation were sunk by subtext. I detected reproaches in everything he said.

One evening Paul placed his hand on my shoulder as I counted in my truck and asked, "Don't you ever smile anymore, Vincent?"

And since I heard—in spite of his own smile—more professional rebuke than fraternal concern, I answered honestly, "What's there to smile about?"

He looked hurt and walked away shaking his head.

In the retelling all this indirection, the suspected innuendos and coded meanings, seems foolish, as any language might to a foreigner—or to a native speaker who's chosen to renounce it. But I took it very seriously then. Over the course of three years, nearly all of my interaction with Paul—or the part of it we both took to be substantive and significant—had been reduced to this, to Torno Bros. business.

One morning in the middle of July the route pad waiting for me in the office was only half as thick as usual, and as I flipped through the stops I couldn't believe my good luck. My truck was lightly loaded, and I hurried through my route with the idea I'd get home early and read. Instead, I finished, returned to the warehouse, happily counted in my truck, and was put to work in the yard.

Along three-quarters of the yard's chain-link fence stood tall tilting stacks of old pallets, blackened, filthy, broken. Some must have been as old as the warehouse itself. Paul led me to the more recently discarded, near which, in anticipation of my early return, he'd placed a bag of nails, new wood slats, and a hammer. Then he showed me how to repair them, punctuating his instructions—issued in a strong clear voice straight to the pallet he worked on—with pauses, during which he raised his head and looked steadily into my face with eyes tightly asquint, though the sun was behind him.

"Okay?" he asked finally, handing me the hammer.

"Yeah," I said, trying to put all my displeasure into it.

For a few minutes after he left I sat on a low stack of pallets, shaking my head with disbelief. It was a hundred and four degrees— beautiful Strickland summer!—and he had me out in the yard with rotten pallets! Then I went to work, hacking at the broken slats of a pallet with the swallowtail end of the hammer, splintering the wood, cursing to myself. Sometimes this kind of destruction exorcises anger; sometimes it exacerbates it. It exacerbated mine. I untucked my uniform shirt, unbuttoned it completely. My body was covered with sweat; dust from the pallets settled on my skin, making it itch and sting.

If I'd allowed myself any doubt that I was misreading Paul's actions that summer, it was completely gone. All at once I knew exactly what Paul was doing: he was punishing me. Never before had he so clearly devised a job just to keep me from going home early. But this summer it had become an undeniable fact that I would get out of the business. I was going to escape, and he was jealous. *I* wouldn't spend the rest of my life in this pit, in this place which quite literally, *symbolically*, made him sick. Three summers of appeals to my pity, to my guilt, hadn't worked. So he punished me. He took his frustrations out on me while he had the chance.

I flung bent nails from the pallets all around the yard. Inspired, I threw one against the tin Quonset warehouse itself, but it made a meager disappointing sound—which made me angrier.

I doubt I repaired three pallets during this tantrum; tearing off broken slats was more satisfying than nailing on new ones. Out of spite I destroyed some pallets completely. Then I decided to quit, and I smashed more pallets until I'd worked myself into a fury, beyond reason and hesitation. I was actually out of breath as I walked through the warehouse, out of breath as I passed through the open doorway into Paul's office, where my panting caused him to raise his head from the papers on his desk and present a face filled with such concern that it nearly routed all my resolve. I halted, doubting in those moments whether I would be able to leave at all. Then in a burst of clumsy and desperate motion, I removed my shirt, balled it up and pitched it at the back of a chair beside his desk, and— suddenly near tears—told him I quit. I backed out the door, saying as I left, while he sat staring, "I don't have to take this, I'm not going to take this, I'm not going to let you ruin my life, I'm not going to let you drag me down, I'm not going to let you drag me, I'm not going to."

Bare-chested, I walked to my car on the silent, fiercely hot street in front of the warehouse, opened the door and both windows— burning myself on the vinyl interior—then got out again to look in the trunk for something to cover the driver's seat. I found a beach towel. I spread it over the seat and sat down, and Paul came out onto the sidewalk. I started the car. He held up a hand for me to wait. I waited.

He leaned down to the window, his chest heaved, then his words came out evenly and so low that without thinking I turned off the engine to hear.

"What have I done to you, Vincent, what have I ever asked from you? To act like a brother? To be of some help? I never even wanted you up here. Dad sent you here. I didn't ask. It was his idea. I could care less. I was getting along fine. Nine months out of the year I get along without you, I can get through the summer without you. It's Dad's idea. I could care less what you do, I won't *drag you down*. Drag you down! I could care less. I ask you to work like everyone else, that's it. While you're here. That's it.

"You're not that much help, anyway. Don't kid yourself. You're fine. But all this summer you've gone around like I'm killing you. My worst driver is friendlier than you are. Strangers are friendlier. Poor Vincent! Poor, smart Vincent. He's too smart for this job. The English major, humping cases! Oh, that's bad. Three months out of the year! You're on the Dean's List, after all! My God. Three months out of the year. You choose whatever major you like. No one asks, *What are you going to do with that? What use is that? Are you crazy? Who does that? What kind of man does that?* You have no idea, Vincent. You're afraid *I'll* ruin you life? You have no idea. *I'm* going to keep you here?"

"What?" I said lamely. "What are you talking about?"

"Nothing." He shook his head. "It doesn't matter. Just go home. I'm not stopping you. Do whatever you want," he said, then turned his back, walked to the warehouse, ducked beneath its large door, drawn low, and disappeared.

"YOU JACKASS!" my father said, more astonished, at first, than angry after I admitted I'd quit. Home early from work, not expecting to find me home yet, he stood just inside the door of my bedroom, where he usually never came. "You spoiled little . . . *punk!* You . . . you . . . Jesus!" He struggled for words, shaking his head, flabbergasted. "Goddammit! You can't quit! You're working for your brother, you damn fool! You can't *quit!*"

He immediately made me call Strickland to apologize. He stood close beside me in the kitchen, panting with disgust, while I waited for Paul, who said only "Hello" when he finally came to the phone and nothing else as I assured him that I'd be back at work the next day and mouthed an unfelt remorse entirely for my father's benefit.

But I think I knew even before my father came home that I'd be back in Strickland the next day, stuck there through the rest of the summer—and for the following one as well. Until I had graduated, until I had clearly become the thrall of some particular career, I knew there was no escaping. I think all of us—my father, Paul, and I—knew this. Yet even after I'd gone back to work, my father couldn't get over what I'd done, or tried to do. For the rest of that summer at dinner, without any apparent provocation, he'd start to shift uncomfortably in his seat, as if he found himself upon a chair of nails, and I'd prepare myself for another of his outbursts:

"You decided to *quit!* What were you thinking of? You can't quit! He's your brother!"

The fact is, I worked harder after my attempted resignation than I ever had. Spitefully hard, with a stern professionalism that Paul adopted, too, in all of our limited interactions, each of us making certain the other had, at work, no reason to complain. Otherwise we had nothing to do with each other. Neither one of us was capable of something like Uncle Joey's subversive buffoonery; we were too much our father's sons. Impeccable professionalism, taken to its most rigorous, perverse perfection: that was the way Paul and I chose to punish each other—and, it occurs to me now, our father too, who spent the last couple years of his life painfully aware of the breach between us, but powerless to really do anything about it.

COUNTERPARTS

DIRECTLY ACROSS WESTON AVENUE from the Tornos' house was a
brand-new shopping center, a vast, grotesque jumble of white
building-block shapes roofed in some kind of plasticky turquoise
material. Vincent could never get used to it. On each of his infrequent visits home his first sight of it came as a disorienting, offensive
surprise. During his childhood, and for twenty-one of his twenty-
three years, an almond orchard had been there. On bright fall mornings before school a crop-duster biplane used to sweep low over the
orchard and the Tornos' house. Vincent used to run outside and
watch, unmindful of the drifting chemical overspray, which he remembered, nostalgically—waiting in his old foreign coupe for a line
of cars to pass so he could turn into the house's drive—as settling
upon him as gently as a benediction.

His mother was not at home. His father had been dead eight
months. At the front door he pocketed the large ring that held the
keys to his car, his apartment, his mailbox, and the office he shared
with five other English department graduate students, and took out
a smaller one (usually kept in the back of a desk drawer) with just
three keys: one which deactivated the blinking red light of the house
alarm, another which let him in, and a third for the door of the
mausoleum in which his father lay, high up, behind polished marble.

The house was still and cold and dark on this late afternoon in December. Vincent opened curtains, turned on lights, turned on the central heat, made the house seem inhabited. He carried his suitcase into his old bedroom, where he found one of the twin beds stacked with boxes and brown paper bags, all of them smelling a little of dust, as though they had sat there for a long time. He used the bathroom, washed his face. Then he went to his father's bar and filled a tumbler with Scotch and ice. Through one of the front windows he saw his sister, Mary, pull her car into the driveway.

A week before, on the phone, she had let him know she thought he was a failure as soon as he told her he was leaving the Ph.D. program in San Diego, a third of the way through his second year. For this he had been immediately grateful, since he knew there was no point in a gesture meant to betray early promise if no one took any notice of it. But then Mary always took notice of such things, and she fretted about them, too, which was why, not five minutes after she'd come into the house and happily greeted him with an awkward slap on his shoulder (they were not a hugging family), she returned to the subject with an impatient directness both gratifying and annoying.

"I still think you're making a big mistake, leaving school," she said, apropos of nothing except her own preoccupations.

"Well, that's your right. Think what you want. But I'm not going to change my mind," he said simply, with a pretense of calm self-possession which he knew would irk his sister much more than any histrionics. Then, with the same calm, he picked his drink up off the end table where it had sat unnoticed and took a sip.

"What's that?" Mary asked.

"Scotch."

"*Scotch?*" Mary smirked. "You drink Scotch now?"

"Sometimes. You get a taste for it," he said (at which Mary couldn't help but make another face). "Especially after a long day, like this one."

"Then I should have some, too."

"Go ahead."

"No. Just kidding."

"How about a beer?"

"No. Really, I don't want anything. I'll leave the drinking to you," she said, with a slip of disapproval which could easily, Vincent knew, be made to bloom.

He took a pack of cigarettes out of his shirt pocket. "And the smoking, too, I'll bet," he said.

"Great," she said, and as he put on his jacket (they both agreed he shouldn't smoke up the house), then as they went out the back door, she reminded him how bad smoking had been for their father, her voice ranging along the same scale of tones she'd used on the phone the week before, from censorious to cajoling to pleading, while Vincent nodded and smiled and indulged himself in her comfortable, familiar, longed-for disapproval.

ON SUMMER NIGHTS when the walnut trees were so thick with leaves that no moonlight reached the earth beneath them, the orchard behind the Tornos' backyard became a terrifying mass of monstrous black shapes. As a boy, Vincent would not have ventured near the first row of trees for all the money in the world. A bulb in a tin dome shade rigged on one corner of the house's roof marked the circular boundary of his nighttime play; he used to keep safely within it, forgoing the pleasures of his swingset at the back of the yard where the light was dim. One of the nastiest tricks Mary sometimes played on him then was, from inside the house, to turn off the backyard light, leaving him in sudden darkness, panicked and scrambling for the back door. This was how she got even with him on those days he had been particularly obnoxious.

The trees were bare now, though, Vincent saw, as he sat down in a wrought-iron patio chair, across a round glass-topped table from

Mary. It was winter, of course, but many of them were bare in summer, too, killed by a disease that had been spreading through the
orchard for years.

"Did anyone pick walnuts this year?" he asked.

"No. It wasn't really worth it, there's so few now. Though I did
think about it, and I probably would've done it—if nothing else, just
for old time's sake—but Mom's been so bad this fall, and it's taken
so much, just trying to keep her out of the hospital. Which really
did a lot of good," she sighed.

Vincent drank from his Scotch. He took a drag from his cigarette,
held it, and exhaled slowly, watching Mary try not to watch the
smoke pluming into the air—his vexing *panache*. "How was she today?
he asked.

"Terrible. She wants to come home now, but she's not ready."

"That's a relief. The drive up from San Diego was a killer today.
I could use some time to get ready for her."

"Well, you don't have to worry," Mary said, her voice colored more
by disapproval than reassurance. "It'll be a few days."

"Good."

Mary looked at him unhappily, seemed about to say something
unpleasant, then stopped herself. She reverted to a casual tone. "I
thought she was doing better today. She looks better. She looks
good. But then she started on Dad again. Out of nowhere. You know,
the same old thing. Nothing's *her* fault, she's not responsible for anything. She just tore Dad down until I couldn't take it anymore. I'd
change the subject, but she'd always change it back. Finally I said, *If
you don't stop talking like this I'm going to leave and not come back. I mean it.*
And when she started it again, I left. I did."

"And you're not going back?"

Mary looked at him, made him wait a few moments for the answer
he expected. "No, I'll go back," she said quietly, before adding, "But
I won't take it. I think I've shown her that. It'll give her something
to think about."

"I guess."

"What?" Mary asked defensively. "*It will.* What am I supposed to do, *sit there?*"

"No, no, no," Vincent corrected her, "not at all. I think you should've left. I think you should leave her more often—and not go back."

"Well, *that's* not that easy. Not for me, at least," she couldn't help adding.

"Yeah, right," Vincent said. He drank.

"I just don't think," he continued, after deciding not to take up the argument, "she thinks about much. I don't think she cares. About anybody but herself, that is."

"No, I think she does. Believe me, I see her almost every day. She calls me every day—it drives Dave crazy. She does. She's worried about you now."

"Really?" he laughed. "Why?"

"About leaving the program. You know."

"No, I don't. When I told her, she didn't seem to care at all. Completely perfunctory—*Hmm, well, I'm sure you know what's best for yourself. Everything will work out.*"

"That's just how she is. She thinks about it, though, believe me."

Vincent raised his eyebrows and nodded.

"But why are you leaving the program?" Mary asked again, obsessively, unreasonably, still not willing to accept everything he'd already said. "Only half a year before you'd have a master's. Why now?"

"*I've told you.* I've had enough."

"At least get your master's."

"Why? What am I going to do with it? It's worthless."

"Paul said you can get a teaching job with it."

"Has Paul been reading *Lingua Franca* lately? How does he know?"

Mary paused, as unfamiliar with the title as Vincent had hoped, then pushed on. "You used to say you wanted to teach," she objected.

"That was just something definite to say. It sounded good—

enough. Going to grad school's like enlisting in the Navy—it may not be much fun but at least you pretty much know what you're going to be doing for the next few years. But the Navy's not for me." Exasperated, feeling the Scotch a little, he leaned his head back in his chair, turned his eyes upward, and found not the sky above him but the close dark canvas of a superfluous once-yellow sunshade. It sprouted from a hole in the center of the table, and filthy and faded from having been left outside in all weather, drooped dun-colored above them on this damp gray day like the head of an old mushroom.

IN THE LATE afternoon of April 3, 1986, Paul Torno, Sr., told his wife he was not feeling well and that they should go to the hospital. He had not really felt well since his heart attack, over three years before, and in late December he'd caught a cold, which turned into pneumonia, then back to a lingering cold, but he generally tried to say little about his health—except sometimes to wonder with a darkly humorous disgust, as twice a day he tapped a hill of prescription pills into the palm of his large hand, if what was left of his life was worth the trouble. Hoping to end such grim musings by changing, at least a little, his daily pill routine, Lucy Torno bought him a plastic seven-day pillbox, a twin companion, though larger, for her own pill container, which had sat alone for years in its own place in a rear corner of the kitchen counter. But he wouldn't use it, refused it as though she were pushing furry slippers or some other intolerable humiliation upon him, and continued to clutter the top of a bureau near their bed with his regiment of pill bottles, arrayed according to height in one neat line.

Paul Torno, Sr.'s, last trip to the hospital was not his only unscheduled visit there since his heart attack. Irregular heartbeats had put him back into the hospital twice in three years. It was during the first hours of the latter of these stays that he had his run-in with the defibrillator, which he told Vincent about in one of their rare one-to-one conversations—so rare that Vincent figured the transcription of every single one of them would hardly fill a pocket-size spiral-bound notebook. The doctor attending him in the emergency room that time (not his regular cardiologist) had, after "fussing around" with him in an attempt to slow down his frantic stumbling heart, told him to close his eyes for a minute and breathe deeply and try to relax, and then had brought "those damned paddles" down upon his chest. "I've never felt anything like it," his father said. "I never want to again. I'd rather die. Really. I've gotten shocked while I was repairing some wiring at the warehouse, but this was something else. Like my whole body contracted to the size of a brick," and he acted as if he held one in his hands, turning them incrementally to indicate dimensions. "No legs, no arms," he laughed ironically, "no head— just a little block. Of lead. All I was was a little block of lead. In-credibly dense. *Unbelievably*. Packed, packed, packed"—again mod-eling with his hands a little cube in the air above his lap—"to that size. Everything compressed, in a flash." He shook his head. "It worked. But I'd rather die."

Vincent wondered if they had applied the paddles the last time his father went to the hospital. Almost everything he knew about that day came from Paul, and he was tempted to ask Mary. But the sight of her across the glass-topped table, bundled up, her shoulders narrowed as if it were much colder than the mid-forties, made him pity her. And also made him angry. A frequent feeling since his father's death; beginning, it seemed, two days after the funeral, in a professor's office, where he'd gone to explain his (unnoticed, as it turned out) absence from the previous seminar and ask for an exten-sion on a ten-page paper due in three days. Vincent's anger began bubbling up as the young professor blithely launched into an only slightly abridged version of the three-hour lecture Vincent had missed, then "strongly encouraged" him to hand the paper in on time, "regardless." Vincent repeated, "My father just died," but the "regard-less" remained. So Vincent wrote the paper in a barely controllable

fury, on Henry James's *The Ambassadors,* filling it with what he thought
were not-so-subtle insults to the professor's ideas and even to his
person (could a reference to "pencil-necked pedants" really be con-
strued as applying only to some indeterminate others?). But, infuri-
atingly, not a single one of them was noticed by his target.

Mary saw him staring vacantly at her and shivered for his benefit.

"Please," Vincent sighed. "It's not even really that cold."

"I'm cold. Wait. Listen."

From inside the house sounded the ringing telephone.

Mary didn't move.

"You want me to get it?" Vincent asked.

"I don't know."

"Maybe it's a Catholic Daughter. Isn't Mom involved with them
again? I haven't talked to one of those in a long time."

"Maybe. It could be Mom."

"She has a phone?"

"Not her own. Out in the hallway."

"I'll get it if you want," Vincent offered again, showing no sign of
moving.

"It could also be Dave." She looked at her watch. "He probably
just got home from work. I left a note I'd be over here after I visited
Mom."

Vincent put both hands upon the arms of his metal chair as if to
push himself up, but otherwise didn't move. "Last chance," he said.

"No. It's okay. If it's Dave, he can wait. He'd just complain. *Where
the hell are you? You gonna spend all night with your family?* He doesn't get
enough attention lately. Poor boy."

For good reason, Vincent thought, the Torno family must have
seemed like an ongoing trial to Dave Hibbert. Through none of his
own doing, his easygoing manner, his loose-limbed slouchy walk,
and his small fair perfectly round child's head, which had once inspired instant suspicion in Vincent and Mary's father and seemingly

instant affection in Mary, had become, during the last phase of his father-in-law's ill health, greater and greater liabilities. Until now, Vincent noticed, Mary was by rapid turns hypercritical and hyper-defensive of her husband. And Dave, who must have been shocked to find himself still in the cold shadow of his now dead father-in-law, had become temperamental. It had been just a couple of months since Mary's idea of taking back her maiden name made him so angry that he stormed out of their house and didn't return until the next day.

To annoy Mary a bit and keep her off the subject of graduate school, Vincent asked, "Does Dave still shop across the street?"

"No, he doesn't shop there. God! One time he goes over there to get Mom some whipping cream and I've got to hear about it the rest of my life."

"Well, I'd never go there. Not even once. I wouldn't buy a gumball from that place."

"Me neither. And neither would Dave—after that once. But," dropping her voice, "you know Mom shops there. I get so mad at her. She says it's convenient."

"Of course. I've decided Mom really is the perfect, the *exemplary* American—whatever's most convenient. It doesn't matter to her that the developer made her eat dust for six months after he leveled that orchard and paid off the city for the zoning changes. All completely forgotten. Dad already couldn't breathe that well. And Rhonda Nollins, before she had to move—that old lady was about ready to die from the dust. But, you know, just forget it."

"She says, what good would it do not to?"

"Of course. That's the spirit. The perfect Reagan American—most comfortable when there's a corporate boot on their throat. They should put her on a postage stamp."

"Well, I can't stand it. I try never to look at that place."

"That's impossible."

"No, it's not. Not completely. As much as I can, I don't see it."

"So," Vincent asked, "if I told you there's a huge Albertson's across the street from this house you'd be completely surprised?"

"No, of course not. You can't miss that. But all those small shops. I have no idea what's over there."

"You're really missing something. A baseball card shop, about as big as a closet. A Hallmark card shop. A McDonald's . . ."

"You've gone and checked them out?"

"No, no. I've never been within a hundred yards of those places, but you can't miss them. I don't really want to look either. But I *have* to. From a safe distance. How can you not? That's our world now. That's everyplace."

"No, I can't believe that. It's awful. But it's not everywhere. You know, Dave and I have been talking about moving someplace around Santa Cruz. Up in the mountains. Felton. Up there. Someplace out of this traffic and everything."

"That would be nice."

"I don't really want to. I do . . . but . . ." She trailed off, then in a minute became suddenly angry. "Why do they have to wreck everything? Why do they have to do it right across the street? This is my home! Why *right here!*"

"Someone's making money from it. . . ."

"They destroy everything!"

"I don't know what to tell you. *The jig is up*—isn't that the saying?— that's what I think. It's all over." He shook his head and stood up. "I'm getting some more."

"You have to see Mom tonight."

"I know."

"So why are you getting drunk?"

He rolled his eyes at her, said, "That's a dumb question. But I'm *not* getting drunk. One more glass. Then I'll take a little nap. Get something to eat. Pay a nice visit to our mother. Do you want something?"

"No. Nothing."

"Nothing? Not even a glass of red wine to warm up?"

"That doesn't warm you up. Going inside warms you up."

"In a few minutes. One more cigarette. The air's nice." He drew in a breath. "Wood smoke."

"Cigarette smoke is all I've been able to smell. I'll kill you if I catch a cold sitting out here."

"Not a half glass of wine?"

"No. No thanks."

ON APRIL 3, Vincent's father insisted on driving, though the fact he'd even mentioned how bad he felt meant that something was seriously wrong. Ralston, like most places in Stanislaus and San Joaquin Counties during the early eighties, was flooded with new inhabitants. In a matter of a few years, after housing costs in the Bay Area had shot beyond middle-class means and stagnant wages and a tight job market had made the once unimaginable idea of a four-hour-round-trip daily commute seem no more unreasonable than, say, reelecting a president who claimed that trees caused air pollution, Ralston had grown by fifty thousand. Unless one counted the indoor mall off Highway 99, there was still nothing *to do* in Ralston, no place really to go, but the mass of traffic on the roads to nothing and nowhere was truly astonishing. To get from the farms on its western outskirts to the farms on its east, even if one avoided the center of town, now required as much consideration of the time of day and probable traffic conditions from the once-rural Ralstoner as a trip from Century City to Santa Monica automatically triggered in the wily Los Angeleno. The trip from the Torno house to the hospital, on a distant edge of town, during rush hour, took Paul Torno, Sr., nearly an hour—about three times what it would have taken at the same time of day five years earlier.

Vincent heard about the trip's length from his mother. All of the rest of his information regarding that afternoon came from Paul, who'd gotten it from their mother. There wasn't much. By the time his mother's direct experience had filtered first through the old-fashioned decorum, emotional incapacity, and sedimented layers of love, hostility, and bitterness that filled her own tightly coiled system, then through the extraordinarily convoluted, constricted, and scruple-packed psyche of his brother, the "facts" that dripped through to Vincent were meager, watery, vague. He knew that his father and mother had walked into the emergency room together. He didn't know if his father had had to wait to be seen or if they took him in right away, just that he was seen and ultimately given a shot of some kind and told that he could go. Just outside the door of the hospital, though, his father told his mother that he still wasn't feeling right and had better go back in. They took him into the emergency room again. His mother was told to wait outside the emergency room. While she waited, she called Mary and Paul at their places of work. His father never came out of that room. He was dead before Mary or Paul arrived.

That was everything Vincent ever found out. He didn't push for more, since Paul seemed incapable of saying more. Everyone in the family, Vincent included, liked to emphasize their father's control over his last hours—he'd driven *himself*. They didn't talk about the little emergency room, where his control, and his life, left him. (Except for one late addition to the story, a day after the funeral— something that Vincent hadn't asked for and Paul, obviously, if he could have helped it, would rather not have said—both of them, ultimately, wishing it was something they didn't know: that it had been very difficult to get Mary to leave the body alone so it could be taken out of the emergency room and away.)

WHEN VINCENT RETURNED to the glass-topped table, Mary had her arms crossed over her chest, her jacket zipped up to the very top of its upstanding collar, and her chin and the lower third of her face ducked down inside it, turtlelike.

"God, what is *wrong* with you?" Vincent asked, after he'd sat down.

"Nothing," she said; then, quietly: "I'm pregnant."

"Really?" he asked, out of habit half acting as if she might be pulling his leg. "That's why you're so cold?"

"No—that's not why I'm cold—but yes. Really."

"That's great . . . isn't it?"

"Yeah," abashedly, as embarrassed as if she'd been caught boasting of some great personal accomplishment.

"God damn! Congratulations!" Vincent said. "Why didn't you tell me before?"

"I don't know," Mary said, actually blushing and squirming a bit in her chair. "We were talking about other things." She told him that she had been to the doctor the week before and had waited to tell him until he got home.

"Is this a . . . you know, a surprise?" Vincent asked. "I thought you guys used to say you didn't want kids."

Mary shrugged. "We didn't want to have them anytime soon. I don't know. I'm not sure that Dave wanted to yet, but after Dad passed away . . ."

"After he passed away what?"

"It seemed to be the thing to do. I realized I really wanted to. Have a family. My own. Like I had when I was a kid."

"You mean an unhappy one?" Vincent joked.

Mary was serious. "We weren't unhappy."

Vincent said, teasingly slow and doubtful, "I don't know . . ."

"We weren't. I had a good childhood." Then, responding to a look on Vincent's face, she insisted, "I did. I wouldn't trade it with anyone. Especially not with *Dave*. You should see his family!"

Vincent laughed. "Well, if you're going to prove your point with comparisons! That's easy. There are plenty of miserable families around."

Mary shook her head. "I wasn't miserable. And neither were you."

He laughed again. "This is silly. This is nothing I want to get into. Whatever you say. I'm not talking about this."

"You're the one who brought it up. You always bring it up—how unhappy the family makes you. You did on the phone last week."

"I don't remember that."

"You did. Something about how Dad thought that children and donkeys should be trained the same way."

He laughed. "What was I *bringing up*? I wasn't complaining. That's just a fact. You don't remember how he'd go on about that—that joke he liked? That you needed a two-by-four to get a donkey's— and a kid's—attention?"

"He wasn't serious."

"No, of course not—not literally. I didn't say he was. You're the one who's getting all offended." He sighed and lit a cigarette. Since his father's death, every talk Vincent had with another family member, regardless of its subject matter, was really about his father. Even talks about their mother, how she was doing, how she should be treated, were governed by an implicit ever-present sense of how their father had indicated he wanted her cared for after his death. Now even Mary's pregnancy had to do with their father—or a certain version of him.

He said to her, "You're reminding me of something Kris said after Dad's funeral. I don't remember how it came up, I just remember how big she was. In maternity mourning—some combination—with Paul Jr. Or Paul the *Third*, I should say. No, wait, Paul the *Fourth*, if you count old Paolo. Much nicer sounding—*Paolo*—I wish they hadn't felt the need to Anglicize all our names. Anyway—sorry, I am feeling this some." He lifted up his glass. "Anyway, Kris said, *You'll see, your dad'll become like an angel in your mind. You won't remember any of the bad things that happened, only the good.* She said that's how it was after her mom died. Her mom started to seem perfect." Vincent laughed. "I didn't disagree, but even then, I knew *that* probably wasn't going to happen. But I couldn't say it to her. Because that's probably how she needs to think of her mom. So she doesn't have to think of other things. Like those pesticides her father sprays all over his apricots. And herbicides. Still. And how her mother, living right in the middle of that ranch, a nonsmoker—what? forty-eight?—comes down with lung cancer. That's what I'd think about. I don't think I could stop thinking about it. You know? But then, that's me."

"What good would it do to think about that?"

"It might be the truth."

"And it might not be. You'd never know. And anyway, to her, it's not the important thing. She doesn't want her memories poisoned with all that. That's her right. She doesn't have to think that way."

"No, of course she doesn't. You're right. She can forget about everything unpleasant that ever happened, and just imagine her mom up on a cloud if it makes her happy. But the pesticides and herbicides are still being sprayed out there, aren't they? And other people are breathing them in now. And eating them."

"I don't know how that applies to us anyway." With one hand she made a vague gesture toward their little walnut orchard, said dryly, "Maybe her father's herbicides are what we needed out there."

"We tried them! You don't remember? But forget about that part. What I mean is, even if you refuse to remember what happened in the past, it doesn't make those events disappear. They still have consequences."

"Obviously. But remembering's one thing. To talk about them . . ."

She didn't need to finish the sentence. It was a Torno family superstition that a dreaded future event might be magically forestalled, a current event diminished, or the memory of a past event vanquished, if not a word was said about it. As though the worst facts fell short of full being, of complete incarnation, as long as one did not name them. As if it was language that condemned one to misfortune, and that by keeping one's mouth shut, by withholding one's words, one could somehow at least half escape from the worst. This was a belief Vincent seemed to have been born with: as unalterable as his blood type—even though it had failed him again and again. It remained still. But in an increasingly compromised state, since Vincent, unlike Mary, had been infected at some point in his childhood with a susceptibility to words, and a growing sense of the other effects they could have.

Vincent smoked his cigarette and looked at the low gray sky darkening evenly all over—no setting sun, but a dimmer switch, somewhere, turning slowly toward *off*.

"So are you going to move back to Ralston for a while now?" Mary asked, with a smile and a lighter tone meant to suggest she was moving the conversation onto a new track.

But Vincent didn't believe it. "No," he answered immediately. "Not a chance."

Mercurially, she became sad. "You hate everything about this place, don't you?"

"Not at all," he insisted, knowing what, or *who*, she included in her *everything*. "There's just nothing here for me. You said yourself that you're thinking of leaving."

"I'm thinking of the best place to raise a family. . . . Someplace like this place used to be."

"Good luck. If I were you I'd look for someplace a little better. . . . But I don't hate this place. Not the way you're taking it." He finished his Scotch. "Listen. You know the last time I saw Dad, last year, I went for a walk with him. One of his twice-daily walks he was doing before he died, that Mom always told me about on the phone. She used to tell me about the new running shoes he bought, the pulse monitor. I'd get off the phone and think, What a trendy, eighties kind of guy Dad has become. My father is finally starting to act like the people on television—a happy semi-retiree. So I came home and went for a walk with him. Though, to be honest, I didn't really want to, since my whole TV idea of family life began to crumble as soon as I got here. It's not like Dad and I could talk to each other. But we went. And we walked down Collier, on the dirt shoulder, with all the diesels rumbling past, the traffic, the trash under our feet. All of it, worse than ever. Or, I should say, as bad as ever, *but even worse*. More traffic. More trash. And the acres across from our house all paved. The almond orchards along Collier all gone. Instead, that stucco coin-op car wash, that cheesy 'fitness club,' that the visit before had been a vacuum cleaner shop. That aloe-vera place—whatever that is—in that tin building. That lumberyard, that crappy chain, with its crappy wood. All that stuff. That was our walk. That was the walk he took, twice a day. It made me feel sick. And it made me realize he was an old man. Not even sixty-five yet, but old. I hadn't seen it before then, hadn't realized it. Everything around him had gone to hell, everything looked like shit, and he walked through it twice a day and didn't say a word. He didn't complain, or lose his temper. It didn't seem to drive him crazy, or make him sick, like it made me. Or if it did, he didn't say a thing about it. He just took it. And not in that way he took other things. Not stoically. But helplessly. Like he resigned himself to it—*had had to*, because he didn't even have the energy left to complain. And then, you know, I realized—and it was a surprise—that for the first time in my life I wasn't afraid of him. He didn't scare me like he used to. So I didn't hate him like I used to. And then I realized that I didn't even hate him as he *used to be*. In fact, I missed him as he used to be—that father who'd scared me so much. I wanted *that one* back, the one I'd grown up afraid of, because *this new one*, this old man walking alongside me—this perfectly, proudly, helplessly erect old man—this one I had absolutely no idea what to do with. And everything in the world, as if every object had once been alive—the blood seemed to drain out of everything."

"You could have seen him more," Mary said. "You could've come home more often. He wanted to see you."

"Really? He never told me that. Besides, what difference would it have made?"

"He had more time. He wasn't working—much."

"Because he couldn't. He was reduced to not working, and when he wasn't working he wasn't even the same person. I felt sorry for him. I felt pity, and that didn't seem right. He wouldn't have liked that. And then the few times we did talk—not about anything really, just business, or school, or some stupid thing Uncle Joey had done recently . . . only for a few minutes, that's all we could manage. When we did talk I'd feel such excitement. . . . It embarrasses me to admit it. But I'd feel so *thrilled*, like some very bright light, a ball of light, incredibly dense and hot, was expanding in my chest, and warming even the tips of my toes and fingers—I couldn't stand it. I'd start to hate *myself*. For twenty-two years, I'd think, there's nothing between us. He hardly notices me. Which is okay, since when he does it usually means I'm in trouble. But still, after twenty-two years of this, he can have this effect on me—make my whole body seem to glow. It was awful. Like I was a child again. Or a dog. I'd sit there, intensely happy, hardly able to stand it, and I'd think, to feel *nothing* would be better than this. To feel hatred even—something I was used to— would be better."

"But why?" Mary asked. "Why when you had the chance—"

"What chance?" Vincent interrupted. "Because he was dying? That's in the movies, Mary—you must watch too many movies. Everything was supposed to be better because he was dying? That's crazy!"

"That's not the way to think about it. You could have made him happy."

"I did, I think. Don't worry. But don't make me pretend that it made everything before it okay."

"I'm not *making* you do anything. No one can do that. You do whatever you want. You always have."

"Sure I have."

"You have. You're like Dad in that way—stubborn as he was. But he always knew what he was going to do. He always had a goal. He supported his family."

"In some ways. With money."

"More than that."

"I guess."

"He did. But you. I don't understand you. You were doing so great—"

"Stop it, will you?"

"But you were."

"Stop!"

"Okay! It's just that everything, everything, is a mess now. I thought you'd become a professor. Dad was so proud of you. You never came home, but that was okay because I knew how much work you had, and how hard it must have been. But now. Everything is falling apart. Nothing is what I expected. I saw Uncle Joey last week and his eyes were *so much* like Dad's. . . . I wanted to hug him. I almost started to cry, right in the middle of a supermarket. Though I know he's a pig. I know how he treats Paul at work. And how he was to Dad, at the end. But I miss Dad so much, I can't help it. I saw him, I saw those eyes, it was like Dad was alive again and everything else went out of my head. Everything. I wanted it so much to be true."

"I know."

"No, you don't," she said quickly. "Not from the things you've been saying, you don't. I would *never say* I *hated* him. . . ."

"I'm sure you thought it sometimes. How about when you and Billy Ramsey—"

"You say it over and over." She raised her voice to cut him off. "Over and over." Then, when she was sure he'd stopped: "I miss Dad so much, I can't tell you."

"Yes," Vincent murmured. He lit a new cigarette from the nub of the old one. "I miss him, too. I do. Believe me. I dream about him every night."

"I do, too."

"But dreams—you wake up and they're gone. You get up, start working, they vanish. They're not what bothers me, what sticks.

What *sticks*, what is constant, is this one image. You know the big brick wall at the Almeda Park tennis courts? I used to ride my bike there when I was in seventh and eighth grade. For a couple of years I was really into tennis and I'd spend hours there, by myself, playing against that wall. Smacking a ball for hours, playing imaginary games. I didn't really know how to keep score, and I had no idea of the right way to hold a racket. I just loved hitting the ball and I loved the sweet *swack* sound it made against the brick wall, so solid, massive. The physicality of the game, the rebound of the ball—immediate, strong, anticipated. So wonderful. *Swack!* Back and forth, again and again, chasing the ball down and sending it back. So when I hit the ball too high and it sailed over the wall there was such a strange, instantaneous disappointment—before I got mad, before I thought, *Damn, now I have to go out the gate and get it back*, before that, a more immediate disappointment. Like a kind of loss, this *nonoccurrence* of anticipated, expected, gratification. Along with a sudden surprise that I had missed the wall. I mean, a wall that big—two courts wide—that tall and massive! Such a huge, solid, physical *fact*, how could I miss it? It seemed impossible. But I was a terrible player, I'd never had a lesson, so I did miss it, and the ball, instead of rebounding to me, like I expected—*knew it would*—would simply vanish without a sound, sail over that wall into empty space, and stop me in my tracks." He looked at Mary but could not make out her face in the darkness. "Do you know what I'm saying?" he asked.

She didn't answer.

"You know, the sweetness of anticipation when the outcome is certain? That certain, inevitable rebound? The huge, immovable, impenetrable, resistant fact—*presence*—right in front of my face, filling the whole horizon? You know? When Dad died it was the same as if that wall had vanished during the middle of a game. So I'd be there serving ball after ball into unresisting, infinite . . . emptiness. Do you see what I mean?"

After a few moments she said, "Yes, maybe."

"The thing is," he admitted suddenly, "I don't know what to do now."

"I know," she said. "I don't either," and silently they sat together in the dark for a few minutes, until the telephone began to ring and Mary quickly shoved her chair back from the table (glad for the distraction, as if she'd been waiting for it), saying "It must be Dave," and hurried into the house, while Vincent, unmoving, a little drunk, looked out at the dead walnut trees, skeletal against the dark sky, and longed for the sharp *fleeting* panic that their full summer shapes had once inspired, ready to exchange for it the panic he felt now— steady and pervasive and, he was sure, unending.

He sat there until Mary turned on the backyard light, opened the door, and called him inside, telling him, "It's Mom."

SCHMERZHAUSER

I

THOUGH THE SEED of our estrangement—of two estrangements, per-haps—would be planted in a matter of minutes, my first sight of Jon Schmerzhauser since our college graduation in 1985, as he walked out of the jetway and into Sea-Tac Airport, brought with it only an overwhelming sense of the familiar, and after six years of just letters, postcards, and infrequent phone calls, we renewed our face-to-face acquaintance with all the pleasure and ease, and as little hesitation or surprise, as one feels sinking into a warm tub after a long day of strain.

Schmerzhauser was the final visitor in what, when we were in the mood to anticipate a long future together, Kate and I agreed to officially label "the Year of Visitors." In actuality it had been a little more than a year and a half, ever since we moved from San Francisco, where we'd met and dated for about eight months, to Seattle, which seemed to be everyone's favorite place to visit. The initial influx of guests, mostly from San Francisco, coming while I still worked at Elliott Bay Book Company, was welcome—since Kate and I had found Seattle to be the kind of place where everyone we met was invariably friendly, but never seemed to develop into friends. But in our last half year there, once I'd finally decided to make a serious effort to become a writer, quitting the bookstore and taking a twenty-five-hour-a-week job as a commissioned telemarketer for Seattle Opera (just a few blocks from our apartment), I hated to have my morning writing time interrupted; and because my desk was against the short fifth wall of the large living room—on the cold hearth of a bricked-in fireplace—in the same room as the sofa bed, every recent visitor sent me huffing off to the public library or simply made work impossible. It wasn't so bad for Kate; she didn't work at home, and her career in stage design was, as they say, "progressing quite nicely." It had brought us to Seattle and was leading us, in about six weeks, to New York. But I'd been drifting since my father's death. I'd seemed to spend the last few years in a restless but deep slumber, and only recently had I begun to feel myself in the shallows of this sleep, from which I could vaguely imagine one day awaking.

However, for Schmerzhauser I was happy to take a Friday off from pitching season-ticket packages to opera fans, and I readily put aside any thought of writing over the weekend.

"Jeez, what a flight!" Schmerzhauser began, after a mere nod of greeting, as if we saw each other every day. "I sat next to what had to be one of the fattest men on the Eastern Seaboard. I'm *flattened* up against the window. As soon as the plane takes off he starts making these little burping sounds—down in his throat. *Urp. Urp.* Like that. And smacking his lips. Luckily, I had Ella on the Walkman. But, of course, just my luck—really, this could've been predicted—my batteries run down. Halfway here." He said all this in a confidential undertone, leaning toward me, with cautious sideward glances at the passing clumps of his fellow passengers: a mixture of polite deference, in case his seatmate was anywhere near, and sneaky but utter disdain. Then he hung his head and shook it in wide slow comically pitiful sweeps, and it was a gesture, following naturally enough upon the old weary and bemused voice, redolent of Schmerzhauser's corner dormitory room—unchanged through four years, with its mealtime view of the girls on their way to the dining hall—and a particular, achingly passive way of letting the hours slip by.

We didn't shake hands. It would've struck both of us as somehow artificial and making *too much* of our meeting. It was already too much for Schmerzhauser that I offered to take either the small canvas duffel bag from his right hand or the backpack from the other—"I'm not your granny," he said. But I persisted, goading his humorous annoyance, since all of his ironic exasperation and muttered dismay deepened the bath of familiarity. After all, annoyance and dismay had, from the outset, been the ground of our friendship. We had met on our second day at a dull Midwestern Catholic university which, like a microcosm of the whole country during Reagan's first term, was positively flatulent with a desperate, aggressively retrograde exuberance. In the midst of such shrill insistence upon our new university's extraordinary "spirit," its specialness and superiority, the deflating sarcasm and deep disappointment we revealed to each other in no more than a few exchanged words, in the tone of our voices, in the disillusioned and bored expressions we both wore, established as strong and sudden a bond between us as the secret handshake of two Masons. Its strength was not diminished a bit when I moved off campus after my sophomore year or when I became serious about my studies and had less time to lounge around with him. Nor by my graduate school pretensions, which were easily outlasted. It persisted even with three thousand miles between us, this bond or connection, as a kind of imaginary retreat for me from everything in my life that required effort or demanded ambition or dangled rewards: a lotus land resting upon our shared bedrock of disillusionment and despair. But in the Seattle-Tacoma Airport it was shaken to its core by a single momentary look from my live-in girlfriend, Kate Linton.

Having become impatient with Schmerzhauser's late-arriving plane, she had gone for a stroll around the terminal. When she returned, I was standing beside Schmerzhauser, where I'd stepped to make a better grab at his duffel bag, and I spotted her small dark figure as she strode briskly through what looked to be an extended family reunion. Then she saw us, and her first brief disparaging assessment, hardly more than a severe twitch of the brow and mouth, a wrinkling of her face's fine small features, transformed me in an instant from participant to observer. I looked at Schmerzhauser and seemed to see him for the first time, as I supposed Kate saw him: large and lumpy, disheveled, looking a little unwashed, and painfully unstylish. For the first time that day, perhaps for the first time since I'd met him, his immense physicality came out of the deep shadows cast by familiarity; it *registered*. He was in fact huge, at least six foot three, even with his shoulders in their habitual hunch, and—for all his scorn for the "fattest man on the Eastern Seaboard"—Michelin Man round. His mouse-brown hair was very fine and very thin on top, and only now did I notice that its longish "comb-over" strands, after several hours in the plane's dry cabin, floated free and electric above his large fleshy pink face—which made me as embarrassed and anxious to smooth them down as if they'd been my own, discovered in a public mirror, levitating above my own head.

Kate put out her hand and introduced herself before I managed to produce a word. In our nineteen months in Seattle she had grown increasingly more assured in public—charming and perfect and sometimes, as I felt in this case, perhaps a little too smooth. She had very clear blue eyes which, I must admit, rarely failed to unnerve me—their very brightness reminding me of how muddled I was—and short artfully tousled hair: black, like most of her clothes. Standing there before her petite trim figure beside my sloppy overstuffed college friend I felt myself somehow hugely exposed.

Meanwhile, taken by surprise, Schmerzhauser's first response to Kate's welcome was, to my further dismay, a nervous, sunny-faced blundering. She startled him out of his usual weary sarcasm; he met her instead with a wide awkward unbecoming grin, which he seemed to thrust up before himself in a defensive panic. "My flight was fine. Just fine," he answered her, nodding his head and grinning. He had never had an easy time talking to attractive women, but it struck me that he was also responding to something specific to Kate; to a certain glossy assurance, which I usually liked. It was this, I think, that accounts for the way Schmerzhauser responded almost guiltily in those first few minutes with uncharacteristic cheeriness—as if trying to dispel any suspicion that he might be anything less than "well-adjusted"—with one bland lie after another. "I don't mind flying at all," he told her (I knew he *despised* it). I snatched his duffel bag from his hand, stepped between them, and led them both away from the gate.

An almost painful silence gaped between us on the subway train connecting Sea-Tac's various terminals, but all three of us relaxed a little during the long walk to the parking garage. In the car Schmerzhauser and I avoided the shameless reminiscing we almost certainly would have fallen into had Kate not been in the backseat, but otherwise he and I talked easily. I pointed out the Boeing factory west of the highway. I told him how everyone left the city on Friday to go camping; how every Sunday night our apartment house's laundry room was filled with drying tents, drooping from ceiling pipes and makeshift laundry lines like synthetic skins shed by our neighbors' departed weekends. "Sounds like my kind of town," he said sarcastically. When I happened to look over at him I discovered that his electrified flyaway hair was, of course, shooting straight up to the roof—but there was nothing I could do about it. I looked in the rearview mirror at Kate. Luckily, she wasn't paying any attention to us. Her gaze was out the side window, her head tilted, her eyes steady: the very image of bored, professional appraisal as the range of I-5's scenery—evergreens, sparse or in dense black-depthed profusion; shopping centers and chain restaurants, fleeting roadside tableaux—passed before her.

II

TRAFFIC, AS ALWAYS, but especially on Friday afternoons, was clotted in either direction around the narrow waist of Greater Seattle.

When we got to our apartment on Queen Anne Hill, in a two-story Tudor brick building from the 1920s, Kate stayed just long enough to lead Schmerzhauser, nodding his head and wearing the faint smile of someone trying to conceal motion sickness, on a tour: the large long living room, the dining room, the bedroom, with its rickety French doors and cramped cement balcony looking up an overgrown hillside, the small kitchen, and the tiny bathroom, whose door, she warned him, never locked, and during the wet months barely closed at all. Then she left to help with that night's production at the theater down the hill at Seattle Center, and Schmerzhauser, discarding those social graces which had suited him like clinging polyester, collapsed onto the couch with warm praise for the "homey" feel of the apartment—"I don't know why you'd want to leave this place for filthy New York"—and a contented expression on his face that suggested if pizza and beer were brought to him he might not move for the rest of his weekend visit.

Inertia, I don't think it's unfair to say, was the guiding principle of Schmerzhauser's life. We never talked about his quietly maintained Catholicism—I was careful not to sneer at his weekly church attendance, and he was careful never to give me the chance—but I don't think it could hold a candle to the power of Inertia in his daily life, and the extraordinary *lack* of faith underlying it. He generally stayed wherever he found himself, not because he believed that it was the best place to be—like many other people I've known, he always suspected that almost any *other* place would have been better—but because he had no faith that any effort he exerted would improve things. He still lived in Pennsylvania at home with his retired father and stepmother (though for the last six months she'd been encouraging him to move out and threatening to sell the house and take his father to Arizona). And he still worked in the same soda water bottling plant that he'd worked in during college vacations. He'd returned to it after graduation, *temporarily*, he'd said, while he lackadaisically looked for the kind of high school post that his English B.A. and teaching credentials qualified him for, but he accepted the job of Quality Control Supervisor as soon as the bottling plant offered it to him. They liked him at the plant—he was smart and reliable, and had a great memory—the pay was fine, and it was "easy enough" to monitor the carbonation, fructose, sucrose, and citric acid levels of soda water. "I'd just as soon be doing this," he once told me, "as teaching." But that wasn't, when I thought about it, saying anything, since more than anyone else I've known Schmerzhauser escaped being stretched on the torturous rack of time between a desire and its fulfillment by assuming at almost every desire's inception that fulfillment was a mirage. Either such fulfillment didn't exist at all, or up close, after much effort, it inevitably revealed its true form: Disappointment. All of which hopelessness justified a great deal of drinking and lounging around. And all of which, I'd say now—without any of the abstracting, generalizing rhetoric we used during college to make our lives into both much more and much less than they were—had everything to do with the particular concrete fact (mentioned to me only once) of Schmerzhauser's mother's death, after two years of withering illness, on his twelfth birthday.

I brought a beer to Schmerzhauser, comfortably boneless-looking on the couch, then sat down with my own bottle in a chair near the front window. Late-afternoon sunlight stretched in long bright sharp-edged quadrangles across half the length of the pale blue living-room rug, and the sounds of rush-hour traffic, just below us on Queen Anne Avenue, came with a soft breeze through the open windows. I asked him how his job was going, and he grimaced, then said, reluctantly, "It's still going." He took a drink of beer. "Let's leave it at that. *Going*, though not gone. Unfortunately. They're trying to promote me again. But now's not the time for such ugly topics. I'm on vacation."

So I mentioned some of the usual Seattle sights most visitors were interested in, while Schmerzhauser looked with drowsy approval at the wide old-fashioned arched doorway across from him, between the living and dining rooms, drank his beer, and said nothing. "We could go up the Space Needle this evening. Take the monorail downtown," I said.

He shrugged. "I don't care. Don't put yourself out. I'm happy right here," he said.

"But you came all the way out here for only a weekend."

"Ah, well, on a free ticket. It was use it or lose it by the end of the year. I came out to visit you," he said matter-of-factly, and I knew he wasn't just trying to be a courteous guest. That was always the thing about Schmerzhauser—the flip side of his awkwardness with Kate—he couldn't manage empty politeness, and wouldn't even attempt flattery. I could trust everything he said; and I knew he would never change. So we sat for over another hour, drinking and talking while the sunlight quadrangles shifted over the rug and hardwood floor, and the slung-back twin uprights of electric buses, trailing along their cables, glided past the window, and the sound of the traffic, of all the workweek weary finally released from their labors, soughed outside—peaceful beneath our lazy talk—like wind through a forest. We talked about college and mutual friends and sports, saying nothing that would have been remarkable to a third party and nothing that, in itself, was even very remarkable to either of us. There was scant *news*. It wasn't what mattered to us. Most of our recollections had been previously recollected, much of what we said we had said before; the pleasure we sought together came, as it had during our college years, from predictability, from the repetition of familiar things and the assurance of sympathy.

Nostalgia, carefully conjured, enveloped us like a cloud that first evening, cushioning our short walk up to Olympic Pizza, for dinner, at the top of Queen Anne Hill, and filtering and determining everything. There was a "buzz" about Seattle in the early nineties; most of our guests during the Year of Visitors came to see particular, recommended sights. A lot of them came as prospective residents to give the city the once-over. But not Schmerzhauser. If I needed any more proof of how uninterested he was in seeing the city, he gave it to me as we finished eating, telling me, when I asked him what he wanted to do, that he'd packed a deflated football and a small air pump in his duffel bag. "On the phone you mentioned a nice little park with a baseball backstop," he said. "I couldn't fit a Wiffle ball bat in my bag, but a football was no problem."

On West Highland Avenue, as we walked to the little park, tossing the football underhand between us, Schmerzhauser stopped in front of a huge U-shaped four-story brick apartment house, set on a large well-tended grassy lot: the Victoria, built in 1921.

I told him Kate and I had looked at an apartment in that building when we first got to Seattle.

"It's great," he said.

I agreed. "The apartments are beautiful. But it cost a little more than the place we got, and it was a little smaller. And, plus, it's too much like a dorm."

"Yeah, exactly," he said, in a tone that contradicted my conclusion.

The postcard view from Kerry Park, a little farther down West Highland, interested him much less. He took it all in—the Jetson-like Space Needle, the modest family grouping of downtown skyscrapers, the concrete bunker of the Kingdome; Mount Rainier to the left, holographic, shimmery, in a horizon-wide pink wash; Elliott Bay to the right—with the look of someone determined to be unimpressed. And he looked at me with a little embarrassment, and perhaps even some derision, when I asked, "Beautiful, isn't it?"

He turned his back on it and walked over to the large outdoor sculpture in the center of the long terracelike park: a large diagonally bored-out cube atop a larger open-sided hollow cube, both of them more air than metal. He read aloud from the plaque, *"Changing Form,"* and made a face of profound distaste. Then we walked down one of the long flights of concrete steps at the end of Kerry Park to the little park I'd told him about. Sheltered by the verdant hillside rising above one edge, the broad beautiful profile of an old two-story frame house at either end, and tall venerable trees on all four sides, with a small chain-link backstop in one corner and a basketball half-court in another, it was more like some boy's ideal backyard than it was a park.

We just played catch at first, stiffly, out of practice, enjoying the last low light while we had it, since it was almost eight o'clock. But after a while, as the light still remained steady in the sky, and we'd warmed up, we started throwing passes to each other on the run. One of us would take an imaginary snap, and a five-step drop, or roll out in a bootleg, while the other ran a crossing pattern, or a deep slant, or a "post." It was all very informal and fluid, no line of scrimmage, no planned routes, no huddles—we never came within ten yards of each other—but there was never any confusion. When we were winded we'd pause and talk desultorily at a distance about college or professional football, but we were not winded very often or for very long. We made a big deal out of impressive catches or amazing throws, trying to outdo ourselves. And Schmerzhauser was, as he'd been in college, surprisingly, even startlingly, light on his feet. When he ran it was as if all his bulk was artificial and insubstantial: foam padding, protectively distended, over the swift undeveloped body of a boy. And sedentary as I knew he typically was—and even after four beers—he didn't seem to tire. The amazing Seattle light stayed and stayed, as though the earth and time had stopped dead in their tracks, and we kept at it like two kids, with no sight or sound of any other humans, seemingly without any particular effort and no thoughts of quitting, until nearly ten o'clock, when darkness fell upon us suddenly and we could no longer see the football against the sky, and could barely make each other out.

III

KATE, NOT SURPRISINGLY, was not home when we returned from the park, so Schmerzhauser and I showered and changed and went out for more pizza—at the bottom of the hill this time—and more beer. At two in the morning when Schmerzhauser and I dragged ourselves back up the hill, Kate was still not home. I was ready to stay up and wait, but for Schmerzhauser's body, running on Eastern time, it was 5:00 A.M., and he wanted to sleep. So I went to bed, lay down and waited, obsessing on every detail I could recall of a slimy German assistant to a visiting director who'd blatantly flirted with Kate, right in front of me, at a recent party. Then I fell asleep.

In the late morning when I woke, Kate, lying beside me, said, "You certainly were affectionate last night."

I had a vague memory of squeezing her tightly and talking and kissing, but it was indistinct enough, and weightless enough, to have been a dream. I covered my eyes with a hand. "It happened again?"

She laughed. "Yes, it did."

I groaned.

"You were so . . . *ardent*."

"I'd been drinking," I said, but both of us knew that it had nothing to do with that. I did it when I was sober too, and fairly often of late. She would come to bed after I'd already fallen asleep and I would wake up only partially, my mind all airy and light—as it is when one is just drifting off—all clear of its usual burdens and shadows, and I'd begin to tell her how much I loved her and how much I needed her. Stupidly, I'm sure—though she was kind enough never to describe it this way; repetitively and simply and insistently as a child, if I remember correctly. And I'd kiss and hug her, and generally maul her. One night I had awakened from this state to a profound puzzlement at the questions she repeated: "Do you mean this? Are you awake?" But most of the time I had only the vaguest dreamy memory of it, and of rolling over and going back to full sleep.

As she began to get out of bed I uncovered my eyes to watch her, wearing very little, and caught, with relief, before she turned her back, a glimpse of a smile as she said, "I wish you'd tell me those things when you're awake."

Often this wish came out as a complaint, in all seriousness.

All three of us had oatmeal together. Schmerzhauser's hangover seemed to temper his awkwardness around Kate.

"Don't forget, we have that play tonight," Kate said.

"Oh, no, don't worry," I said, speaking for both Schmerzhauser and myself. "We talked about it last night. We're looking forward to it."

"I haven't been to a play since college. But I saw the movie they made with Albert Finney from that one play of this guy's—*Tenants*, or whatever it was called," Schmerzhauser said. "It was okay."

"Do you want to eat out before it?" I asked.

"No. I said I'd make dinner," Kate insisted pleasantly, "I'll make dinner."

I shrugged. A perfect hostess, as always. But with Schmerzhauser it struck me as too much trouble to make dinner, and I felt vaguely embarrassed, though on whose behalf I wasn't sure.

After our lunchtime breakfast, Schmerzhauser and I turned on the television and lay around for three hours watching our Alma Mater, with her high-paid, quippy little Jesse Helms–supporter coach, get the crap kicked out of her in football. I would have liked to ask Kate about the previous night but never had the chance to find out anything more than that "they"—the cast? the crew? the sleazy German assistant?—had insisted she go out with them after the play, since she would be leaving Seattle in just a few weeks.

After the game, Schmerzhauser and I walked around the neighborhoods of Queen Anne: the fancy, expensive ones, but also the solidly middle-class, with yard sales, and homeowners putzing around in their planters or garages or under their cars. In these latter areas Schmerzhauser wore a constant, pleased little smile, said hello to children, petted a dog.

I said, "I can't believe it, but you look like a guy who's thinking about moving to Seattle."

"Oh no," he laughed, "not me. But you have a very comfortable situation here. You've got it made. I can't understand why you're gonna move. Nice neighborhood. An almost-wife."

"*Almost* being the key word. We're not married."

"It's only a matter of time."

"I'm not so sure about that. But what about you, Mr. Domestic Bliss? You have your eye on anyone?"

He shook his head, walked along, then shyly said, "There's a woman where I work. . . ."

"A secretary?"

He shook his head. "She runs the filler."

"You're going out?"

"No. I don't know. It's nothing. . . ."

Schmerzhauser had had no shortage of "crushes" in college, but except for a couple of arranged dates for what were called "Screw-Your-Neighbor" dances in the dorm, he almost never even managed to speak to the women he really liked. Once I had teased him about his timidity around a particular woman and he'd said, "Look at me—fat and balding at twenty. What do you think my chances are with her?" and I never teased him again. He was not ugly—nothing like the Quasimodo he seemed to think himself—but he wouldn't risk rejection. As far as I knew he was still, at twenty-eight, a virgin. The woman at the bottling plant, he told me, reluctantly, was older, divorced, with a son in the Navy. "She's nothing," he repeated. "She seems kind of interested. But I'm not," he quickly added. "No thanks," he said, suddenly becoming more definite, shaking his head almost vigorously. "Nope. No way."

I took him to where he'd have a good view of the Olympic Mountains and Puget Sound. He crooned, *"The bluest skies you've ever seen are in Seattle . . ."*

"Who's that?" I asked.

He looked shocked. "You don't know? Perry Como, of course."

When he was in a good mood he had some corny old song for every occasion, and it usually came from further back than Perry Como. I had gathered that Schmerzhauser was a late, unplanned addition to his family and, as a result, he was nostalgic about cultural remnants from decades before his own birth. Of course, this longing for the unexperienced past afflicts pretty much all of America, but Schmerzhauser's connection to such stuff was immediate and *lived*, not just neurotically fantasized. He had been raised amid the relics of his parents' distant happy youth—those songs (including one of his favorites, from the twenties, I think, which began "Three little fishies in an itty bitty pool . . .") were played in his house. And given the capaciousness of his memory, and his proclivities, I wouldn't have been surprised to learn that his stockpile of such recollections dwarfed all four of his much older brothers' combined.

But when he was depressed, this stockpile nearly crushed him. I'd find him listening to his tapes of old music in his darkened dorm room, lying fully clothed on his back on his narrow bed, as heavy and motionless as if he were buried up to his neck in sand.

Later, while Kate was preparing dinner, Schmerzhauser and I walked to Safeway to buy beer. There was shelf after shelf of unusual brands—"designer beers," Schmerzhauser called them—and we drew out as long as we could, with all kinds of fatuous considerations, the pleasantly dull and diverting process of making a decision of absolutely no importance. By the time we returned to the apartment with two six-packs, Kate had been holding dinner for twenty minutes and was silently furious. She had devoted a good deal of time to making a special, exotically spiced Middle Eastern vegetarian dish—one of my favorites. I told her how good it was. Schmerzhauser said nothing about it and hardly ate, regarding it with a stereotypical child's—or then-president George Bush's—aversion to broccoli. He did talk, however, as comfortably as he could around a good-looking woman: mostly about his first impressions of me in the dorm, before he met me. He made me sound, in spite of the banal facts he worked with, more interesting than I was. Kate listened with a half-smile, her eyes returning obsessively to his fork as it piled up and smoothed out and rearranged the food on his plate. Fortunately, we couldn't linger at the table; we had the play to attend.

The play, in its world premiere run, was quite weak—not painfully bad, but shallow and obvious and dull.

Afterward we went to a café, just beyond the boundaries of Seattle Center and usually quite pleasant. It was crowded and we were seated in a rear corner at a small round French café table with a bad wobble.

Kate started in on the play as soon as we were seated: "Well, I apologize. That was terrible."

Schmerzhauser shrugged. I asked her, "Why should you apologize? You didn't write it."

"I'm the one who got the tickets. I suggested it. I had no idea it would be so bad."

"About the level of the average movie," Schmerzhauser said.

Kate flashed a dismissive glance over him; I said, "That's not too good then."

"Everything was just so *bland*," Kate continued. "I don't know what they thought they were doing. To have all that money to spend and to come up with that! God, that set . . . !"

Kate had definite ideas about stage design. She'd recently had a large hand in a production of *Measure for Measure*, which was fortunate to receive both a fair amount of praise and the kind of prurient criticism that sells tickets. It drew heavily upon the iconography of fascism, both Italian and German, but it was set in no particular historical time. Much of the costuming was recognizably Nazi-like, but the rigid authoritarian character, Angelo, was cast to look and act like Mussolini, the minor character of Marianna was got up in a rigid and distorting semi-Victorian outfit, and contemporary surveillance and communication technology was everywhere. The sets, too, were a grab bag: mostly German and Italian fascistic, but also—best of all in my opinion—there was one set, with a heavy coffered ceiling, that strongly suggested the Metro stations of Washington, D.C. (Though when I complimented Kate on this acute piece of political commentary she looked a little offended—she'd meant to suggest Rome's Pantheon.) There were also the mandatory S&M elements and nude writhing bodies, and, hanging over the whole thing, a foggy Foucaultian air. I thought the production reeked of my first year of graduate school, where the most interesting theoretical ideas were applied ham-handedly to produce the most predictable results.

In any case, coming out of that kind of aesthetic, Kate didn't spare the detailed, old-fashioned sets we'd just seen: a fully realized alley, a shabby two-room apartment, and, for the majority of the play, a pawnshop picturesquely crammed with junk and warmly lit, with dark moody shadows. This is what I'd always liked about Kate: she got worked up after plays or movies; she wasn't shy; she had her own ideas. She didn't wait, either blatantly or secretly, for me to give her direction. She had her own career, and was good at it. She was, in other words, nothing like my mother. With few interruptions, she held the floor until the beers we'd ordered had arrived, and Schmerzhauser, after absently taking a drink from the bottle instead of his half-full glass, sighed and placed it back down with a heaviness that set the table wobbling and all three of us clutching at our suddenly tipsy, sloshing glassware.

When everything and almost everyone had settled again—Schmerzhauser was too large for his round-seated wood chair; he struggled to sink back into a comfortable slouch and find a place, out of the waitress's path, to stretch his legs—he said, "I guess I didn't mind the sets that much." It came out very matter-of-factly, soft and harmless as a bun from the oven—but it was impossible to take that way.

Kate and I waited, but he didn't continue.

"You didn't mind them, but did you like them?" she prodded. "Did they do anything for you? For the play?"

"For *me*?" Schmerzhauser repeated with a chuckle, as if putting it in those terms would be far too artsy and indulgent for a regular guy like him. "I don't know. . . . But for the play I thought they worked. Well enough. Created a certain mood."

"A pretty vague one. The whole thing was so mushy. So *nostalgic*"— pronounced, as always, with the utmost scorn. "But do you have any idea how much money they spent? It's unbelievable. Why didn't they just use the sets from some old Clifford Odets production? You know? They make a big point of billing it as a *world premiere*, a *new* play, a *new* production, and then they give us that tired old stuff? I feel totally ripped off."

Schmerzhauser sat slouching back in his chair, his eyes down on his stretched-out legs. He didn't say anything. The waitress came and we all ordered more beer.

"I didn't like the play, or production, at all," I said, leaning forward to try to get out of the corner I was sitting in. I looked at Kate. "I agree with you. But I guess I can see how you could argue that the realistic sets, all the detail, the heaviness—just all those things sitting around—acted as a contrast to the total insignificance, and empti-ness, of the characters. The sets are so solid, while the characters are so nebulous and lost. That's the drama. That's what's supposed to break your heart."

"Oh, come on!" Kate exclaimed. "That's so tired! You want to see that, go see Chekhov. No one's done it better. But can't we do some-thing else now?"

"I didn't say *I* thought that," I said. "*I* thought the whole thing stunk. There was nothing to it."

Kate smiled and leaned forward to pat my knee. "It would have been okay if you did. Don't worry, I wasn't attacking you. It's just that that kind of soggy nostalgia is so dangerous. . . ." And as she continued I looked at Schmerzhauser, listening with what seemed to be amused irritation and again trying to get comfortable. There was just too much of him for his chair, and the more he tried to relax into his usual slouch the more uncomfortable he looked, and the more effort it cost him to maintain his habitual angle of careless repose. When the waitress brought more beer he hunched forward, rested his forearm against the table, and again set it awobble—luckily catching an empty bottle before it hit the floor. Then he leaned back and just drank, the hint of a smile flickering now and again at the corner of his mouth, especially when Kate was speaking energetically, in that way that a lot of people (myself included) found rather captivating. If, when I was speaking, I turned in his direction he'd raise his eyebrows a bit in acknowledgment, but he gave no sign that he wanted to participate. On the contrary, his features gradually settled into a distant wry expression. I felt embarrassed for him and angry, but also very self-conscious, and even the most mundane things that Kate and I said began to sound very pretentious to me.

When he'd finished his beer and Kate and I, preparatory to leaving, sat silently finishing ours and smoking, Schmerzhauser hunched toward the table and gingerly placed his empty bottle upon it, then pushed his chair back even farther from the table and hulked with his elbows on his knees.

He shook his head and said, very slowly, the voice of common sense, "I don't know, *somebody* must have thought that play was pretty good. That playwright's pretty well known. And a couple of those actors sure work a lot in the movies. And even the set designer. I'm no expert, but from what I read in the program it seems like he works everywhere. London. *New York.* I don't know. What's the use of all this talk, you know? I'm not gonna argue. I'll admit, I don't know."

"Yeah. Sure," I said, trying to attach, retroactively, a benign tone to what he'd said. "That's the thing—we're just talking. It's not life and death." It didn't work. Kate took an audible drag on her cigarette, then she turned an angry look on me which made me continue, "But it's Kate's job. And she's really good at it. It's why we have the chance to go to New York." I snorted with self-deprecation. "It's not like *I'm* doing anything that could have gotten us there."

"I understand," Schmerzhauser said, with a strained effort at calm. "But since you mention jobs, I'll tell you something I know from my job. As a *Quality Control Supervisor.* You see that Sprite that woman's drinking over there? Or that club soda? Or even our beer? You know how little it costs to produce this stuff? Of course you know how much cheaper it is in stores than here—but you know what it costs to *produce?* Practically nothing. *Nothing.* You pay two bucks, or four, or five bucks here. You think that *play* was a rip-off? This *place* is a rip-off. It's all a rip-off. Everything. A great—big—fuckin'—rip-off."

IV

THE NEXT DAY, Sunday, Schmerzhauser and I did touristy things—I didn't care whether he wanted to or not.

Though it was too late to salvage Kate's opinion of him, I liked being able to tell her that morning that Schmerzhauser and I were going to Pioneer Square, that we were going to take the monorail; that, in other words, we were going to do "normal" things, the things you expected to do with out-of-town visitors. (She declined to accompany us, and demonstrated obvious relief when I told her we wouldn't be back until after dinner.) I also thought it would be good for Schmerzhauser to do something other than just hang out. And, most of all, I felt the need to get out and about myself, to mix in with other people and everyday randomness, after what now struck me as two days in the company of a guy for whom practically every moment seemed preordained: every action, every thought, stifled in the amber of the past.

Once again it was warm, the sky bright and blue. We drove first to see Lake Washington and the University of Washington. The lake did nothing for him, but he seemed to like the campus, beautiful and built of brick—rather like the college we'd graduated from. And having spent so many hours watching televised sports, including college football, he perked up at the sight of Husky Stadium. He did a pretty good imitation of the ABC announcer Keith Jackson's hokey down-home patter: *"Yessiree, we done got ourselves a real rootin' tootin' shoot-out here in Husky Stadium, with All-American quarterback Sonny Sixkiller leading a fine Washington team...."* He asked me, "You remember Sonny Sixkiller?"

I shook my head, "Not really."

After lunch we drove through Fremont, over the drawbridge, and back to Queen Anne, then parked and walked down to Seattle Center. Pointing to the long line, he refused to go to the top of the Space Needle. "I'm not going to see anything I didn't already see from the hill."

"But you come all the way out to Seattle and don't go up the Space Needle?"

"Yeah. What a deprivation."

We went downtown on the monorail. "Just like Disneyland," Schmerzhauser sighed. I took him to Pike Place Public Market; we walked through it, looked at all the other tourists. Then he stood out on the sidewalk watching and nodding his head, "Okay," he said, "guys tossing fish. Got it. Now I can die happy." We caught a free bus to Pioneer Square. At the edge of the logoed and labeled, T-shirted and sports-capped jam of foot traffic we sat down among the homeless, draped on benches, on planters, in drab dirt-blackened clothes like the disavowed shadows of that desperately emblemized crowd. We stared at the totem pole. I took from my pocket a flyer I'd picked up at Pike Place Market advertising a tour of old underground Seattle and promising *Sex! Scandal! Filth!*

"Oh God, don't make me," Schmerzhauser said, after he'd looked it over. "If they've got to resort to this kind of corny hype, it's bad news, believe me."

We browsed Elliott Bay Book Company for a while, then I suggested we walk to Shorey's to look at used books, but we ended up in a dark high-backed booth in an old saloon on what, during Seattle's logging days, was known as Skid Row. With an exaggerated sigh, Schmerzhauser settled in. Here, where no particular reaction was expected of him, where there was nothing by which he was supposed to be impressed or charmed or amused, and nothing that required analysis or thought, where a Seahawks game played on the television above the bar and a wide selection of beers was available, he was content.

In the middle of the summer he'd sent me a postcard of Duke Ellington which read: "I have no excuse for not writing you other than sheer laziness. Nothing is happening in my life. Absolutely nothing." Then, about a month before his visit, another postcard (Frank Sinatra): "Still nothing happening. I'll keep you posted." But I also recalled that one summer during college he had written me, "Without any hope that even *I'll* be able to bear reading it, I've started writing a novel." I was driving a beer and wine delivery truck at that time in hot and filthy Strickland, California, near the San Joaquin Delta—hardly reading, much less writing—and I remember how envious I was, and how I cursed myself for being stupid and incapable.

"Hey," I said, to get his attention away from the football game, "what ever happened to that novel you were writing?"

He was drinking, and he quickly lowered the glass from his lips, bulged his eyes, and acted like he was on the verge of choking. "*Novel?* What novel?"

"You wrote a letter to me one summer saying you were starting a novel. Maybe after sophomore year."

He shook his head. "No. Uh-uh. I wouldn't have done that."

"You mean you wouldn't have started a novel, or you wouldn't have told me?"

"Both. Neither."

"But you wrote that you were."

"No," he insisted. "If I wrote that I wasn't serious."

"You took that creative writing class."

"Yeah, but from old 'A-B' Slabey. How could I not? Do *no* work and you're guaranteed a B. Do a little, a *smidgin*"—indicating with the thumb and forefinger of one hand—"and get an A. That's my kind of class."

I looked at him dubiously.

"Really," he said, turning back to the game. "You're the sensitive writer, not me."

"Ah, fuck you," I said, half seriously.

He smiled without taking his eyes off the game.

It was no use. My friendship with Schmerzhauser had always centered around the dimming of lights, a muting of noise. One morning he'd told me of his mother's death: we had sat drinking all night at a lifeless party in an old house off-campus, had stayed on despairingly and from utter, stubborn frustration long after everyone had left or gone to bed, and we were crunching back over the frozen snow to our dorm, all wrapped up against a bitterly cold wind, with the sky beginning to lighten in the east, and he asked, as of himself, his voice weak and strange, muffled by a scarf, "If your mother wastes away for two years . . . if you wake up, your twelfth birthday, and she's dead . . . what are you supposed to do?" He didn't want a response from me, and I didn't say anything. But I knew then that I could have told him about my own mother, her breakdowns and hospitalizations—and it was the only time and place I ever felt tempted. I never told other friends—nor, later, even Kate, who only met my family on a few afternoon-long visits—because I didn't think it was anything they needed to know, and I didn't trust that they would understand. I didn't tell Schmerzhauser, though, because, mystical as this may sound, I never doubted that he—without knowing—already understood. What I've referred to as our "muting" and "dimming" was an effect, or evidence, of this understanding. But these last three days with him reminded me of how sick I was of such a drowsy, reduced life.

One last time, though, I sat and got drunk with him. We watched the end of the game and then started talking about the long-vanished Seattle Pilots baseball team and our boyhood trading card collections, and he would have stayed there all night, until his flight in the morning, if I hadn't insisted we leave.

As we waited for the bill I made us both laugh by shaking my head very seriously, didactically raising a forefinger, and pronouncing with mock solemnity, "But Jon, now seriously, the thing that's so dangerous about this kind of soggy nostalgia . . ."

IN NOVEMBER, KATE and I moved to New York. We rented a sunless one-bedroom in Chelsea, and she continued to do very well in her career and I continued to write, taking a telemarketing job like the one I'd had in Seattle for an opera company in New York. Although he lived just an hour outside the city, Schmerzhauser and I never managed to get together. Twice we spoke on the phone, but after the second conversation, when he seemed scornful of everything good I had to say about the city, I decided I couldn't afford phone calls and would stick to the mail. I wrote him a brief letter or two, but he didn't respond.

In the meantime, Kate and I began to have trouble. Our twenty months in Seattle had been almost like a long vacation, something less than "real life." It seemed like we were always showing visitors around the city, always doing touristy things with some guest, and we never really moved beyond that odd, infatuated-but-detached state of newcomers to the city—and to each other. We were living together for the first time but yet, like the cost of living compared to that in the city we'd moved from, everything about our life in Seattle seemed to be a little *less*: less serious, less threatening, less permanent. New York, with all of its expenses and pressures, didn't allow us such pleasant distance. In Seattle, no matter how often you take them, the monorail and the little underground train circling between Sea-Tac's terminals always seem a little like amusement park rides—no one, no matter how Disneymografied Times Square and 57th Street become, can maintain such feelings in a New York City subway.

There were more opportunities for jealousy in New York; countless reasons for Kate to suddenly turn on me—or worse, away from me. But, more important, I began to seriously dislike her work: her kind of reckless, meaningless cherry-picking of history. I decided she *was* pretentious, and superficial. She was continually rummaging through the junkshop of the past. She knew her way through it like a pro, and knew everything by sight—but only by sight, not context—and how much it was worth in the marketplace of commercial culture. She could create sensational effects, but no significance. (*Frisson*, unfortunately, became one of her favorite words; Jean Baudrillard her new hero—though I never found any of his writings around the apartment.) Worst of all, though, were the times when the historical images she appropriated—and the suffering represented in them—were demeaned by her usage; as, for example, when a kitschy hipper-than-thou play about a "white trash" family's visit to Graceland unfolded amid projected images of Biafran babies, Hiroshima radiation victims, and a loop of that infamous Saigon street execution. (Of course, this is now commonplace in advertising: an image of a dying skeletal AIDS victim to sell clothes; an image of rag-wrapped battered feet beside one of high-couture heeled sandals to sell a certain newspaper . . .) In such cases I couldn't stop myself from being openly critical of her work, and then, ignoring whatever argument I offered—even if I cited Baudrillard himself—she'd react to me as if I were Jon Schmerzhauser in that crowded café in Seattle.

But I suspected I had become Schmerzhauser-like for her at other times too. She began to complain about my moodiness—as if she'd never noticed it before. She complained that I never showed her my stories anymore. That I didn't like to go out as much as she did. And then one night, after she surprised me by bringing home three of the most pretentious, artsy, empty-headed dilettantes I'd ever been forced to spend an evening with, the silent distance I kept from her new friends made her proclaim the comparison outright: I was, she said furiously, "as hostile and rude as that big, bloated, balding, do-nothing friend of yours."

In short, things got rather ugly between us. After less than a year in New York we split up—not long before she took a job at VH1.

And during this time not a word from Schmerzhauser—and none since. I made sure to send him a card with my post-Kate New York address, but after that I became too busy to concern myself with his continued silence. I started work on a series of connected stories, started to contribute an occasional book review to a rather ramshackle weekly paper, and of course I still had my paying job at the opera company. What I know about Schmerzhauser's life since his Seattle visit I learned by chance, when I ran into an old dormmate from New Jersey one slate-skyed winter afternoon in 1993 near the Lincoln Center fountain. He had also maintained sporadic contact with Schmerzhauser after graduation, and he was able to tell me that Schmerzhauser had gotten married in the winter of 1992 to someone he'd met at work. He couldn't tell me if the bride was a filler operator. Nor could he tell me—and he seemed to find it odd that I asked with such interest—if Schmerzhauser's stepmother and father had moved to Arizona. Nor, finally, did he know how it was all working out, since the letter mentioning the marriage, received the year before, was the last he'd had from him.

When I asked him if Schmerzhauser seemed happy in the letter, he shook his head in bewilderment, shrugged his shoulders. "You know Schmerzhauser," he said.

I don't doubt that someday I will get the answers to these questions from Schmerzhauser himself. I think of him often, but I don't yet feel any particular urge to reestablish contact. Someday I know I'll call our college alumni association, or otherwise track him down, and I'll find out if, as he put it in his last postcards to me, *nothing, absolutely nothing* has continued to be the only thing happening in his life since the last time we saw each other. But for the present it seems better to keep things as they are: our friendship relegated to the protected space of memory, where it was always most at home . . . the two of us running patterns in the lap of Seattle's long twilight, pale eggshell fragile—within a stop-time spell we don't dare mention; pausing to look up and all around us at the light—still fantastically there, *still*— with wonder and gratitude.

The great plain around Ralston is some forty or fifty miles wide
from east to west, and to both north and south stretches to
the horizon, literally as level as the sea and seemingly as
boundless.

—*William H. Brewer, April* 1862

THE FIRST LONG-DISTANCE call, immediately following the surgery,
had been to let me know that everything had gone as expected,
without any complications.

"Mom's fine," Paul said, from the lobby of Ralston Memorial Hospital. "She'll be laid up for a while, of course, but then she'll be as
good as new. She'll be able to walk again without pain. In fact, the
doctor was surprised she'd been able to go so long without the surgery. The hip was in such bad shape most people wouldn't have been
able to stand it."

"Well," I said, "that's Mom. She's tough. In a weird way."

I hadn't been able to leave New York for the operation. Within
my first year in the city I'd discovered that selling opera season tickets over the phone in New York, even to those who'd bought them
in previous years, required a masochistic impulse I lacked, and after

months of inadequate commissions I took a full-time job that opened up in the development office, composing grant proposals, mostly. My boss there was kind enough to let me start a little later than usual on Mondays and Tuesdays—which, with the weekends, at least allowed me four good consecutive mornings of writing time—but she was quite rigid when it came to unscheduled time off. Paul assured me on the phone that night that I hadn't missed anything; "Mom's fine," he repeated. He didn't want me to feel bad. But his very kindness inevitably raised feelings of guilt. I wondered if I should have been more insistent with my boss, and if I hadn't underreacted to news of my mother's hip replacement, like a sound sleeper half-awakened by a telephone who immediately plummets back to the depths as soon the ringing stops. But that's a misleading image. Rather, I usually felt wide awake in New York, and my family's calls tended to break upon my life in the city like waves of sleep—sometimes nightmarish, sometimes quite sweet—in which, either way, it seemed dangerous to stay too long submerged.

During the second long-distance call, the next day, I spoke to my mother herself. She sounded remarkably well.

"I feel so much better," she told me.

"You're comfortable?" I asked. "No pain? The stitches don't pull or anything?"

"No, no. Just fine."

Paul and Mary and I had been anxious about how she'd handle the operation, since in the past her emotional balance—always wavery, and becoming ever more so with age—had been upset by ailments and events much less severe. A head cold, the flu, a couple consecutive nights of poor sleep, even short vacation trips could send her reeling into what we called one of her "episodes"—weeks of frantic pointless activity—or sink her into depression. But on the phone that day she was cheerful. And not too cheerful.

I was all ready to talk about the trauma of being opened up by some strange surgeon, of having a piece of yourself removed and replaced by plastic. I couldn't get over this idea. I was ready to be sympathetic. But she didn't want to talk about the operation and her brand-new hip. Nor about the long recuperation time, to which she—who so often obsessed upon the unpleasant—seemed to have given no thought. She good-naturedly but firmly rebuffed each of my approaches.

Other matters occupied her mind.

"You think you can take back those records of yours this time?" she asked—a puzzling non sequitur.

"What records?"

"In that front bedroom closet. You've got boxes of record albums in there."

"I don't know, Mom."

"And other stuff, too. In the garage. Books and things."

"I don't know," I repeated. "I haven't really thought of it."

"Well, think about it," she advised me, agreeably enough. "Maybe there're some things you want. Otherwise everything's going. Maybe you could bring home an empty suitcase."

"Maybe," I said. Then I concluded our conversation as quickly as possible, hung up, and sat for a few minutes completely bemused in the humid August dusk of my rented studio apartment, until the phone on my lap made my thigh begin to feel sweaty. I got up, closed the window, turned on the noisy air conditioner and a light, sat down again with the newspaper, glancing absentmindedly over its lead story on the wide gap between Clinton and Dole in the polls, then belatedly came into a profound chagrin.

I no longer felt any guilt about not being in Ralston for her surgery. "To hell with her," I thought first; then, "There's nothing back there I want."

Though, to be honest, five days later I was at La Guardia with some open space in my luggage—just in case.

*   *   *

IN FIVE YEARS in New York I had become something of a city-dweller cliché. I wasn't so bad as those New York natives who supposedly never venture outside of their own neighborhoods—after all, I lived on East 81st, in an ugly tenement-style building, and while my rent was surprisingly better than it would have been in other areas, I couldn't afford to purchase all of life's necessities on the Upper East Side. But I almost never left Manhattan.

When I first met Risa Templeton at a party in a mutual friend's apartment, she was astounded to hear I hadn't spent even an hour outside the city for fifteen months; not since I flew to California for my grandmother's funeral in July of 1994.

"Don't you miss nature?" she asked. "Don't you miss *trees?*"

"I go to Central Park."

"I mean trees without a backdrop of apartment buildings."

I shrugged and told her, honestly, that it never even occurred to me to miss them.

What I didn't tell her that night—though even then I correctly sensed I eventually would, or could—was that I had whole orchards in my head. That trees were the chief, inescapable feature of my childhood landscape. That I had not only raked and played in their leaves, climbed (almost daily) and once even napped in their limbs, but I had trimmed their branches, felled them whole, both shaken and knocked their nuts and then picked them up. That a walnut tree's catkins were as familiar to me as my own fingers (though catkins smelled more like toes or feet or dirty socks). That, on the spot, I could have drawn every subtle phase of a walnut's maturation: from its first huge green fruitlike look to its familiar wrinkled hard-shelled guise (and even its occasional spoiled, blackened, spiderweb-filled end). Or sketched out how a walnut tree twig, if split correctly, reveals a chambered pith similar to the inside of those dry old cocoons you sometimes find clinging to them: those ossified casketlike remains of caterpillars who, for reasons no one in my family could ever explain, never made it to the next, winged, stage. None of which information I much valued or wanted to carry around with me—but there it was. As far as I was concerned I had a lifetime's fill of trees. What excited me still, almost daily, was the city's right-angled, architectural solidity. The feel of concrete beneath my feet. The way the late-afternoon sun gilded the massive brick fronts of East 79th Street apartment buildings—their countless windows' repetition and regularity superimposed like the stanzas of a poem upon the unseen, unknown lives within.

AT SAN FRANCISCO International Airport I rented a car for the drive to Ralston.

I was always met at the airport while my father was alive. It was one of those things which, in my father's imperative-ridden world, one simply *did*. Even when his health was failing after his heart attack, he'd be waiting with my mother (and sometimes Mary or Paul) at the gate—smiling and eager—at one o'clock in the morning. These were the happiest times of my college breaks. Set far apart from the city and suburbs, from anyplace where people lived bounded and bothered by the quotidian, the airport seemed as charged with pure possibility as an empty stage. It was a utopia of comings and goings, arrivals and escapes; a sterile *no place* in which nothing contravened or refracted or dissipated whatever persisted between my father and me—whatever needs or desires or sentimentality could still make us happy to see each other again.

Once my father died, though, that was the end of being met at the airport. My mother, even if she'd wanted to, couldn't have managed the ninety-mile drive from Ralston to San Francisco, and Paul and Mary were always busy with their children or work. Beneath such excuses, such "practical considerations," we all agreed to partially conceal the judgment rendered by their absence. The truth, I thought, that Saturday as I crossed the brilliant sparkling Bay on the San Mateo Bridge, was that I'd abandoned my mother and family by moving to the opposite end of the continent, and so they, as a kind of punishment, had abandoned certain of their obligations to me. If I didn't feel compelled to live close enough to them to help care for my mother, they didn't feel compelled to practice familial duties such as picking me up at the airport. It was petty and unspoken and fair enough. And the thought of it filled me with a kind of happy resentment. After all, in my family, such shallow hostility induced far less guilt than sympathy, forgiveness, and magnanimity would have. Understanding of that sort would have been paralyzing.

The wind buffeting in the open windows grew steadily hotter as I drove east until by the time I saw the white windmills lined singly, toy-soldier-like, across the uppermost curves of the Altamont Pass I was sweating. But I left the air conditioner off. The dry heat was familiar, reassuring, while the windmills—which had begun to sprout sixteen years before as I began thinking about college; symbols, I'd thought, of a brave new future—were the worse for wear. The "egg-beaters" in particular, I discovered as I drove in among them, were eaten with rust, their tall elliptical blades idle. Then, sooner than I expected, between two parched hillsides, the irrigated green patch-work floor of the valley opened up before me—an ancient inland seabed, now tinseled with canals and aqueducts, overflowing with smog; I took my foot off the gas and coasted down the steep descent into its stifling heat.

At the outskirts of Ralston I turned off Route 132 and cut over to Weston Avenue, near its dead end. Out there, at its farthest reach, it was still a country road—but only for a short stretch. As I headed toward town I passed housing tracts with names like Quail Gardens and Vintage Estates (with its Chardonnay Lane and Cabernet Court) where there had once been, respectively, a horse farm—with neither gardens nor quail—and a rickety secret dog track, its rails almost entirely hidden by weeds, where greyhounds were trained (according to Paul) for Florida. Before I could ride a bike, he'd "give me a pump" out there (I'd sit on the seat while he stood pedaling) and we'd watch, unseen, from the roadside. All the way up Weston I squeezed meager satisfaction from knowing what had once been; a bitter, sentimental satisfaction which peaked as I approached Collier Road and came to the strip of stores, opposite the Albertson's shopping center, where my family's house and acre of walnuts had once been. There was no longer a trace of them. The trees, many of them dead, had been torn out. Mary had wanted to move the house, but it wasn't worth the expense. It came down. The shed too, its cement foundation jackhammered into bits. One day my father had written my name for me in that cement, saying kindly that it would always be there. But he was wrong. It was gone four years before this visit; he himself was gone six years before that.

My mother had moved to the center of town, where my father would never have agreed to live. The narrow streets and smallish lots would have aggravated his claustrophobia. The pitiful Waspy pretension of the neighborhood, its streets named for Ivy League schools, would have grated upon him. In truth, though, the new house ("new" forever, regardless of its construction in the fifties and of how long she lives there) is very much like the one in which I grew up: a ranch-style, with exactly the same number of rooms, distributed in much the same way. Three bedrooms and three bathrooms, too, though my mother lives alone and almost never has overnight guests. But its superficial similarity to our house on Weston counts against it: it has neither distinctive charm nor any memories.

Mary dislikes it so much that during my last visit, for my grandmother's funeral, she tried to persuade my mother to move into my grandmother's house, which is less than a mile away.

My mother wouldn't hear of it.

"I have my house," my mother said, "finally. This is exactly what I've always wanted."

As I pulled into its driveway I said to myself sarcastically, "Home sweet home."

* * *

"HELLO. HELLO," I heard my mother calling, after I'd hardly gotten in the front door, not yet having introduced myself to the round, red-headed woman who'd opened it for me.

"Hello," my mother repeated in a strong voice. *"I'm in here."*

"Is she up?" I asked the woman, with surprise.

"Oh no." She smiled. "No. Come and see."

She, my mother's twenty-four-hour attendant, led me into the brightly sunlit living room, where my mother lay propped against a hillside of pillows in her large bed in the very center of the space.

"Hello, Vincent!" my mother said, raising her arms ambiguously, as if at once to call for a hug and to gesture at her privileged place in such unusual surroundings. "How do you like this?"

"Wow," I said, and I stepped around furniture to her bedside, where I leaned down and hugged her.

"I'm glad to see you," she said.

"Yes," I answered.

The Queen Anne–style furniture had been bunched together to either side of the bed, and the television from her bedroom brought into this normally little-used room.

"It's been so long," my mother said.

"I guess," I said, "though it doesn't seem that long. Two years."

"You look the same. Still too thin." she smiled. "Sit down, sit down."

I sat in a straight-backed chair beside the bed.

"How are you feeling?" I asked.

"Pretty good. I wish I could get out of this darn bed more often! But otherwise . . ."

"How long do you have to stay down?"

"Five more weeks," she said. "If I'm lucky, maybe less. I hope, for once, I'm lucky."

"Oh, you've got it real tough here," I teased her, and she smiled again. "Look at this setup!"

"Yeah," she agreed. "It's okay. Nicer. When I first came home from the hospital I was in my bedroom, and it was so dark. All day long, no matter how bright it was outside—and we've just been having beautiful weather. Like a tomb. So Paul moved me out here." She raised her arms again in that same gesture, habitual or rehearsed. "I'm not dead yet," she said.

"Far from it," I agreed.

She politely asked me how my flight was.

Then she pointed toward the large plate-glass windows and sliding glass door opposite her bed. "Doesn't the backyard look nice?"

I nodded.

"This hip was giving me such trouble I had to have a gardener do most of it this year, but didn't he do a good job? Now *that's* the kind of yard I always wanted. Only had to wait forty-odd years to get it. Look at that."

"Those roses are beautiful," I said.

"Aren't they? Those are new. I'd started some from clippings from the old house, but they weren't any good. They weren't any good there even! I don't know why I bothered. I had to tear them out. But these I bought. These are new. They're beautiful. I like that backyard a lot now," she said, her hands folded and resting, self-satisfied as a child's, on the sheet. "It could be in *House Beautiful*."

"At least the Ralston edition of it," I said, aiming to check her a bit, since the new yard wasn't much different from the one at our old house. I smiled.

"Well, I'm sure it's nothing like the places they've got in New York," she retorted, smiling also.

But, as I'd suspected, the roses were simply the first entry in her Catalog of New Acquisitions, and she wouldn't be diverted from it for long. "And did you see that lamp I got before I went in for the operation?" she asked.

"Ah," I nodded, as if she were showing me a Brancusi.

"And that?" she asked. I looked where she, from her place in bed, directed. She could have been five years old, pointing out her newest purchases and saying *mine, mine, mine*—or more simply *me, me, me*. There were artificial flower arrangements, unrecognizable landscapes, a new chair, and a large oil painting of a glowing Aryan child. After I'd responded appropriately, with neither disapproval nor any questions about cost, she turned her attention, for a time, to me.

"Seen any operas lately?" she asked.

"No. It's not the season."

"The job going okay?"

"Fine. Nothing exciting. It pays the bills."

"Are you still writing?"

"Yes."

"When do I get to see something?"

I made a face.

"What?" she asked.

"I'm still working on the collection of stories."

"You've sure been working on it a long time."

"I'm trying to teach myself to write. It takes a long time. . . ."

Embarrassed for me—by my secretive, perverse persistence at something that would never pay—Mary and Paul scrupulously did me the favor of never mentioning my writing, but my mother sometimes, still, surprised me with her interest. I was tempted to let myself go, to say something without irony or sarcasm, but I hesitated too long at the edge, not risking it.

She gestured toward a glossy hardcover, a hugely popular sloppily written suspense novel, on a coffee table near the bed. "I'm reading that. It's awfully violent."

"You like it?"

"It keeps you reading. It's entertaining."

"Then you wouldn't like what I try to write," I said, lamely trying to recapture her attention.

But it was already too late.

"It's a page-turner," she said. "It's pretty clever."

I nodded, then we sat silently a few minutes.

"I'm so glad you're here," my mother said.

I nodded again.

She wasn't yet sixty-five, but she looked at least five years younger—her face firm, lined only lightly—and acted ten years older. Her hair was blonder—dyed—than I ever remembered seeing it; "like it was before any of you were born," she told me and Mary later in the week, in a tone we both took as accusatory.

She began to talk about her plans for the front yard.

Then, luckily, the doorbell rang twice in quick succession, the front door crashed open into the wall, and there was my four-year-old nephew, doe-eyed and dark-haired, grinning and giggling in the doorway of the living room.

"Hello!" I said, getting to my feet, and he fled, shrieking excitedly, back in the direction of the front door. A few moments later he reappeared with his mother, making a show of clinging to her as she walked in, tripping her up. Mary said, "Justin, will you knock it off! Look at you! Will you? Justin!"

I thought, could my father have ever imagined he'd have a grandson named *Justin Hibbert?*

"Do you remember Uncle Vincent?" Mary asked him.

Then my nine-year-old niece came in last, carrying a bunch of flowers. She shyly, dutifully hugged me as soon as she entered.

"Sandra, you remember me," I said.

"*Yes,*" she answered, as if I were a fool to doubt it.

She held the flowers out to my mother. "I picked these for you, Nonna," she said.

Justin climbed onto the bed with my mother. "Careful," Mary told him. "Justin, careful. Calm down. Don't hurt Nonna."

After the flowers had been put into water, and Justin had been coaxed into shaking my hand, we all settled around my mother in her bed, in her glory. Mary asked about my flight, then she started telling stories about the kids, while my mother acted as her unruly chorus, interjecting comments, interpretations, sometimes threatening to completely derail the narrative. I was happy to listen. They are pretty kids, normal kids. As I listened—in spite of my mother—I forgot I was sitting in a living room which looked like a furniture warehouse, and the sickroom air was dispelled by the health and vigor of the children. They brought out their stash of toys and we played awhile.

Then I went to use my mother's bathroom and was confronted by all the modifications for her new, *physical*, infirmity: the handrails in the tub and beside the toilet; the grotesquely heightened toilet seat. *Christ!* I exclaimed, laughing at my surprise. But I couldn't quite shake it. The toilet seat suffered from elephantiasis; a foot and a half tall, thick—though obviously hollow—and beige-colored, as if dingy from use. I knew it was there because of the hip replacement, nothing else. But it evoked so much more embarrassment. All the stupid things I wish I never knew.

I left the bathroom without using it and closed the door behind me, thinking, the children shouldn't see this.

"NOW'S THE PERFECT time to introduce the idea of someone living here with Mom," Paul said. "We can just let the present arrangement carry over. Like it's no big deal. The most natural thing in the world."

We'd spent the afternoon of my first full day in Ralston pretending the only thing wrong with my mother was her hip. Paul and Kris and their two sons, Paul Jr. and Robby, and Mary and Dave Hibbert and their kids, along with me, devoted ourselves to entertaining her. We got along pretty well. I knew how to act around them. I rarely mentioned New York. When I did, telling about a famous tenor who'd waddled into the office and caused a huge stir, or the beauty of Central Park in the spring, Paul and Mary inevitably flashed skeptical deflating looks, as if to say, "But *you're* from Ralston too. Don't forget it."

After dinner, Paul asked me to go for a walk with him, and as we walked past one neat still yard after another, ranch-style house after ranch-style house, he revealed the real situation.

"We can't do it anymore. We can't take care of her. It's a full-time job. Ask Mary. Ask Kris. They're really the ones stuck with it. I'm at work too much to be much help, but those two. *Every day*," Paul said, his voice high and wheezy with exasperation and allergies. "*Every day*. They're over at the house. Always some emergency or crisis. And she can be *mean*. She's so sweet today, with the kids and everything. Don't believe it," he scoffed. "Do everything she wants, she'll still stir up trouble. Kris does her shopping for her, brings the groceries home, puts the change on the table, and Mom sits down and *counts the change!*"

Walking along beside him, I silently shook my head. His dark hair had receded, emphasizing the broad level hairline he'd inherited from our father, and had become gray at the temples, as my father's had been around the time I was born. Paul had managed, after many years, to put the Strickland warehouse into the black; had managed, as our father had, to dutifully compensate for the laziness and stupidity of Uncle Joey (*and* his son, *and* two of his daughters: employed in Ralston as salespersons and a secretary). But Paul was not our father, and our mother was all too much for him. His words poured out:

"And the money she spends. She thinks she's Howard Hughes. I can't keep enough in her account. Someone has to be around. Because it's all the time now. Not good periods and bad. But pretty much one bad spell after another. The doctor says that's how it goes as they get older. The cycles speed up, get closer together, even overlap. And she doesn't eat right. She eats junk. Someone has to live with her. She can't live alone anymore. She can't do anything for herself."

None of this was news. I'd heard these things for years. At my safe distance I thought something should have been done two years before. But in Ralston, Paul and Kris and Mary bore my mother with *santa pazienza* (as my grandmother would have said)—the patience of a saint—fortified by a certain amount of simple denial: it's not easy to admit that your mother is helpless and can't really act like your mother anymore, nor the grandmother of your children.

"I've told her how much per year she has to live on. It's more than any single person needs," Paul continued. "But nothing helps. I've tried to work with her. She eats with us at least once a week. . . ."

I nodded sympathetically, but we had arrived at the neighborhood around my grandmother's house and I became distracted by the smell of freshly mown lawn in the day's last heat, by the tree limbs arching over the narrow roads, and the shadows, not nearly as deep as those beneath the walnut trees on Weston; by flower scents so fleeting as to seem wholly imagined, by the smell of wet sprinklered sidewalks— not fields; by all those sensations whose first experiences seemed to have remained entire but desiccated in memory and which now re- acted to this repetition of themselves as a certain gimmicky business card once brought home by my father reacted to water: with a sur- prising, thirsty, spongelike expansiveness—almost crowding out the present. As a child I'd firmly believed this beautiful old neighborhood of two-story houses around Almeda Park was immune from the chaos and unhappiness of my home on Weston Avenue. I was now almost ready to believe it again. But Paul raised his voice as if he'd noticed I wasn't listening—or maybe just in conclusion—and kept me from slipping completely away from the present.

"It can't be avoided any longer," he said. "It's the best thing." He shook his head, his eyes on the sidewalk. "We have to do it. We have to do it," he repeated.

I knew he wanted me to tell him he was right; to absolve him of his guilt and become implicated in it. But he was also half hoping I'd say he was mistaken.

"You're right," I said, "we have to. We should all talk about this." When we returned to the house, though, we didn't mention it. At one point just before the party broke up, when the kids had become variously cranky or exhaustedly overexcited, subject to tumbles and tears and sudden animosities, and my mother in spite of the noise was nodding amid her pillows in what I'd taken to calling "the Throne Room," Paul, Kris, Mary, and I left Dave to watch the kids while we stole conspiratorially into the front yard. But in the driveway we discovered one of Justin's sneakers and readily gave ourselves over to laughing and wondering how long he'd been running around with only one shoe. Then we ended up discussing the plans for dinner on the forthcoming Friday.

The night was calm and not too hot and none of us really wanted to spoil it.

THE NEXT DAY, Dede, the round, redheaded woman, helped my mother get ready for her walk. Then my mother and I set off, at a snail's pace.

I had to remind myself that my mother was *not that old*. It wasn't just the hip replacement, slowing her, which led me to think otherwise. For ten years at least, since my father died when she wasn't even near sixty, she had seemed elderly: peevish, and tormented by a self-absorbed aimlessness—her own "second childhood," which, however, had nothing to do with senility. She'd call me on the phone to tell me of her latest short-lived interest—flower arranging, pinochle, quilting, the junior college's theatrical productions—but she couldn't help but conclude by revealing the futility of it all.

"Look what I'm doing!" she'd call to say; then end up, almost always, asking, "What *should* I do?"

Sometimes I made the mistake of trying to answer. From this elderly child I tried to shape the mother I'd always wanted, suggesting interests I'd wished she'd had—my own interests—none of them right for her.

As we walked she kept a hand on my arm to steady herself; she talked, I listened. She told me what she wanted to do with her front yard. She commented on her neighbor's yards as we slowly passed.

"There," she said, "see that? That planter? How it curves like that with those different levels? That's what I'd like to do in front of my house."

"You've got your work cut out for you," I said.

"Well, I'm going to have to hire a landscaper. When this darn hip . . ." She broke off with an exaggerated sigh, suggesting good-natured frustration.

Then, out of nowhere, she asked, "Have you had a look in the garage at those books of yours?"

"No, Mom," I said. "I haven't really thought of it yet. What are they?"

"Mostly schoolbooks, I think. Some magazines."

"Well, I probably won't want them."

"Paul wanted his. I made him come take his a few weeks ago."

"I don't think I want mine. I've got no use for textbooks."

"But there're those records in that closet. All your old albums, two or three boxes of them. In the front bedroom."

"I don't even have a turntable, Mom. But I'll look at them."

"Other stuff, too. You should see what you want. The rest I'm throwing out."

"Fine," I said.

"You've got a lot of stuff here," she persisted.

"Oh, come on!" I said. "Not that much. I live in New York. I don't exactly have storage space."

"Well, I'm not going to be your warehouse."

"Who's asking you to? I've hardly left anything. What's the problem, Mom? I'm not asking you to keep a bedroom here for me. This house has nothing to do with me. But a corner of the garage? Two boxes in a closet?"

"There's more than that," she said. "And it's my house, isn't it? Why do I have to explain to you?"

I threw my hands upward. "You don't. That's fine. That's right. You're absolutely right. Okay? Let's drop it."

But I couldn't yet. In a joking voice I said, "Besides, if you make me clear out all my stuff I'll have no reason to come visit."

"Let's go back now," she said abruptly.

"Mom! I was just kidding."

"It's not that. I can't walk very far yet. We've gone far enough. Let's turn around."

We turned around. She kept her hand off my arm and we walked back to the house in silence.

I'd been in California less than forty-eight hours. In Ralston, with my mother, things always went south in a hurry.

ASIDE FROM PERSONAL touches like the potted plants on the wide front step, Mary and Dave Hibbert's house was indistinguishable from the houses around it. It was the lot that had sold Mary on it. From the orchards on the eastern edge of Ralston that the eight-year-old tract had replaced, a single massive old walnut tree had survived, and it stood in the center of the Hibberts' large backyard. Mary and I sat in its shade in lawn chairs late Tuesday afternoon, watching Sandra and Justin rummage about in the garden, which ran along one side of the plank fence.

"Have you seen Mom's new watercolor?" Mary asked.

"No. Paul mentioned it, too. But I haven't noticed it," I said.

"It's in the hallway. It's awful."

"I can't believe she didn't tell me about it," I said. "She told me about everything else she's bought since last time I was here."

"Don't worry, she'll get to it. And when she does, maybe you can find out what happened to Dad's baby picture that used to be in that spot. I haven't been able to get a straight answer out of her."

"Did you check the garbage?"

"Don't even joke about that," Mary said. "Around Christmas I found her wedding album out in the garage, on top of some boxes she'd put out for the Salvation Army."

I couldn't help laughing. "That's nice."

"Isn't it? She claimed she didn't know how it got there."

I laughed again. Mary gave me a quick censorious look.

I tried to put on a straight face. But how long can one be outraged by the same transgressions? Sometimes I couldn't help but laugh at the vista of hopelessness revealed by my mother's actions: the foreground barren, the background, if I dared look, even grimmer. It was one thing to think that photos and other objects so fetishistically charged for us held absolutely no meaning for her; it was even worse to believe they were equally loaded for her and *that* was precisely why she got rid of them. In the former case, I'd discover a troubling, seemingly pathological disaffection; in the latter, I made out dark forms of hostility, hatred, vengeance. This landscape would appear suddenly before me, foreground and background occupying me in turn. It required an effort to shut it all out.

I halfheartedly made that effort: "Maybe she didn't realize what it was."

"It would've been awfully hard to mistake for anything else," Mary said. "When she does things like that, I want to grab her by her shoulders and shake her—say, '*Snap out of it!* What's wrong with you? Isn't there *anyone* home?'"

"No, there's not. Not really."

"I don't know. I still can't believe it. . . . If she'd *try*. Maybe if she'd stop thinking about herself for a change. Feeling sorry for herself. I know I sound like Dad, but *if she had a little ambition. Discipline.*" Mary smiled self-consciously. "*Something.*"

"But that's just it—that *something* is what she doesn't have. That's what the illness is."

"It's hard to believe. How can anyone not—"

"Or more specifically," I interrupted, "how can *our mother* not . . . ? That's the thing."

Mary gave me a look. "You know what I mean."

"I do."

"Okay. It's just that it doesn't make . . ." Then she stopped as Justin approached.

"Look," he said, "I found one." He held out a zucchini hardly longer than one of my fingers.

"Wow!" Mary said, overly effusive. "That's really nice."

Sandra, a few feet behind her brother, one arm akimbo from her snake-slim trunk, observed her mother's reaction with a supercilious air.

"I found it myself," Justin said.

"Neat," I said.

"Boy!" Mary exclaimed, taking it and looking at it. "But, you know, I told you we picked all the ripe ones this morning. I don't think this one's big enough to eat yet."

"I told him that, Mom," Sandra said.

"It's okay," Mary told her. "It's cute, isn't it?"

"Yeah," Justin agreed.

"But let's wait for bigger ones," Mary said, and reassured him, so that he returned to the garden without embarrassment, though all the while Sandra followed him, shaking her head and her long sun-lightened hair and saying, "I *told* you. I *told* you."

"*Sandra,*" Mary called after her. "Come on. Leave him alone." Then quietly she said to me, "She thinks she knows everything lately, and she never lets Justin forget it."

"She's very precocious."

"Yeah, but she can wear you out with it."

We watched them in the garden a minute, then I asked Mary, "Well, what about getting someone to live with Mom?"

She sighed.

"We have to do it," I said, echoing Paul.

"I don't know. . . ."

"What don't you know?"

"She's not going to like it."

"She'll like the alternative a lot less," I said.

The corners of Mary's mouth turned down at this, as disapprovingly as if I'd named the alternative—which, in this case, I was still too much a Torno to even consider uttering.

"We should all meet with her before I go, and talk about it," I said.

Mary sighed again and kept her eyes on the kids.

"Mom!" Sandra yelled from the garden, interrupting us. "Look what Justin's doing!"

"What?" Mary asked, quickly standing.

"*What?*" Justin asked also, perturbed.

"He's planting the squash," Sandra said.

"I am not," Justin said.

"You are," Sandra insisted.

"I'm burying it," Justin corrected her.

"Oh God," Mary said. "It's okay. Leave him alone, Sandra. He's not hurting anything."

Mary sat back down. "He's on a kick. He buries everything now."

"Like he's a dog or something?"

"No, no. You don't know about Lime Sherbet? I never told you this?"

"No. Lime sherbet?"

"That was Justin's parakeet. He was green. Not green like lime sherbet, but you know. . . ." She shrugged. "Justin had Lime Sherbet out one day, playing with him. His wings were clipped. I don't know why. They did it at the pet store. He was playing with him, all overexcited, running after the poor bird, and—I shouldn't laugh. It's not funny. But he stepped right on him."

"That's horrible!"

"I know. It was horrible. Justin was heartbroken. And Sandra was, too, and furious. It was terrible. They were crying. I didn't know what to do. So we ended up having a big funeral for Lime Sherbet. Graveside prayers and everything. We wrapped up his crushed little body in a paper towel and dug a hole. It was very touching."

"I bet."

"I felt so bad for them. I felt so bad for the bird! But the ceremony seemed to help. We talked about Lime Sherbet in Heaven. With Nonno, Sandra said. Yes, with Nonno. She never knew him, of course, but one day she wanted to know why she didn't have two grandfathers like her friend. So, with Nonno. And we were very serious. Very serious. Then Justin asked, 'Is the paper towel in Heaven, too?' "

"Now there's a good question!" I laughed. "A Catholic theologian in the making. Or a heretic. What did you tell him?"

"I said—not to get too complicated—'Yes, the paper towel's in Heaven too.' " She laughed. "I didn't know what to say!" She shook her head. "I don't think Sandra bought it. She didn't say anything, but she kind of rolled her eyes. But Justin seemed to find it comforting."

Mary and I never returned to the topic of my mother's living situation. There were too many distractions; even when the kids didn't interrupt us, Mary's attention inevitably wandered to them. When Dave came home from work I suggested to her that we go someplace we could talk, but she pretended not to hear me and walked off with Justin to help him look for something in his closet.

After dinner I played pool with Sandra on the table that used to be in our house on Weston Avenue. It was much too large for Mary's living room and Dave absolutely hated it, but Mary couldn't stand the thought of getting rid of it. She'd never forgotten, she said, the night my father surprised everyone by bringing it home on the back of a one-ton stake truck.

*   *   *

MY FATHER WOULD have called Dede an "Okie": meaning she had a
country accent, little money, and no apparent ethnic affinities. From
my father's vantage point in the bigoted Ralston social order this
would have placed her near the very bottom; well beneath the Portuguese, who were the butt of every relatively good-natured joke,
and just above the level of Mexicans and blacks, who were the sub-
jects of more vicious and cowardly ones. Portuguese jokes and some
Okie jokes were told in front of women, children, Portuguese (or
Porta-*ghees*, as they were called by nearly everyone in Ralston), and
some Okies. Whereas jokes about Mexicans and blacks were passed
only between whites, since they embodied a real malevolence. I never
heard my father tell a joke about blacks or Mexicans. He would've
felt it demeaned him in my eyes. But this didn't mean he wasn't a
racist. Whereas my mother, as much as was possible, was not bigoted.
Though sometimes I cruelly wondered whether this had more to do
with neediness and revenge than principle. It was her own suspicious
family—me, Paul, Mary, the ghost of my father—whom my mother
distrusted; she wholeheartedly accepted Dede as she'd accept any
stranger who from unfamiliarity, politeness, or professional duty gave
credence to her every word and complaint. And the more un-Torno-
like Dede was, the more my mother was charmed.

One night during dinner Dede announced to me, "I'm a cowgirl,
you know. I'm from Oakdale."

I didn't immediately recognize the connection. I glanced at my
mother, but her eyes rested pleasantly upon Dede and she gave me
no help. "You ride, you mean?" I asked.

"A little. When I was a kid. But no, not for a long time. I go to
the rodeo every year, though. I *love* the rodeo!"

"Oh. Right," I nodded. The Oakdale Rodeo. I'd driven past the
empty grandstands once when I was in high school. I remembered
the roadside billboard: OAKDALE: COWBOY CAPITAL OF THE WORLD.
"They still have it?"

"Oh yeah. Going strong. Good as ever."

I nodded and smiled.

"You've never been either?" she asked.

"No."

"So close and never been." Dede shook her head. "Well, I already told your Mom I'll take her next year if she wants to go. If you're home, I'll take you too."

"I've always wanted to go," my mother said, sounding convincingly deprived.

I smirked at her.

"I have," she insisted, so I didn't remind her that she'd always professed a great fear of horses—of any mammal, really, much over the size of a cat.

I had a much harder time than Dede did in engaging my mother's interest. I avoided any topic really important to me, since I was sure her reaction would be disappointing, and I waited futilely instead for her to reveal some facet of her "old" self. To this end I suggested we play Scrabble one night after dinner, as we had often done when I was a boy. But it quickly became apparent that my nephews and niece had gotten their hands on the game. A lot of tiles were missing, particularly, for some reason, vowels. Much sooner than expected, our game came to a standstill. We were helpless to form any words from the odd assortment of consonants left on our trays. I said, "Tomorrow I'll go buy a new game." But I didn't.

Instead, most nights I ended up at the video rental chain, looking for a movie that wasn't serious or depressing. My mother had never liked serious movies—by my teens I was convinced that depressing movies or books were actually dangerous to her emotional health—and now she insisted on completely upbeat titles. The cynicism and transparency of most of these movies disgusted me, but when I lived in San Francisco for a couple of years after dropping out of graduate school I'd worked in a bookstore and learned that this childlike appetite for sugarcoated fare wasn't peculiar to my mother. So I'd select a suitably banal video and she and Dede and I would watch it to-gether. I'd slump in an overstuffed chair on one side of my mother's bed, Dede would sit in a straight-backed chair on the other, and in front of the glowing screen we'd pass time together without the slightest exertion. It was not unusual for my mother to fall asleep, nor for Dede to wake her with her loud laughter; in this way they made a good pair. We'd watch obstacles overcome, lovers and fam-ilies reunited, and the magical working of some beneficent generic Spirit. All things were possible. Sadness and failure were anomalies.

It made me want to spit at the screen.

At the end, inevitably, Dede would say, "Now that was a pret-ty good movie," and I would think, *I came here for this?*

I didn't know what I wanted to happen, but by midweek I was dying for *something* to happen.

My mother would nod in agreement with Dede. I'd hit the rewind button on the VCR and flee that house's numbing overworked central air as quickly as possible.

WEDNESDAY AFTERNOON MY mother again mentioned my still-unsorted books and records.

I snapped, "What is it, Mom? You want your house clear of every trace of me?" and then had the rare pleasure of a concrete reaction. She looked a little taken aback.

That night I called Risa.

At one point in our conversation I overheard someone stomping up the stairwell outside her apartment. "I miss noise like that," I said.

"Yeah, isn't that amazing? Sasquatch lives upstairs from me."

But I was serious. I told her the first couple of nights in Ralston I'd had a hard time sleeping; it seemed so unusually quiet to me that the silence assumed a certain mass and pressed like water upon my eardrums.

"You're really weird," she said.

"Yes. But you already knew that."

Thursday I ate dinner at Paul and Kris's house.

The wall beside the stairs in their house was covered with family photographs. I stopped before it after dinner, looking over them generally at first, then trying to detect some order in them. The photos were of various sizes, many of them in their own frames, others—snapshots—in large frames whose matting had precut squares and ovals. Most of the large standardized frames were devoted to a single event: Robby's birthday party, the marriage of Kris's sister, Paul Jr.'s first days of life. I walked up and down the stairs, considering who was at the top, who at the bottom. Was there some kind of generational order—familial descent paralleling that of the stairs? No. My father's grandfather, the oldest photo on the wall, appeared two-thirds of the way down. Some notion of progress as one ascended? And where was I?

I'd only meant to pause a minute, but this was much more diverting than Scrabble or Hollywood movies.

Then Robby, as blond as his mother had been at his age in a photo I'd just seen, appeared at the bottom of the stairs. "Dad sent me to see if you got lost," he said, smiling, flirty still at six years old.

"No, no," I said, "I was looking at the pictures. I saw your birthday party."

He just smiled and leaned rubbery-legged against the lowest upright of the railing.

"He didn't get lost," he reported happily, as we both reentered the kitchen where Paul and Kris and Paul Jr. sat at the table.

"So there's no order to the pictures along the stairs?" I asked.

"What do you mean?" Kris said.

"Some kind of temporal progression, maybe," I said. "Oldest photos to most recent . . . some kind of narrative . . . ?"

Paul and Kris had in common a vexed look involving a certain tilt of the head—they gave it to me when they thought I was being willfully odd. They both gave it to me now.

"*Narrative....*" Paul repeated with half-serious disdain.

"I don't know," I said, then decided to make the whole thing into a dumb joke. "Maybe they're arranged in terms of virtue. Moral qualities. Then, of course, you'd put all my photos at the top. Something for the kids to aspire to."

"Oh sure," Kris said, rolling her blue eyes.

"I don't think you'd be anywhere near the top," Paul agreed.

We were all comfortable with this kind of talk.

"Now, I know," I said, "that as an uncle I'm a role model. Right, Paul?"

But my bored nephew had been looking out the window, wanting to go outside into the sultry evening. He turned toward me a delicate version of his father's face, a distant version of *my* father's, high-cheekboned, but with no trace of ethnicity, no darkness, and smiled distantly, uninterested.

"Well, we do sometimes use you as an example . . ." Paul said. "Though usually not a good one."

I laughed.

The period in my early twenties, before my father's death, when Paul and I had hardly spoken to one another had evolved into this kind of careful, not especially witty banter. Once, at the Strickland warehouse, we'd displayed our anger toward one another, and neither of us wanted to do it again. Out in the open like that it had seemed too much to overcome. So we gave it to each other in small doses, maintaining our resentments and our relationship at the same time, our affection never quite clear of recriminations.

Which is why, after dinner, when the kids had run into the backyard to play, and while Kris and Paul did the dishes, I raised the subject of my mother—trying to demonstrate filial concern and responsibility.

I asked, "When do you think we should talk to Mom?"—a question that emptied the air from them both.

"I don't know if this is the right time," Kris answered.

"Well, while I'm here," I said, "I thought it might be a good time. All three or four of us can do it. So she can't blame one person. Get paranoid about one or two of us. Try to play us off each other. You know how she does."

"Oh, I know all right," Kris said.

"I'll do it myself," I said. "I don't care. Mary doesn't want to talk about it either. At least she wouldn't talk about it the other night. So why don't I just do it? Things aren't so great between me and Mom anyway. What's it going to hurt?"

Paul dried the dishes, eyes on his work, head down heavily. Standing on the far side of Kris, he seemed to droop under the weight of the topic, so that his wife, her brown hair bursting out in a high ponytail, tanned, athletic, but a good three inches shorter, seemed taller than he.

"Can't we let the poor woman get out of bed first?" Kris said. "I think we should."

"I won't be around then. I'm just trying to help you guys while I'm here," I said.

"That's okay," Paul said at last, since I wasn't giving up. "Now's not the time."

"It seemed to be the time the other night," I said. "You were talking like it was pretty urgent."

"I was just letting you know," Paul said.

"Let her get out of bed first," Kris repeated.

"We have time," Paul said.

"I don't," I insisted. "I'm leaving in a couple days. If you want me to be any help. I'd like to get it done. Be in on it."

Paul gave a sarcastic laugh. "You'll be in on it. You'll be the first person she calls."

"To try to play me off you," I said, "and Mary. I don't want that. If we present a united front . . . Or, like I said, I'll do it myself. I'd like to have it over with before I leave."

Paul shook his head.

"I really don't think there's any hurry," Kris said. "She'll be in bed at least four more weeks."

"I won't be here, though," I said once more, weakly. But it was no use. You were either *in* Ralston all the time, or you were out. They would not be rushed. Perhaps Paul and Kris were right about not bringing up the subject while she was bedridden (not that it went smoothly after she was up), but my frustration led me to suspect this wasn't their main motive. I was in Ralston looking for some sense of accomplishment, some sense of involvement. They would not allow me the satisfaction. While Mary had avoided the topic of my mother because it drove her to despair, Paul's refusal to discuss my mother seemed punitive and self-interested. Having attained a certain authority from long years of suffering, he wasn't about to let an interloper dictate the time and terms of the discussion.

FRIDAY, WHEN I had delayed as long as I could, I reluctantly walked out into the garage—and discovered something like a world. To my surprise, in the first minutes of my sorting, it came to meet me, rose up all around me. As my mother had said, most of the books were high school texts, and they were worthless and outdated, with end-paper maps of vanished countries and a truncated cosmos. But I found them irresistible. With them in my hands I lost track of time and became pleasantly confused about place. The garage lost all its strangeness. I pulled a dusty geometry book out of a box and more memories than I could sift came to me: old teachers, old classrooms and classmates. A fifth-grade reading book, with a primitive gyne-cological drawing in a margin, brought back Harry Burnet, who'd died in the early eighties after driving his TR6 into a telephone pole. A brittle paperback *In Dubious Battle* reminded me of how important my brother, Paul, had been to me. I'd inherited the novel from him, read it at his urging, and all its righteousness, the clear sense of justice transcending every particular cruelty and wrong, had thrilled me. I

even found my father's old cardboard cigar box which I'd adapted
for use as a treasure chest. Somehow its scrap of pale blue corduroy
lining had vanished, but my First Communion rosary, coins, and
arrowhead were still there, recalling to me what was long gone: the
two medals Hammy Oakes had given me—the only two of my hidden treasures which, for a time, I firmly believed I couldn't have done
without. And Hammy himself: almost as distinctly and vigorously
with me in the garage as he'd been as a boy—even though his present
whereabouts (upon the earth I assumed, and not, like Harry, closed
within it) remained, as they had for twenty-three years, a complete
mystery.

For four hours that afternoon I felt safe within the aura of a sen-
sible past: details lost, but the *air* of each memory all around me,
vague and palpable. I seemed to breathe the distilled essence of each
remembered scene, sweet now—no matter how bitter it had once
been—and welcome. At moments I would have sworn it was as simple a thing as pulling aside a sheer curtain to find myself back with
my father and mother in the Weston Avenue house. The thinnest
permeable membrane separated me from that place—its comprehen-
sibility guaranteed by my father, *if only I could learn enough to read it*—
and I longed to penetrate it, to be back *then* once more. Everything
I picked up reinforced the immanence of this past, everything seemed
to be a valuable souvenir, and only late in the afternoon, after my
imagination had grown so weary that practicality could once more
assert itself, did I finally begin to see the things themselves and realize that very few of the books and records were actually worth
saving. These I set carefully aside. The rest I packed up and stored
as inconspicuously as possible, hoping my mother might overlook
them the next time she took to discarding the past.

Then, after a shower, I sat in an overstuffed chair in the bright
living room, near the corner of my mother's bed. I thought she was
sleeping, for her eyes were closed; I read the *Ralston Bee*. But all of a
sudden she asked, "Why are you in such a good mood?"

I started a little. "Am I?" I laughed.

"You look like it. Better than you have all week."

I considered. "It's a relief to be done after putting that off, I guess."

"Well, I told you," she said. "Get it over with. Clear it out. It makes you feel better, doesn't it?"

"Yeah," I agreed with a shrug, though she had it all wrong.

But I really was in a good mood that night.

Paul and Mary and their families arrived, and my mother joined us at the table for dinner. The children entertained us. Justin and Robby were funny and made everyone laugh. Sandra, with little urging, showed off her ability to add single-digit numbers in her head. I rattled off long lists of them but couldn't throw her. She was impressive and proud—and she didn't sit at the end of the table, with the other three kids, but right in the middle of the adults. The lasagna Dede had volunteered to make from my mother's recipe turned out surprisingly well. It was a pleasant, uneventful time. I was leaving the next day, not to be seen again for perhaps another two years, and the anticipation of a long absence put us on our best behavior.

Tolstoy famously wrote that "all happy families resemble one another, but each unhappy family is unhappy in its own way," but I don't believe it. A friend from college who once visited during a Thanksgiving break was amazed by how sedate and quiet my family was at its happiest. He said, "If I was home right now, my brothers and father would have drunk too much, the television would be blaring a football game, turkey scraps would be scattered all over the table, everyone would be shouting. . . ." Tolstoy's maxim is doomed by its absolutism. I can't conceive of some complete distinction between happy and unhappy families, because I can't imagine that a family's happiness is ever unrelated to its unhappiness. So my friend's family, two generations of underachievers meekly fulfilling the duties of their dull office jobs, really "let loose" on the holidays they spent together. While my family, never reconciled to the unpredictability of the world and each other, tried to celebrate special occasions with the utmost order. From one holiday to the next, there was a great resemblance between my family's happiest days.

As there was between their disruptions.

After dinner my mother resumed her place in bed. We arranged ourselves around her. The course of the kids' play carried them all through the house and out into the backyard, but Sandra, for the most part, stayed among the adults. She sat quietly and listened while we, of course, talked about the kids. It was *always* the kids, or else the past. At times it was really too much; I'd feel as if I sat among the dead who, devoid of any present life of their own, could only rework the past or consider the prospects of their descendants. But on that Friday evening the aura from my afternoon's work still lingered, everything, still, was softened by nostalgia, and I was content to let them talk about the same old things. All the kids were doing well in school, in sports, in everything. Paul was refinishing that picnic table my father had built from scratch, still amazingly sturdy after thirty-five years outdoors. And, in as direct an acknowledgment of my current life as I would receive that night, hadn't my parents once gone to a convention in New York and stayed at the Waldorf-Astoria?

Then my mother said she was tired, and all of us left her and, since it was still early, went into the den. Paul Jr. and Robby were already there, watching cartoons on the twenty-four-hour cable kids' channel. We closed the door and spoke in low voices, but within fifteen minutes Dede came in and told Paul, "Your mom wants you guys to leave. She's trying to sleep."

"Oh, sorry. Can she hear us?" he said. "We'll be more quiet."

Dede left.

A few minutes later I heard my mother calling for Dede. Then Dede came into the den again, where we were quiet, and said, "You really have to go. Don't frustrate her now. Get going."

Mary smiled in disbelief. "We'll keep it down," she said.

"No, really, I think you should go. She wants you to."

Mary stared. A half-smile nonsensically remained, but she was angry. "Now listen, I don't think this is right—"

Paul interrupted her, "No. It's okay. Let's go."

"*Paul*. Because *she* says so?"—nodding toward Dede.

"Because it's what Mom wants. We'd better go."

"Jesus," Mary said. "I'll go talk to Mom . . ."

"I wouldn't if I were you," Dede warned.

"Forget it, Mary," Paul said. "You know how she is. Let's just go. Come on."

I watched silently. Paul and Kris began to rouse their sons from their gape-mouthed place on the floor in front of the television. Mary asked, "Where's Justin and Sandra? Where'd Dave go?"

I went with her to find them. As we walked through the Throne Room to the backyard, Mary said, "Thanks, Mom. This is really great," to my mother's back, curled in bed, unresponsive, beneath a sheet.

Dave and the kids were in a corner flower bed, looking at two ladybugs. Dave picked up Justin and went inside with Mary, but Sandra lingered.

"Come on, Sandra," I said. "We have to go."

"*Why?*" she asked, still kneeling amid the plants.

"Nonna doesn't feel well," I told her.

That captured her attention. I followed her into the house, then turned to close the heavy sliding glass door.

"*Nonna* . . . ?" Sandra began, behind me, with a voice of comfort and concern.

"Go, will you!" my mother said viciously. *"Get out!"*

Sandra didn't move. I put a hand upon her shoulder and led her out the front door, where she shook free of me and went and clung to her mother, who stood with everyone else in the driveway, trying to figure out what to do next. Justin, unaware that anything was wrong, had his father chasing after him on the front lawn. Paul's boys stood side by side near their parents' car, looking a little dazed, though not because of anything to do with my mother. They hadn't noticed a word of that. They'd been yanked away from the stupefying medium of television, and they gasped a little, like newly landed fish.

It was not yet eight o' clock. The heat was still stifling, but the sun had dropped from sight; its last rose brightness bled across the sky above the neighborhood's dark trees. We could not stay at my mother's house, but no one wanted to go home yet. In two cars we drove to a nearby Dennys. Then while two waitresses pushed and tugged two tables together to make one large enough for our group and an elderly couple seated nearby admired the children, Paul and Mary and I stood together, smiling sheepishly, avoiding all eyes, embarrassed by our own embarrassment, because still, after all these years, none of us had ever really gotten used to our mother arbitrarily, with a sudden surge, washing what seemed like the very earth out from beneath our feet.

We had always tried to pretend that we were natives of solid ground, of the old certainties of our bullying and frustrated father: us and them, right and wrong, the virtue of hard work and the evil of laziness, responsibility and blame; that whole logical, comprehensible, illusory world. We held on to our souvenirs—books and records, photographs, that massive pool table—as evidence of a stability which, however, was always predicated upon absence. Which arose, compensatory, desired—and like writing itself—only after the confusion, the anxiety, the meaninglessness of the moment had passed. So that my mother could throw out all those things and yet we'd lose nothing really and she'd escape from nothing. The past would remain no more nor less solid in our minds than it had ever been, shifting with each of our moods and needs—our comfort and curse— forever untouchable, while we were left, whether we liked it or not, alive, in the puzzling mess of the present, with each recalcitrant, impossible other. Left, as we had always been, with our mother.

Later that night when I returned to her house she'd call to me and

I'd find her slouched in bed, propped up by pillows, alone, penitent, teary-eyed. I wanted none of that. I was angry. *"Why did you do that? Why do you act like this?"* I asked. She straightened and smoothed the blanket over her lap with both of her small hands, her eyes upon them. "I don't know," she said simply, her tone unreadable and flat with either disaffected obfuscation or unadorned honesty. I've never been able to decide which.

But in Dennys we tried, in a familiar practice, to make the best of the situation, to take it all in stride. We were very kind to each other and tried to be cheerful. The adults had coffee—but no appetite for dessert. The kids all had huge sundaes. Except for Sandra, who didn't want anything. She sat quietly and very close to her mother, with an injured look I would not get out of my head for days, even after I returned to my life on the granite-based island of Manhattan.

Welcome to the family, is what we should have said to Sandra that night.

Instead, we all tried to cheer her up.

Mary told her, "Nonna just doesn't feel well. But she'll be okay. She was half asleep. She didn't know it was you."

But Sandra was too smart to believe that: smarter than she'd thought she was, and smarter, at that moment, than she probably wanted to be. The abruptness of my mother's nasty turn had really shaken her—the first bolt of illogic amid all the obscuring assurances with which she'd been raised—and for that night at least, while it was still fresh, before she conjured her own defenses against it, nothing any of us could say, no simple explanation, no cheerful mystification, none of the usual lies, could console her.